THE
DEFENDER

Also by Bill Mesce Jr.

The Advocate
Officer of the Court

THE
DEFENDER

———— ★ ————

BILL MESCE JR.

BANTAM BOOKS

THE DEFENDER

A Bantam Book / October 2003

Published by Bantam Dell
A Division of Random House, Inc.
New York, New York

Book design by Lynn Newmark.

Library of Congress Cataloging-in-Publication Data

Mesce, Bill.
   The defender / Bill Mesce Jr.
      p. cm.
   ISBN 0-553-80239-9
   1. World War, 1939–1945—Fiction. I. Title.
PS3563.E74627 D44 2003
813'.54—dc21

2002030549

Manufactured in the United States of America
Published simultaneously in Canada

10 9 8 7 6 5 4 3 2 1
BVG

THE
DEFENDER

CHAPTER ONE

★

Before the war, Glyditch had been a small, nondescript hamlet, a few rows of walk-ups and shops hugging the southern shore of the firth midway between Edinburgh and North Berwick. Unprepossessing as it had been, it had managed a lovely, serene stillness, a calming view of the water, and comfortable enough accommodations to meet the needs of some of Edinburgh's posh crowd looking for a bit of quiet and rest-up for the weekend. But what had been nondescript yet quaint before the war had now taken on the qualities of disuse. Glyditch wore the same wartime drabness that much of Britain had taken on as its uniform in those days. And certainly, the chill winds off the North Sea and the whipping winter rains did little to dispel the air of Glyditch being a forgotten, dying place, and the notion that Glyditch was a place to pass through, not stay.

Among the weather-beaten establishments overlooking the firth was a narrow five-story, the flats long abandoned by tenants who could no longer survive the faltering economy of Glyditch. In their place a small cadre of American officers and their support staff had installed a warren of cramped, paper-filled offices and tended to some of the more innocuous elements of the great war against the Hun.

Lieutenant Colonel Harry Voss occupied one of those little cubbies. Sitting at his desk, poring over plat books and land leases, his reading spectacles parked far down the bulb of his nose, a cigarette dangling from thoughtfully pursed lips, huddled inside a heavy sweater and scarf of fine Scottish wool, he seemed less a military officer than a figure from "Bartleby the Scrivener."

There was a knock at his door which he did not answer. The visitor was obviously experienced; he didn't wait for a response and immediately entered. Harry glanced up from the plat books and over his reading spectacles just long enough to identify the intruder as one of the staff orderlies, a young private whose child-like form was lost in the folds of his Government Issue uniform. He was pushing a serving cart ahead of him, navigating the cramped confines of the office unsuccessfully, avoiding a collision with the desk by clanging into one of the overstuffed file cabinets.

"Happy Thanksgiving, Colonel!" the orderly chirped in some Great Plains drawl. "They all missed ya down in the mess! Yore missin' out on a helluva party!"

Harry resettled his spectacles on his nose. "I'll muddle through."

The orderly awkwardly piloted past reefs of piled files until he docked the cart alongside Harry's desk. He made a show of lifting each of the plate covers and declaring the scrumptiousness of the food with a loud sniff. "Mmmmm-mph! The cooks did a right good job, Colonel! Tried to make it just like home! Even got cranberry sauce! It's that glop comes out a can, but it's still cranberry sauce. Got some— Well, I don't rightly know what it is, some local sheep thing. A 'joint operation' 'tween us 'n' the Scots, ya might say! Don't look like much but smells yummy. Well, kinda. You should get inta some o' this while it's hot, Colonel."

"Thanks."

Without looking up, Harry could sense the youngster's disappointment, and his puzzlement that such a mouthwatering invitation could be so dispassionately rebuffed. "They didn't really have 'nuff turkey for ever'body," the orderly confessed, attentively re-covering the plates. "The junior officers got a lot of chickens mixed in. Turkey don't seem to be so big over here." The young man seemed to be looking for an excuse to maintain a conversation. He leaned over the studious Harry, peering out the office's one narrow window. A gust of wind sent the pelting rain against the pane sounding like thrown gravel. "Funny how quiet it is ever'place else. I mean, it's a helluva wing-ding they got goin' downstairs! 'N' out there—"

"It's just Thursday to them."

"I guess."

"A rainy Thursday."

"Yeah."

"A cold, miserable, rainy Thursday."

"Hey, maybe it'll catch on."

Harry turned to study the orderly's earnest, open face over the rims of his lenses. *"Catch on?"*

"You know, like they celebrate Christmas. Why not Thanksgiving?"

Harry sighed and returned to his paperwork. "They've been celebrating Christmas a lot longer than we have."

The orderly was not so naifish as to miss Harry's dismissive air: he began to back out of the office. "Well, enjoy yore dinner, Colonel."

Harry nodded a thanks and sighed pleasurably when he heard the door shut.

But only a few minutes passed before he heard footsteps again creaking along the hardwood hallway floor toward his office. "You forget something, Private?" Harry growled impatiently.

No response. Harry sat up curiously. "Is somebody out there?"

Then, in an unreservedly artificial *basso* that echoed up and down the empty corridor: "*Who knows what evil lurks in the hearts of men? The Shadow knows!*"

Of all the people on earth with whom Harry Voss was acquainted, only Joe Ryan would have refined the ability to balance himself on the doorknob, allowing his upper body to swing into the room while his feet remained in the doorway, and only Joe Ryan would have believed the hours spent in refining such a flourish were a worthwhile investment.

"My God! *Joe!*" Harry tossed his glasses on the desk and shot to his feet, his face opening in a welcoming smile as he grasped the hand of Colonel Joseph P. Ryan, Judge Advocate's Bureau.

"Harry-boy!" Ryan clasped Harry's hand warmly in both his own. He stood back a moment, his bright green eyes squinting in study at the shorter, thicker officer in front of him. "That's a rounder shadow than I thought Lamont Cranston would have."

"Drop dead. What are you doing here? Are you AWOL?"

It was a dashing smile of perfect white teeth that Ryan flashed, a smile befitting the looks that made him look several years younger than the man across from him, though they were of the same forty-odd years. "Colonels do not go AWOL." Ryan emphasized the point with a leather-gloved finger. "Colonels conduct operations at their own discretion."

"Sit down, you dirty so-and-so!"

Ryan glanced about the cluttered cubby, glared at the one visitor's chair bristling with files. "No mean feat, Harry-boy."

Like a contrite housekeeper, Harry hastily made room.

"Who'd you piss off to end up in this rat hole?" Ryan pretended to dust the seat with his gloves before setting himself and his trimly tailored Royal Navy–styled bridge coat down.

"I like this rat hole," Harry retorted, returning to his own chair. "I think it's cozy."

"You think anything that reminds you of home is cozy." Ryan leaned toward the serving cart, peeked under a cover. "Need I remind you that you lived in a tenement? Oof!" Then, in a horrible imitation of an Irish brogue, "Would this be our loverly Army cooks be havin' a try at proper holiday victuals?"

"I hate when you do that." As Ryan opened his coat, Harry noted the steam-pipe fit of the colonel's Eisenhower jacket. "Did you lose weight?"

"Living in the field makes you hard, Harry."

"I thought you wrote me you were living in a hotel in Liège."

"That's close enough to the field for me. C'mon, let's go."

"Go where?"

"You've got to show me some sights."

"What sights? Have you *seen* this town? There *are* no sights."

The room was close enough that Ryan could lean back, snag Harry's coatrack with a finger, and pull it near enough to where he could bob Harry's cap free of its hook. "Let me put it to you another way." He tossed Harry's cap onto the desk. "Let's get out of here."

With a sigh, Harry scooped up his cap and reached for his jacket. "I don't know what you think you're going to see. It's raining. And there's a blackout. Did I mention the rain?"

"You can be such a killjoy, Harry-boy—a wet-blanket-sourpuss-pain-in-the-ass killjoy!"

In the doorway, Harry frowned and nodded toward the serving cart. "What about that?"

Joe Ryan smiled and made an inviting gesture of his arm. "Little mice, little mice, wherever you are . . . *bon appétit*."

There had been a small establishment—a café of sorts—over-looking the beach where the tourists—in those days when there had been tourists—could purchase some refreshment and lounge about on the roofed patio, watching the waters of the firth roll into shore. Like the rest of Glyditch, it had not been much to look at, but along with lemonade and assorted snacks, there had been a modest stock of champagne and brandies, Swiss chocolates, tins of caviar, and other unexpected delicacies. But years of abandonment, the untreated damages of one winter after another, had left the place derelict, decaying, picked over by scavengers.

It had been but a walk of a few minutes from Harry's office to the seaside café, but even in that short time, wrestling their umbrellas against the muscular wind, they found their trouser legs sopping by the time they reached the shelter of the patio. They folded their brollies and left them on the barren serving counter, shook the drops from their shoes and cuffs, huddled together against the wind to nurse a flaming match against a pair of cigarettes.

Ryan took a deep draft of his cigarette, then squinted against the wind, looking out toward the firth, watching the wind stir the wave tops to a white froth under the last feeble light of the day. He turned, looked at the dreary façades of the buildings along the waterfront. "What the hell're you doing here, Harry?"

"We compile information on land availability, negotiate access and use for estate lands by the military—"

"Harry, what the hell're you *doing* here? You should've said something to me when they assigned you. I might've been able to get you out of it."

"I didn't want to get out of it."

"Is everything OK at home?" Ryan asked, sincerely concerned.

"I hope so." Harry shrugged off Ryan's worry. "It's quiet. I like that."

"All those years of law school and now you're a goddamn real estate broker. Hardly seems lawyerly to me."

"I like it."

"Nobody bothers you."

"Nobody bothers me."

"Oh, so little Harry's learned his lesson."

"He's learned his lesson."

"Keep your head down, your mouth shut, blend in with the walls."

"That's the ticket."

"You are *so* full of shit . . ."

"Flattery was never your strong suit."

"Not true. You better than anybody else know that I am the all-time heavyweight title-holding ass-kisser in the Judge Advocate's. But one kisses ass *up* the chain of command, not *down*."

"Pile it on. I still have a shred of dignity left."

"Harry . . ." Ryan paced a restless little circle. The wind picked up a few knots and the rotting timbers of the café moaned under the abuse.

"If you want to keep abusing me, could you do it someplace that's warm and dry?"

"No. Harry, what would it take to get you to fight one more fight you couldn't win?"

"What kind of fight?"

"Dominick Sisto needs your help."

"Dominick? He get caught breaking into another wine cellar? That cost him his sergeant's stripes, you know, back when his outfit—"

"Was still in Italy, I know. This is . . . bigger than that. And, by the way, he's a lieutenant now."

"Dominick? A lieutenant? I'll be damned! Where is he? We were still in touch when they transferred his division to England for a re-fit. I kept meaning to get down there. I haven't heard from him in a while. I assumed they were sent into France."

"Belgium," Ryan said glumly. "A place called the Huertgen Forest on the border with Germany. Not that far from where I am in Liège. That's how I know about this. My office is handling the case."

Still not expecting anything more serious than a charge of drunk and disorderly, Harry asked, "How much trouble is he in?"

Ryan took a last puff and stamped his cigarette out with finality. He looked out toward the firth with a sigh. "Worst case? Tie-him-to-a-post-with-a-black-sack-over-his-head kind of trouble."

For a moment, Harry thought—hoped—this was a poor jest of Ryan's. But the other man turned to look at Harry with a sad, helpless, confirming nod.

"Dominick?" Harry shook his head, denying, disbelieving.

"Desertion under fire," Ryan explained, "disobeying a direct order—and don't say Dominick again. Yes, *Dominick*. Making a mutiny. They're throwing a load of other Mickey Mouse stuff on his head as icing."

"I know the drill." Harry leaned against the counter. Again, they were quiet. Again, the strange moan of the wind through the rafters of the café. "You said this is up in your neighborhood. You couldn't do anything?"

"Can't. I'm going to be sitting on the trial as law officer. He asked for you, Harry."

Harry shook his head. "Defense Counsel shouldn't come from the Judge Advocate's staff."

"That's the recommendation, but it's not ironclad. You're not a part of *my* Judge Advocate's staff. Right now you're not part of *anybody's* Judge Advocate staff. Hell, Harry, you haven't even done any trial work since you transferred here."

"If the Defense Counsel comes from the Judge Advocate, it risks the *appearance* of impropriety and unfairness. Even if I'm not attached at the moment—"

Ryan laughed caustically. "Harry, we're *way* past the appearance of impropriety! I'm so far out on a limb . . . I'm not even *here* officially! I have to be on a plane back to Liège in a couple of hours so I'm back for reveille. If it gets out that Dominick's judge snuck over here to draft Dominick's Defense Counsel . . . All three of us wind up in the crapper."

"Does anybody there know how well you know the kid?"

"They know I know him, but they don't know I *know* him. If they did, I'd be pressured to recuse myself."

"Who's prosecuting? Anybody I know from the London days?"

"Trial counsel's a new guy, captain named Courie, came on with me in September, just before we shipped out from London. Word was he was some kind of hotshot ADA in Cleveland—*Cleveland* for Chrissakes—before the war. You know, one of those young up-and-coming types. I don't know what that means in Cleveland! For all I know, a major crime there is kicking someone's dog. I think he's thinking of something better when he gets home than being an ADA in Cleveland."

"He's trying to run up a score over here?"

Ryan nodded. "Since I've known him. He's hungry, Harry, and he's a smoothie. Except in the courtroom. Then the gloves come off and there he's a tiger. A maneater! You come out of the courtroom after a tussle with Courie, you'd better count your fingers to make sure you still have 'em all.

"He pushed himself into this, that's how hungry he is. With his pedigree, it would've looked funny if I'd tried to block him. Let me warn you: Courie's sharp, he'll smell something if I don't play this perfectly straight, so don't look for me to do anything more than sympathize once we're at trial."

"Has anybody been holding Dominick's hand?"

"He knew some kid in his outfit that had just passed the bar before he was inducted. Kid's so green, he makes you look like Clarence Darrow."

Harry noted how short his cigarette had burned. He stubbed it out on the counter and dropped the extinguished butt in his jacket pocket. "I'm not his best bet. Like you said: I haven't done any trial work in five months. The few big cases I've been on . . . as you know, they haven't exactly been stellar successes. And I've never handled a felony defense, even back home."

"Doesn't matter." Ryan said it resignedly, sitting himself close by Harry. "Like I told you at the top: you won't win. Even Dominick knows that."

"Is that a comment on my ability? Or is it that open-and-shut?"

"I dropped some notes off at your quarters before I came up to your office. There's some photostats of the Investigating Officer's report, the charge sheet. Try not to let anybody know where you got them. They'll give you a better idea. Sisto's alone, Harry, and this looks real bad for him. He should have a familiar face in there with him. I'm hoping you can do something to justify moderating the sentence."

"What's the trial date?"

"Looking to start jury selection on December eighth. The charges were filed last week."

"That's awfully fast for a capital case."

"They have reasons to close this fast."

"'They'?"

"The powers that be; the brass hats; the rulers by divine right. He committed the cardinal sin, Harry. He's a junior officer who disobeyed a direct order from his superior. I could piss in King George's hat and we wouldn't draw as big a thunderbolt from the Almighty as what Dominick did. Throw in desertion under fire . . . They want him slapped down hard and fast." Ryan paused.

"What's the rest?"

Ryan smiled at how easily his friend read him. "First Army's been bogged down in the Huertgen since September. The casualty numbers keep running up, and nobody sees an end. Right now it's just another part of the war, but if it keeps going on the way it's been going—and it looks like it will—the worry is that the Huertgen is going to get a good look. If it does, the question's going to get asked: Does anybody here know what the hell they're doing? They'd prefer that question didn't get asked. Courie's taking advantage of that. He's trying to shoot this through before a defense can come together."

"Not a lot of time," Harry murmured, as much to himself as to Ryan. "I'm going to need a good second chair to help with the scut work."

"I was thinking maybe Peter Ricks."

"I was thinking the same thing. Except he's in San Francisco."

"What makes you think he's in San Francisco?"

"The last word I got was he'd been wounded at Cassino. Pretty bad. I didn't hear from him after that, so I assumed they'd shipped him home."

"They tried. God knows he was eligible. He fought it. He's down south. England. I already cabled him. He said no."

"I need him, Joe."

"Then go talk to him. I don't think they're going to be sorry to see him go."

"I have to talk with my CO about getting permission—"

"Already approved."

"I need to do something about all that material in my office."

Ryan glanced at his luminous-dial watch. "In about two minutes I'm in my jeep to my plane. I wanted you out of here tomorrow morning." It was clear to Ryan that this disposition did not sit well with his friend. Ryan shook his head, already regretting his change of mind: "OK, I'll give you two days to clean up your crap and try to shanghai Ricks. I'll get your travel authorization changed accordingly. Happy? But that's all you get, Harry. Ricks or no Ricks, I expect to see you in Liège three days from now. You're burning up the clock."

CHAPTER TWO

★

We press joes were all billeted in the same snug *gasthaus* not far off the *Plâce de la République*. The lot of them would loiter in the cozy little bar, cluster round the fire, trying to rub some warmth into their hands and backsides. Some would be fresh back from the field, wearing clods of mud on their boots like medals of valor, heedless of the strained tolerance in the smile of the waistcoated old proprietor who cleaned up after them, feeling their day or two at the front represented a marvel of survival against all odds. They were all so God-blessed young and fresh, bubbling with sensations new to them: the elation of epic adventure, the conviction of serving some grand cause, the exhilaration of having survived weapons discharged in anger. They felt invulnerable and purposeful and flush with the naïve idea that the story would, eventually, have a happy ending.

I would sit in a corner, alone, silent. I'd hear the giddy back-and-forth among them, and it would strike my ear with the tinny, tired sound of an old gramophone record played too often. Each time the record would begin again, I'd reach for my glass with one hand, my bottle of cognac with the other, and therein the tools for deadening the din.

My sole pleasure on those evenings came in the interruption caused by noise of the flying bombs that sporadically sputtered by overhead. As soon as the noise penetrated the barroom racket, the façade of bravado would falter, heads would turn skyward, the collective breath held as they waited to see if the device would continue on overhead to fall on the docks at Antwerp, or perhaps put-put it way farther on to London. But there were times when the engine would suddenly lapse into silence, and every soul in the bar as well as the rest of the city would steel itself and gird for the inevitable detonation and trembling of earth, the sound of sirens, and the clamoring bells of ambulances and fire crews.

Each explosion declared how empty the hope was of the war ending by Christmas. There would be no happy ending.

"You all right, Owen?"

I squinted through my liquory haze to see Colonel Joseph P. Ryan of the Judge Advocate's office sitting across my table.

I nodded at the bottle in invitation.

He shook his head no. "I thought you'd want to know . . ."

"Eh?"

"Your pal is coming to town."

"My . . ."

"Harry. In a couple of days. You should get to bed. You don't look so hot."

Silver-tongued chap though he normally was, Ryan seemed at a loss for anything further to say. Rather than his usual glib fare-thee-well, he merely nodded and departed.

Harry was coming. The wearing sound of the invulnerables

in the barroom had reached an intolerable pitch, so I poured myself another splash. At least for the time he was here, I'd not have to sit through the grim show alone.

As most trains were in those days, Harry's compartment on the southbound overnight was crowded with uniforms: American, British, the odd Canadian or Frenchman. All snored the night away oblivious to the reading lamp over Harry's seat. Spread open on Harry's lap was the file on Dominick Sisto's case. It was not a particularly thick file, though Harry quickly and bleakly determined that considering the contents of the few items therein, it didn't need to be.

Harry's first page of study was headed "Featured Players." Typical of Joe Ryan, the Judge Advocate colonel had spent some time doodling in the heading to make it resemble a cinema marquee, while the actual contents were barely decipherable scribblings:

1 Army
LtGen Courtney Hodges
HQ—Chaudfontaine (Belgm)

V Corps
MajGen Leonard Gerow
HQ—Eupen (Belgm)

28 Division
MajGen Norm Cota
HQ—Rott (Belgm)

(28 now rest/refit
new HQ Wiltz—Lux)

103 Rgmt
Col Henry Bright
(temp attached 28 Div as of Nov)
3 Batt.
Maj Conrad Porter (MIA)
XO Capt Whitcomb Joyce

Harry had actually met Porter and his exec, Joyce, almost a year earlier while Dominick Sisto's unit had been in Italy. He remembered not caring much for either of them.

He turned to the Investigating Officer's report, dated 11 November, addressed to the divisional commander from one "Capt. S. O'Steen":

By order of Maj. Gen. Norman A. Cota, commanding general, 28th Division (Rott), a hearing was held this date to investigate charges forwarded by Capt. Whitcomb Joyce, acting commanding officer, 3rd Battalion/103rd Regiment temporarily attached to the 28th, concerning actions by 2nd Lt. Dominick V. Sisto, acting commanding officer, L Company, 3/103 on 11/7/44 while engaged against enemy forces on Hill 399, Schmidt sector, Huertgen area of operations.

According to Capt. Joyce, in an 11/7 attack on the hill, Lt. Sisto was to lead a special assault detail of approximately 20 members of L Company from Phase Line II against an enemy position at the hill's summit. Battalion CO Maj. Conrad Porter was to accompany the assault detail.

The attacking rifle companies reached the phase line sometime after 0900, and the special assault detail jumped off from the phase line at approximately 1000 under heavy enemy fire. Because of communications difficulties, Capt. Joyce moved to a forward observation post across from 399 from which he could directly observe the special assault detail gain the top of the hill.

At that time, Capt. Joyce ordered a composite reserve company composed of the battalion's I & R, Mine, Antitank, and Ammunition and Pioneer platoons, as well as additional troops from the HQ Company, under the command of 1st Lt. Walter Tully, I & R platoon leader, to advance to the hill and exploit the breakthrough. Despite observing the success of the special assault detail, Lt. Tully refused to advance without first receiving a prearranged go signal from the special assault detail.

Immediately thereafter, Capt. Joyce received radio communication from Lt. Sisto informing him that the special assault detail was withdrawing from the hilltop, and that he was also ordering the withdrawal of all attack forces from the hill. Capt. Joyce issued a direct order to Lt. Sisto to hold his position. Lt. Sisto claimed to be operating under orders from Maj. Porter, who could not be located. When Capt. Joyce attempted to pursue the matter, Lt. Sisto broke off communication and proceeded to bring his men down from the hilltop and withdraw all engaged 3rd Battalion troops from Hill 399. When the attack force regained the original jump-off position, Lt. Sisto informed Capt. Joyce that Maj. Porter was missing and presumed dead.

PFC Avram Kasabian, Lt. Tully's RTO, who was present during the radio communication between Capt. Joyce and Lt. Sisto, confirms that Capt. Joyce issued the order to Lt. Sisto to hold his position atop the hill.

PFC Paul Makris, Lt. Sisto's RTO, was in a position to hear Lt. Sisto's end of the communication and confirms that he refused the order and told Capt. Joyce he was withdrawing all engaged forces from the hill. He also witnessed him cutting off communication with Capt. Joyce.

Because of the disposition of the members of the special assault detail on the hilltop, there are no witnesses to confirm or disprove Lt. Sisto's statement that he was acting under orders of Maj. Porter.

It should be noted that as a consequence of the confusion typical of heavy battle, the statements of some of the witnesses are vague and there is some confusion as to precise actions, statements, and sequences of events. However, they are all in agreement on the substance of the communication between Capt. Joyce and Lt. Sisto, which alone justifies recommending action. The open question of possible orders from Maj. Porter and Lt. Sisto's conduct with respect to Capt. Joyce raises issues that can be settled only by a full formal proceeding.

Recommendation

That 2nd Lt. Dominick V. Sisto be tried for disobedience and the unauthorized withdrawal of forces from battle;

That the case be referred to the Judge Advocate for proper disposition and a formal drawing up of charges on the appropriate grounds supplied by the Articles of War.

Several maps were attached to the report, covering the area of the operation, as was a hand-drawn diagram of Hill 399 marked with symbols and notations indicating the disposition and movements of troops, all in a manner of cryptography which Harry found indecipherable.

Then there was a memorandum from Captain Leonard T. Courie, Judge Advocate General's Bureau in Liège, to his immediate superior, Colonel Joseph P. Ryan:

> Having received advance notice of a case involving a possible capital offense(s) being referred to JAG-Liège, and anticipating the convening authority's desire to see an expedient handling, I studied the IO's report, and responded to 28th Div. HQ queries on appropriate disposition and informed the commanding general that a clear prima facie case on capital charges existed. I have taken the liberty of initiating prelim work and drafting charges that will be submitted to you for approval.
>
> For the sake of consistency both in dealing with the case as well as with the convening authority, I request that I be formally assigned as lead Trial Counsel for the duration of the process. Should this not be the case, the convening authority should be apprised ASAP.

Harry could almost close his eyes and picture the entire scenario that the few typed lines hinted at, see it like an old-fashioned cine film in fast motion.

Courie had caught wind of the case even before it was a case. That network of gossiping lips Americans artfully describe as "the grapevine" would have been exhausting itself with a subject as pungent as the one the IO's report outlined. Once Courie had picked up scent of the incident, he preemptively (and here, another spot-on American colloquialism) "hot-footed" his way from Liège to Rott before the JAG office had been officially alerted to the situation, got a peek at the IO's report, volunteered himself to offer advice and counsel to General Cota and his advisory circle on what to do about the situation, and even offered to get the process started. Having insinuated himself into the case, Courie then turned to Ryan, asked for the official appointment to the case, ending with the deftly veiled threat that should Ryan not do so, he could personally explain to General Cota why that very helpful JAG Captain Courie who, incidentally, possessed a record as a bona fide criminal prosecutor, was no longer on the case.

The true measure of Courie's hunger for the case was indicated by the memorandum's date of 12 November—the date when the IO would have still been finalizing his report. In Harry's eyes, Leonard Courie was already shaping up to be as dangerous as Ryan had claimed.

There followed several other memoranda from Ryan informing concerned parties that Lieutenant Dominick Sisto would be subject to court-martial, that Courie would be lead Trial Counsel, and alerting them to the next steps in the process.

And then finally there was the charge sheet with the notation that charges had been served to Dominick Sisto at 0800 hours on 15 November. *They hit him right after breakfast,* Harry observed.

The charge sheet read:

Charge 1st: Desertion in the face of the enemy in violation of the 58th Article of War.

Specification: In this, that while engaged against the enemy in a leadership role on 11/7/44, and with no authority to do so, Lt. Sisto fled the scene of battle.

Charge 2nd: Demonstrated disrespect toward a superior officer in violation of the 63rd Article of War.

Specification: In this, that Lt. Sisto's actions and language directed at his immediate commanding officer at a critical time in the fighting on the above date and place represented disrespectful and insubordinate conduct, as did his deliberate ceasing of communications with said commanding officer.

Charge 3rd: Willfully disobeyed a direct order from a superior officer in violation of the 64th Article of War.

Specification: In this, that at a critical time in the fighting on the above date and place, Lt. Sisto refused an order to hold his position.

Charge 4th: That he made a mutiny in violation of the 66th Article of War.

Specification: In this, that Lt. Sisto unlawfully assumed command of several companies of his battalion engaged against the enemy and issued orders contrary to those of the lawful military authority.

Charge 5th: Displayed misbehavior before the enemy in violation of the 75th Article of War.

Specification: In this, that Lt. Sisto's actions at a critical time in the fighting at the above date and place constituted an abandonment of an assigned position.

Charge 6th: Engaged in conduct unbecoming an officer and a gentleman in violation of the 95th Article of War.

Specification: In this, that Lt. Sisto's decision to withdraw his unit, to unlawfully assume command of other units, in defiance of clear orders from his superior at a critical point in the fighting at the above date and place, represents a disgrace and discredit to his service and his country.

Charge 7th: Through his actions threatened the good order and military discipline of his unit in violation of the 96th Article of War.

Specification: In this, that Lt. Sisto's abridgment of the chain of command and command protocols, and his exceeding of his own lawful authority by taking command of other commands of his battalion, and his unauthorized withdrawal from the field of battle, and his conduct toward his superior officer, threatened the effectiveness, cohesion, and safety of the 3bn/103 units engaged against the enemy at the above date and place.

Harry dropped his spectacles on the open folder. He watched the words turn to a less discomfiting blur.

You want to feel bad about this? Feel bad later. Work first.

He picked up his reading glasses, pored over the contents of the file, making notes as he went. That completed, he dug into his luggage for his copy of the *Manual of Courts-Martial* and his annotated *The Articles of War.* He flipped his notepad to a fresh sheet of foolscap, poised his pen, opened *The Articles of War,* and began to read.

The window on the other side of the blackout curtain rattled; ripples crossed the surface of their drinks.

Harry was the only one in the pub who seemed to give the explosion any notice. "What the hell was that?"

Captain Peter Ricks smiled. "The UXB squads have a range out on the plain. It's where they take the bombs they dig out of London to set them off." Ricks took a sip from his whiskey glass, then a long draft from his pint of ale. Neither seemed to go down well. "They'll still be digging bombs out of this country when Buck Rogers collects Social Security."

Harry frowned and sipped his tea. "You look like hell."

"Gee, Harry, don't spare my feelings." Ricks's laughter was a bitter sound that ended in a raspy cough bred of cigarettes and liquor and sleepless nights.

Sixteen months before, as an officer on the staff of the London Judge Advocate's Bureau, Peter Ricks presented as very much what he was: the well-bred, well-mannered, well-kept scion of a well-to-do San Francisco family. Always polite, deferential, tidy, I remember him sitting so proper and straight, one would've thought he'd shatter if he'd so much as crossed his legs.

Now he slouched unkempt and rumpled, his once brush-cut hair a barely combed mop. Liquor had thickened and aged the young man's weathered features. And there was the hook.

From his left cuff, the sleeve stained with something sopped up from the pub table, there came the leather sheath that fitted about the stump, and from that base came the shining steel hook. Actually, there were two hooks side by side to form one, the gap between them adjustable, allowing Peter Ricks to grasp and hold. Like the amalgamation of wooden spars and ball joints that had replaced my leg, it was an ingenious if somewhat unattractive contraption.

"Why didn't they send you home?"

Ricks idly scratched at the scuffed surface of the booth table with the hook. "They tried. I persuaded them I could still perform a useful function."

"And what useful function is that?"

Ricks fumbled in his breast pocket for a packet of cigarettes. "That training cadre back in the States doesn't have any more combat experience than the kids they're sending over here."

"So you try to . . . compensate. Joe Ryan dropped a hint that maybe everybody isn't happy with your particular brand of training."

The captain smiled, shook a cigarette partly from the packet, plucked it free with his lips, then went back in his pocket for a light. Harry went for his own matches, but Ricks produced a Ronson and neatly struck it one-handed.

"I have a half-dozen sharpshooters with Springfields and scopes. When these kids come over my course, I have my snipers put rounds so close to them, they damn near crease their helmets. Their COs don't like that. They think it's too dangerous." Ricks's smile took on a malevolent twist. "When they ship out, they'll see what dangerous is."

"You knew Ryan was asking on my behalf, didn't you?" Harry asked.

"You don't need me."

"I haven't even been *near* a courtroom in over five months."

"And I haven't been in one for almost a year and a half. I'm not sure your friend Sisto'd be getting much of a bargain with either of us."

"You're a combat soldier—"

"Was."

"Dominick's a combat soldier. You're going to understand what's in his head better than me. You're going to understand what happened out there better than me."

"I don't understand shit these days." Peter Ricks drained his whiskey glass. He sat for a moment with his head bowed, gritting his teeth, his good arm cradling his middle. When he looked up and saw the concern on Harry's face, he smiled grimly. "Ulcer."

Harry nodded at the empty tumbler. "Maybe you should lay off."

"Can't." Ricks tapped the glass with his hook. "This keeps my mind off the ulcer."

"Why didn't you go home?"

Ricks slouched back on the booth bench. "They won't look

at me the same way they used to anymore. And I can't look at them the way I used to anymore."

"Who?"

"Everybody. Anybody."

Salisbury stands at the edge of the plain, and the pub stood at the edge of Salisbury, just past the Cathedral on the road running west. Standing outside the pub, Harry and Ricks could look out at the endless undulating expanse of gorse and bracken and heather. The wind carried a dampness that laid an ache deep in one's bones.

Ricks pointed to the obelisks of Stonehenge standing along the horizon, silhouetted against the last mauve light that still haloed the rim of the world. "Ever see those?" he asked, hacking his way through the lighting of a fresh cigarette. "They're not really sure what they are. Or even who built it. They think maybe it was a place to pray."

Behind them, Salisbury was gone: the gabled medieval houses, the limestone spires of the Cathedral that had floated ghostly white over the town in the dusk light, the ruins atop the hill marking Old Sarum. The darkness had taken it all.

"Look out there, Harry," Ricks said. "Nothing out there but those stones. The people who built it were already forgotten when the Romans got here."

Another detonation from someplace unseen in the murk settling over the plain; a tremor passed through the ground under their feet. Peter Ricks shook his head. "I think all we'll leave behind is a big, smoking hole. That's what they call progress." He tried to shrug himself deeper into his greatcoat. "I can't seem to get warm these days."

"I'll give you a lift back to your barracks," Harry offered, and they walked across the cobbles to where he'd parked his jeep.

Ricks didn't climb in immediately. He still faced the plain, watching the last color seep from the sky, watching the circle of stones in the distance disappear into the enveloping night. "Harry? The last time I saw you, you were on your way home. Why didn't you stay there?"

"I don't know. Maybe for the same reason you won't go home."

"You ever see it so dark?"

"Pete, this is my first time out of my hole in five months. I don't want to go over there by myself."

Ricks slid into the passenger seat, his hands thrust deep in his coat pockets. "Jesus, I'm cold." A finalizing, decisive sigh. "Let's go get my toothbrush."

Evening comes early in northern Europe during the cold months. Though it was only four in the afternoon, the sun was almost gone by the time the C-47 set down at the aerodrome outside Liège. I was waiting for them when Harry and Ricks set foot onto the muddy field.

It was a warm reunion, the warmest part being when Harry and I clasped our four hands together.

"Good to see you again, Eddie!" Harry had to shout to be heard over the rising and falling din of incoming and outgoing aircraft.

"Hullo, Harry!"

"Just kiss the ugly son of a bitch and let's get someplace warm!" Ricks cracked. "How're you, Mr. Owen?"

I noted the hook hanging at his side. "Ah, I see you've joined the fraternity." I rapped my knuckles on my own artificial appendage. "I must show you the secret handshake one day."

"I thought Joe Ryan would be here," Harry said.

"He's at your quarters," I informed him. "There's a car and a driver waiting. The colonel thought—for reasons I'm under the impression you understand—a public warm and friendly greeting would be . . . impolitic."

"Heaven forfend!" Ricks fluttered the fingers of his good hand by his mouth, as if he were some outraged innocent belle. Then, wryly: "If a guy as political as Ryan did something impolitic, I bet he'd break apart at the seams."

"I think you'll find it cozy enough," I said, leading them through the lobby of my *gasthaus*. "You're already registered. I'm afraid my colleagues have taken most of the better rooms."

"I don't like the sound of that," Ricks said. "That part about the better rooms."

"The only thing available your dear friend Joe Ryan could find for you was a sort of garret—"

Ricks was already peering up the stairwell. "Garret?"

"How high up is a garret?" Harry inquired.

"In this case, four flights."

Which, after scaling, had left the three of us on the topmost landing, gasping for breath. The landing was under the eaves, crimped by the sloping roof, so much so that the top of the door to their room had been cut at an angle.

"This is looking worse all the time," observed Ricks.

To call it a room would be to grant the sleeping space squeezed out of what should have been a portion of attic a dignity it did not deserve. The bed, a washstand, and a narrow wardrobe left little maneuvering room. The only place in the slope-ceilinged compartment where one could stand erect was by the innermost wall, except that area was filled with an uncomfortable-looking folding cot.

Joe Ryan was comfortably splayed on the down-filled bed, propped against the headboard, cap carelessly pushed back on his head, cigarette dangling lazily from his lips, shoes thoughtlessly on the quilted bedspread. "I feel like I've been listening to you fellows clomp up the stairs for *days!*" He flicked his cigarette ash on the threadbare rug. "You really ought to exercise more. Or get a girdle. I see Captain Ricks decided to make the trip after all."

"Hullo, Colonel."

"You cost Harry two days, Captain. I hope you're worth it."

Ricks looked momentarily humbled, as if he, also, hoped as much.

"Enjoy this cozy little nest while you can," Ryan went on. "You boys are on the road tomorrow morning." He enjoyed Harry's confusion for a moment before continuing: "I warned you about Courie, Harry. This guy's got the goods!"

Harry had long ago learned how to deal with Ryan's annoying evasiveness. He sat himself on the cot, crossed his legs, leaned back against the wall, and assumed a pose of infinite patience.

Ryan laughed at the long-missed sight, then grew abruptly serious. "Dominick's gone, Harry. I believe your literary friend Mr. Owen there would use the phrase 'spirited off in the dead of night.'"

"Want to try that in English?" Ricks asked.

"That *is* English, laddie," I cracked. "Your colonial crudity is showing."

Ryan swung his feet to the floor, snuffed out his cigarette on the bedstead, all business now. "The day I snuck out of here for Scotland, I don't know how Courie found out I was gone, but he did, and he took the opportunity to move Dominick."

"Move him where?" Harry asked.

"A castle. No, really! An honest-to-God castle! Between here and Wiltz. The Signal Corps has a radio repeater there."

Ricks bridled. "And what authority did he use—"

"He's the Trial Counsel," Harry cut in.

That didn't seem to clear up the captain's confusion.

"You need to bone up on your *Manual of Courts-Martial*, Captain," Ryan said somewhat snidely, then quoted therefrom, more or less: "The Trial Counsel's specific duties include this and that and blah blah blah *and* obtaining a suitable room for the trial."

"What's so 'suitable' about a room wherever this room is?" Ricks asked.

"It's about twenty miles southeast of here," Ryan answered, "and what's so suitable is that it's close to Wiltz."

"Cota is the convening authority," Harry translated. "Wiltz is where he's headquartered now."

Ricks was shaking his head. "So Courie says he's putting the hearing where it's convenient for Cota to keep an eye on the proceedings—"

"And it's close to where the witnesses are now bivouacked and all that other I'm-just-doing-my-job stuff," Ryan concluded.

"Forgive my stepping in," I said, "but as an objective observer, I understand the *how* at work but not the *why*."

"The why, Eddie, is to be a pain in the ass," Harry told me. "My guess is Courie's pretty well got his case set. But we'll be trying to build *our* case out in the middle of nowhere with no staff, no support facilities, and the relocation alone'll cost us half a day. Hey, Joe, is anybody at this place baby-sitting Dominick?"

"He's still got that fella from his outfit with him."

"Why didn't you just yank the leash on this guy?" Ricks demanded.

Ryan looked ready to bark, but Harry held up a hand and interceded: "Because then Joe'd have to explain to Cota why he wasn't around when Courie pulled this stunt."

"I wouldn't think our sly Captain Courie would have much trouble puzzling out the connection between you two," I said, indicating Harry and Ryan.

"He won't bring it up," Harry replied grimly. "Because then he'd have to bring up Joe's coming to see me in Scotland, which is one kind of misconduct, and his taking advantage of Joe's trip to Scotland, which is another. The short of it is we'd all be off the case then, including Courie, and he sounds like he really wants this one on his résumé."

"Mr. Owen, does it ever bother you that somebody as sweet-natured as Harry seems to understand sneaky sons of bitches like Lenny Courie so well?" Ryan stood. "I'm leaving before sun-up, but you guys get your rest. I'll leave a map at the desk and directions to the motor pool. A jeep and your trip ticket'll be waiting for you there."

"Colonel, will anybody mind if I tag along?" I asked. "I know the ground between here and Wiltz rather well, certainly better than Harry and the good captain. I can help navigate them."

Ryan smiled suspiciously, the respectful antagonist. "I appreciate the good deed, but how is your employer back on Fleet Street going to feel about you walking off the job?"

"Oh, I'll be on the job, *mon colonel*. My bones tell me there's a story worth telling in all this. In the time you've known me, have you ever known me wrong in that regard?"

"Unfortunately, no. Go if you like. But it's up to these two. See you at breakfast, Eddie."

Ryan began to make his farewell, then froze, held up a hand for silence. Overhead, they heard the muffled putter of a rocket bomb slipping by.

Harry looked quizzically to me.

"V-1," I answered, and looked upward at the angled ceiling, waiting until the engine faded into the west.

"You'll be unhappy to know you are now residing in what the boys call Buzz Bomb Alley," Ryan said, delighting in the pained look this brought to Harry's face. "Sleep light tonight, Harry," he added, as he set his hand on the doorknob. "They don't all fly by."

CHAPTER THREE

★

"**What do you** think the chances are I'll get a crappy bed even here?" Peter Ricks shifted uncomfortably on the cramped rear seat of the jeep amidst our piled bags.

We had seen the turrets and pinnacles rising above the barren trees almost as soon as we'd turned past the two moss-mottled stone lions marking the entry to the drive. A few twists and turns, and there the chateau sat atop its motte, in an open field surrounded by thick woods. This was, it should be said, not a true castle, built more as a castellated estate than a bastion. Edged with snow and icicles, the whole affair had a timeless, harmless, fairy-tale quality. Against that particular impression, the vehicles clad in U.S. Army drab clustered just outside the front gate seemed an offensive anachronism, as was the skeletal thirty meters of wireless tower emerging from someplace within the ivy-clad walls.

A figure in an officer's cap appeared alongside the great-coated Military Policemen stationed on either side of the portcullis. "Major Voss!" he chirped as we clambered out of our jeep. "Good to see you!" He had small, dark eyes, his narrow, pointed face already blotchy from the cold. "I'm Lieutenant Alth, Sir. I'm working with Captain Courie as his assistant trial counsel. Leave your baggage, gentlemen, I'll have somebody bring it up later." Alth paused, gave me a curious, wary look before escorting us through the gate and across the inner ward.

"I hope you weren't standing out here in this cold waiting for us all morning," Harry said.

"We had a man looking out for you. From the north tower you can see almost all the way to the main road."

"How delightfully period of you!" I said. "A watchman! 'To the north tower with you, Yorick!' But, Lieutenant: no hot lead poured from the barbican on opposing counsel? Missed your opportunity there!"

To which Alth halted in his tracks and turned to study me again. "Sorry?"

"Just ignore me, Lieutenant. I do have an unfortunate tendency to prattle."

"And you would be?"

"This is Mr. Owen," Harry interposed by way of introduction. "He's a newspaperman."

Alth's little hyphen brows came together, part curiosity, part unsettlement. "Captain Courie didn't say anything to me about, well . . ."

"Colonel Ryan knows," Harry assured him. "Where is he?"

"He came in early this morning, Sir," Alth said, his eyes still on me. "He's in Wiltz with Captain Courie."

"Sight-seeing?" Ricks cracked. "I hear Wiltz is lovely this time of year. How's the skiing?"

Alth finally drew his eyes off me, resetting them on Ricks. The lieutenant, as I was to find, was a rather literal-minded chap. "Sorry?"

"What's Colonel Ryan doing in Wiltz?" Harry clarified.

"He and the captain are both conferring with General Cota."

"I was expecting to do some conferring myself with the colonel and your captain."

Alth started again for the double oak doors of the main keep. "I understand it came up at the last minute, Sir. Mr.—Owen, is it?"

"He's cleared," Harry again vouched. "If you have any question about Mr. Owen's authorization, take it up with Colonel Ryan."

"It's not that, Sir." Alth opened the heavy wooden doors; though not as frigid as outside, the arch-ceilinged entry hall was chill enough for the stained glass windows bracing the door to carry a lacy fringe of rime. "It's the matter of...accommodations. Believe it or not, Sir, we're getting a little crowded. The Signal Corps unit has one wing," Alth explained, "and we brought down a platoon of MPs for security. Then we set aside space for the jury pool. We're expecting at least a few senior officers who require quarters appropriate to their rank."

"I knew it," moaned Ricks, and Harry hushed him.

"The krauts didn't leave much when they pulled out." Alth nodded about the foyer. Where there would normally be wall hangings, perhaps a painting or two, some appropriately medieval instrument of destruction on display, a rug, an entry hall table, there was...nothing. Stone. Bare and cold. Sometimes there remained only the hooks where something had hung, and scratches where it had been roughly pulled away.

"Just whose place is this?" Harry asked. Barren it might have been, but there was no doubting the pedigree of grandeur to the place.

"Now? Now it's the U.S. Army's," Alth answered with a superior sniff. "We don't have a mess detail. The captain's supposed to be doing something about that while he's in Wiltz. I know you've been on the road all morning, so if you gentlemen are hungry, there's plenty of stuff you can make in the kitchen. I'll show you the way if you like."

"First things first," Harry said. "Where's Dominick Sisto?"

"Of course," Alth said impassively, and led us up the staircase that curved out of the foyer to the next floor.

We followed Alth down a corridor that led to a heavy door set into the wall of one of the chateau's turrets. A Military Policeman was posted nearby. Alth nodded at the MP, who unlocked the door and held it open. "I'll leave you to it, then," Alth said, and disappeared back down the corridor.

The room was cozily small and circular, and I took it to have been a private study of sorts, as the walls were lined with bookshelves—empty, of course. Other than a few scuffed chairs and a table and a folding cot, there was no furniture. The tower overlooked the drive leading up to the castle.

Dominick was a smallish sort, so diminutive I found it hard to believe he'd passed muster at his induction physical. Face of a cherub, large, dark, wonderfully bright eyes. But there was an age there, of a kind not counted in years, not measured in wrinkles or gray hairs. It was there in his carriage, in the heaviness about him, a perpetual sadness that seemed to lurk behind the bright eyes.

But at the sight of Harry Voss coming through the door, the heaviness lightened, the sadness dissipated. The cherub face grew wider and wider with a welcoming smile. Quietly, hushed, as if disbelieving: *"Signor Roosk . . ."*

"Hello, Dominick."

They stood apart, unsure of the proprieties.

"Do I salute?" the boy asked.

"Come here." Harry reached out a hand, the boy made to take it, then Harry pulled him close and they embraced.

They held each other long enough that both Ricks and I began to feel uncomfortable. I think they'd be holding each other still if we hadn't heard an embarrassed shuffle from behind the door.

"I better introduce you to this guy," Sisto said, and he and Harry finally separated. "This guy is the saddest-faced son of a bitch you're ever gonna see. Andy, the cavalry is here."

"Howdy. Uh, Sirs." He stepped shyly out from behind the door, a lanky fellow, the sleeves of his windcheater adorned with corporal's stripes. At first glance, Corporal Andy Thom reminded me of cowboys I'd seen in American films at the cine: tall, lithe, a bow to his legs that gave him something of a rolling gait. His handsome face was all clean angles, his dark eyes sharp, his black hair thick and bushy. Yet, unlike those cinema Westerners, his face was unlined. He saluted in Harry's direction. "Corporal Thom, Sir. I'm guessin' you'd be Colonel Voss."

Harry waved the salute away and shook Thom's hand. "Glad to meet you, Corporal. Let me introduce Captain Ricks. He'll be part of the defense team. And Eddie Owen. He's a reporter, so watch what you say and make sure he spells your name right."

Andy Thom shook hands all round. "Boy, you fellers don't know how glad I am to see you!"

"I think Andy was feelin' kinda overwhelmed," Sisto explained.

"Overwhelmed? Hell, Sirs, I was still waitin' on my bar exam scores when I got called up so I guess you could say I was feelin' just a mite *more* than overwhelmed! I practically dirtied myself, I don't mind tellin' ya!"

"I'm really sorry you got dragged into this, *Signor*," Dominick said to Harry. "It was the last thing I wanted."

Harry smiled wryly. "I would've thought the last thing you'd want is for *you* to be here."

"Me? I was drafted. Can you butt me, Signor? I'm out."

Harry's smile turned sad; he shook his head disbelievingly as he brought out a packet of cigarettes. I don't know that anyone else saw that look, or understood it, but I flatter myself that I comprehended. There was still an image in Harry's mind of Dominick at home, Dominick the child sprinting up and down the halls of the tenement where they lived . . . Little Dominick. It was still a great leap to connect Little Dominick to the war-weary second lieutenant asking Harry to "butt me."

"Well," Harry said, shaking off the reverie. "Maybe we better get down to business. Eddie, if you don't mind . . ." He indicated the door with a tilt of his head.

I hadn't expected to be ejected, but I kept up a graceful smile. "Of course."

As the door closed behind me, I heard a sighing Harry ask, "Now, Dominick, what in the hell did you do?"

Harry, Sisto, Andy Thom, and Peter Ricks remained cloistered for the rest of the afternoon, leaving me to prowl about the chateau's icy and denuded chambers and corridors. The three of us rendezvoused that evening for dinner.

The dining hall was a cavernous room scarcely warmed by the blazes in the fireplaces at either end. Harry, Ricks, and I sat clustered at one end of the long dining table—an unwieldy piece that had escaped the Germans' kleptomania or need for heating fuel. Harry, characteristically, had left the head of the table open, sitting by me.

"I've never met Courie and I've spent all of five minutes talking to his little flunky, Alth, and they already give me a pain in my ass!" Ricks ranted. "Left and right cheek respectively!"

I chuckled, but the mirth died instantly as I stirred the

glutinous mess in my bowl. "I appreciate you lads had to make do with what was on hand..." "Supper" was a loose term for the stew pot of mixed rations Harry and Ricks had concocted by picking their way through the crate of 10-in-1, accompanied by a side buffet of open boxes of K-rations. I scooped up a spoonful and watched it ooze back into the bowl. "What has the esteemed *in absentia* prosecutor done now?"

"Alth says that for this meeting of the minds down in Wiltz, Courie had to—he just *had* to—take everything with him to review it with Cota. Depositions, statements...they took everything on the Discovery list with them but Sisto!"

"Rawthah unsporting, wot?" I said, affecting my best Etonian whine.

Ricks flashed a look that said he was not nearly as amused by my apery as I was, then fulminated on: "And now we get this crap about Courie not coming back until *tomorrow*? He's cheating us out of another half-day! I don't know what kind of law they practice in Cleveland—"

"The same kind they practice everywhere else," Harry said with a resigned sigh. He sat with elbows on the table, his hands wearily massaging his brow. He pushed his bowl away and one hand picked through the K-ration boxes strewn between us until he found a fruit bar. "I would just like to point out that this guy from Cleveland you and Ryan don't seem to think too much of is sitting on what I'll bet is a fully prepped case, has managed to shove a short trial date down our throats, and has—legitimately—been cutting down on whatever prep time we have left. So the next time either of you want to make some crack about the practice of law in Cleveland, I hope it is one of respect and reverence."

"Colonel Voss?"

We turned to see Andy Thom hovering in the doorway.

"Evenin', Sirs. I just thought maybe I'd bring some chow up ta the lootenant. If that's OK."

"In the kitchen," Harry said with a nod.

As the corporal disappeared through the kitchen door, Ricks turned to Harry: "Seems like the time to put it to him now that we're all here."

Harry nodded. "Andy!" he called out. "Before you go back upstairs..."

Thom returned, taking the seat Harry indicated next to Ricks.

"Eddie," Harry said to me, "I need to ask you a favor."

"Harry, you know you don't need to ask. Say what it is and it's done."

"You better hear me out. You know we have a time problem. Dominick gave me a list of people in his outfit I'd like interviewed. It's the men named in the hearing report and a whole lot more. To get through them, get the interviews back in any kind of time where we can review and collate them into some kind of usable shape—"

"Back from where?"

"Wiltz. Alth says he can get a message through to divisional headquarters there, have the men brought in from the field, have a place set up for interviews. I was thinking of sending Peter and Andy down there. I've already talked it over with them and they're OK with this..." Harry paused.

"You want me to go with them? Help out?"

He nodded.

"Of course, Harry! Though I should point out: I'm no lawyer. I'm not sure I'd know how to conduct a proper—"

"There won't be anything proper about it," Harry said. "We don't have time for formal depositions."

"Still—"

"You're naturally nosy, Mr. Owen," Ricks put in. "At least that's been my experience. That's the only qualification you need."

"I need them interviewed quickly but thoroughly," Harry said. "All the usual questions: What happened? When did it happen? Who was there? That doesn't sound any different than what you'd annoy the Army with on your own, does it?"

"Well, I resent investigative journalism being referred to as an annoyance, but, aye, that's how I'd annoy them on my own. It doesn't seem like much of a favor, Harry. Why the reluctance?"

"You're here thanks to Joe Ryan. But there's no way I can get him—or anybody else—to swallow a reporter as a legitimate part of the defense team. Handling some Q & A's, I think we can squeak by on that, but not as anything more than background assistance...And I won't violate privilege with Dominick. What he says to me I can't share with you, Eddie. That means you have to do a lot of this in the dark. And whatever you get in those Q & A's... You're working for me, not your paper. You can't use anything that doesn't get cleared by the Judge Advocate and the Public Relations Office."

"It's not the first time you've asked me to keep a secret, Harry."

"It's the first time I've asked you to keep one from your paper. I wouldn't want to put you in a bind with them. If they find out how close you are to this, and wonder why none of it's getting back to them—"

"That'll be their concern, Harry. Not mine."

He smiled. "Then you're off first thing in the morning. All three of you. I'll stay here, work with Dominick, and start plowing through the Discovery material when Courie gets back."

"I'd best get this chow up to the lootenant 'fore it gets cold," Thom said, rising.

"And if it's a bright and early start we're talking about, I'm going to go pack my ditty bag," said Ricks, joining him.

"Do you still have your copy of *Manual of Courts-Martial*?" Harry asked him.

"Didn't have much use for it in Italy, and it's lousy latrine reading."

"Take mine. In whatever spare time you have, get reacquainted. Courie earned his reputation in a *civilian* criminal court. He hasn't been with the Judge Advocate's that long; he might still be learning the ropes. We might be able to find a blind spot there."

Ricks nodded; he and Thom made their good-nights and retired.

We sat silently, just the two of us in the great room, then Harry pushed away from the table and walked slowly toward the nearest fire. He threw another log on, poked the blaze to a new height, though it did nothing to provide more warmth beyond the immediate circle of the hearth. "Not much of a reunion, is it? Seems like all I ever do when I see you is ask you for—"

"I appreciate the sentiment, but the apology is quite unnecessary." I caught the pensive look in his eye. "Worried about the case?"

"Worry comes from not knowing what's going to happen. I am not worried. They've got Dominick nailed. I'm pretty confident I can get the heavier charges reduced, maybe even cut. But he's going to get convicted and he's going to end up in Leavenworth. What's worrying me is not the case."

I walked to him, set a hand on his shoulder. I did not press. I'd wait as long as he needed me to wait.

He took a long breath. "I saw that boy grow up, Eddie. I

remember the first summer he learned to walk, clomping along down the hall on his fat little bare feet." A smile of re-membrance: "Dominick was my . . . practice run before I had my own boys. I think, maybe, he made me want to have kids of my own. And now . . ." The smile evaporated. "Sometimes I wish I could put the whole goddamned human race on trial." Harry's face flooded with moroseness. "That could just as well be one of my boys up there."

"I should think this mess'll be all tick by the time your lads are of age, Harry."

"Maybe this mess. What about the next?"

After Harry had bid me good night, it occurred to me that I could not fix the world's ills, or even ameliorate those of my friend, but I could at least clean the dishes. I was so occupied when Corporal Thom found me later that evening as he duti-fully returned Lieutenant Sisto's empty bowl. Without a word, he removed his windcheater, rolled up his sleeves, and took a stand by me at the sink, drying as I washed.

"If you don't mind my asking, Corporal, with the university years one needs to complete one's *juris doctor*, I'm surprised you were not taken on as an officer candidate."

A rueful smile. "Well, it was *suppose'* ta go that way. Come the end o' basic, I did get put up as a candidate for OCS, 'n' that was all-righty fine with me. But then they folded up the class I was suppose' to be in. The way it was put ta me, they needed more riflemen over here than they needed lawyers. After spendin' the last coupla weeks dealin' with Courie 'n' that loo-tenant o' his, I'm a mind not ta think much o' lawyers myself."

"Might I ask you something, Corporal? Habit of the profes-sion, you understand, always curious."

"All-righty fine with me. Long's it's nothin' 'bout the case."

"Nothing about Lootenant Sisto, I promise. I was just wondering, if you were comfortable with it, if you'd tell me about it. About what it was like on that hill."

It was almost imperceptible, the change in him, as if some mild but distasteful current had suddenly passed through his body. "'Bout like any other battle, I guess. Not that I'd know. It was my first. Colonel says you just 'bout been ever'where, writin' 'bout the war 'n' other stuff. He told me, you know, 'bout your leg. I don't know what I could tell you, you haven't awready heard 'bout some other fight."

"I *have* covered quite a bit of the war. And other things as well. Natural calamities. The odd assault and homicide. One form of ill-doing or another. I've even been under fire. But I've never—not *actually*—been in a battle. By the time I get there it's time to take away the bodies and sweep up the rubble, eh?"

"You haven't missed nothin', Mr. Owen." He stacked up the dried dishes, toted the clinking pile about the kitchen as he poked into this cupboard and that, looking for their proper place. "I wasn't one o' the ol' men from when the outfit was in Italy. I was one o' the replacements come over in July, when they were re-fittin' in England. A lot of us, we'd all been in basic together. By the time we shipped 'cross the Channel, I'd known some o' those guys I guess eight, maybe nine months. Long time. You get ta know the fellers you bunk with pretty good.

"We were all scared, 'n' even if you wanted to you couldn't hide it; that's how scared we were. I don't know 'bout anybody else, but I figgered, well, a situation like that, it made it a little better bein' with all these fellers I knew.

"Then we went up that hill the first time." The remaining plates were forgotten now. His fingers fished about in his breast pocket for a crumpled packet of Camels. His Ronson flared briefly, he took a long draft of his cigarette.

"I look over and there's somebody—one o' those fellers you got ta know over those eight, nine months—and he's . . . well, he's gone. Just like that.

"Sometimes, we used ta talk 'bout gettin' wounded." He shook his head, amazed at their naïveté. "We used to talk 'bout what kinda wound we'd take, like you had a choice. 'Well, a leg wound doesn't seem too bad, walk 'round with a cane for a bit.' This one talked 'bout takin' one in the arm, havin' a sling, somethin' that'd really impress the gals back home.

"It wasn't that . . . that *neat* on that hill, Mr. Owen. Till you see it, you never figger a body can come apart like that."

There was a scarred butcher's block nearby. Thom boosted himself atop it. I got the feeling he no longer trusted his legs. He hung his head, shaking it over a barb of a memory, then he looked up with a strange half-smile. "You ever see tracers in the dark, Mr. Owen?"

"At a distance."

"Kinda pretty. Almost don't look real. When we jumped off, it was 'fore sun-up. The krauts had so much fire comin' down that hill, all those tracers, it looked like some kinda gold rain. Bullet comes close enough ta you, you feel it. Like a little—" He made a small puff with his lips. "'N' you hear a little *snap* when it cuts the air. That's all I heard: *snapsnapsnap*. I thought, 'Andy, just stick your hand up 'n' catch one 'n' you are *outta* here!'"

"But you didn't put your hand up."

"'N' I'll be damned if I could tell you why I didn't, Mr. Owen." Andy Thom slid his feet back to the floor and shuddered, as if shaking off a chill. He rolled his sleeves back down and picked up his windcheater. I think he sensed my guilt over having him relive those three days again. "'S'awright, Mr. Owen. But you do me a favor, OK? Unless it's ta talk about the case . . . you don't ever ask me about it anymore."

By the time I was finished in the kitchen, I was fatigued but felt too restless for bed. I grabbed my winter garb, found a stair turret that let me out on an allure running along the crest of the main keep and walked the castle walls.

Cold clean air whistled through the machicolations. The sliver of moon was enough to set the thin layer of snow aglow on the motte's slopes, and etched the shadowy firs sharply against the star-speckled night.

I was not alone on the wall. I could make out another figure, his Military Police brassard barely legible in the shadows, the white "MP" on his helmet alight with the moon. I nodded a good evening to the sentinel, but the helmeted head hardly moved in acknowledgment.

"A wee bit cold this night, eh?" I offered conversationally.

Another stiff nod. I smiled an apology for troubling him, and stepped off to allow him the walk to himself.

"Well, if by 'wee bit' you mean it's ball-bustin', ass-freezin' cold, I'll second that!" From the other side of the MP, I saw the diminutive silhouette of Dominick Sisto, hunched against the cold, his woolen Army "beanie" pulled low across his ears, hands jammed deep in the pockets of his windcheater. "Hi, Mr. O."

"Lieutenant."

"Look, don't mind Benjie here." He clapped a friendly hand on the MP's shoulder. "He gets nervous. I'm not supposed to be up here. He's just a softie. Hey, Benjie, how'd a softie like you get to be an MP? I thought you gotta have no heart to make it into MP school. How'd you pass the test?"

"I cheated," Benjie grunted.

The smaller man laughed again.

"Ya mind keepin' it down, Lieutenant?" Benjie hushed. "Lieutenant Alth finds out, he'll tell Courie and *he'll* hand my balls to me!"

"Sorry, Benj." Sisto nodded at me to follow him into the shadowy arched entrance of the tower at the far end of the walk. He touched a cautionary gloved finger to his lips. "The guy's really puttin' himself out for me," he said quietly. "I don't want him gettin' in trouble. 'Sides, here we're outta the wind. It really bites you on the ass up on this wall." I heard a rustle of paper in the gloom. "Ya want some gum?"

"Nae, thank you."

In the dark, the crackle of chewing gum. "See, this guy Courie—you know him?"

"We've yet to meet."

"He's a real ass-buster the way he's got me locked up like what's-'er-face. The one with all the hair."

"Excuse me?"

"You know! The fairy tale, the broad with all the hair."

"Rapunzel."

"Right, Rapunzel. Benjie there, he feels kinda bad, so after everybody turns in, he brings me up here for a little air. He gets caught, I mean, hell, I'm up to my ass in the shit now, so I'm jake, what else can he do to me? But Benjie does me a solid, I don't want him—"

"I understand. Mum's the word."

"Thanks. I don't know where this Courie thinks I'm gonna go. Maybe I should start growin' my hair and slip out the window just to bust his balls, huh?" He leaned over the hollow center of the tower and with enviable skill neatly tucked his wad of gum safely in his cheek . . . and spat in the abyss. I could not see his face in the gloom, but I sensed he gained some satisfaction from the distant echoing splat. He resumed his cud-chewing. "Look, Mr. O, the ol' signor—the major—he talks a lot about you. He's got you down as all aces, Mr. O, and comin' from the signor—"

"*Signor Roosk?*"

A flash of a smile in the slice of moonlight. "That's what we call him back in the old neighborhood. Almost everybody was Italian, and here's Harry Voss, this Russian guy, a Russkie, get it? Russkie, Roosk—"

"I see. What did you call Joe Ryan?"

"Joe Ryan."

We both chuckled.

"Anyway," he continued, "I just wanted to say thanks."

"Thanks?"

"Harry told me you'll be goin' down to Wiltz tomorrow with the other guys. You know, to help out. Look, who am I to you? You don't know me from Adam. You're doin' it for the signor. But, so you know, I appreciate it."

"You're quite welcome, Lieutenant."

"Make it Dominick, OK? Friend of a friend and all that."

"All right, Dominick."

"Hey, Lieutenant!" Benjie called. "I gotta be gettin' you back 'fore we turn into pumpkins."

"My carriage awaits!" Sisto said with an unexpectedly fey flourish of his hands.

I followed him out onto the allure. The view from the keep seemed to strike him afresh, and he leaned against the wall, soaking up the sight of iridescent snow and dark trees. "Jee-*sus*, it's somethin' out here, ain't it? The first clear night, I saw those trees and the sky was like this, I thought, 'This is Christmas-tree Heaven.'"

"Lieutenant," Benjie urged.

Sisto smiled regretfully in my direction and began to follow the MP to the far turret.

Something tugged at me. "Lieutenant!" I said quietly, trotting along to close the distance between us. "As you say, I don't know you from Adam. But Harry Voss vouches for you, and that's enough character in my book. I also understand the instinct for self-preservation, and if that instinct should present itself, and do so by deception, and in so doing hurt Harry Voss either professionally or personally . . . I would take strong exception to that, laddie."

I waited for him to bridle at the threat. Instead, he merely nodded. "The signor is like family to me," he said softly. "I couldn't hurt him without hurtin' myself." He gave me an appreciative smile. "Harry's got himself a good friend. *Ciao, signor.*"

CHAPTER FOUR

★

There was a knock at the door.

"Aye, come in."

He poked his head round the edge of the door, not so much shy as cautious. Dark-complected, spindly, twenty or so.

"And you'd be?"

"PFC Kasabian."

I searched through the roster of those to be interviewed. "Kasabian, Avram C.?"

He nodded. I beckoned him into the room and put on what I'd hoped was a disarming smile.

"I thought there'd be a, you know, an officer or somethin'."

"I'm the sexy civilian assistant," I replied.

"They must be rationin' sexy."

As Wiltz's limited stock of cozy little inns and hotels had been commandeered by one unit or another of the 28th Division's headquarters staff, the arrangements concerning Peter Ricks, Andy Thom, and me consisted of installing us in the six-hundred-year-old chateau that commanded the ridge overlooking the Wiltz River, which divided the town. A field hospital unit was operating in the chateau, having converted a number of the larger chambers into wards. However, there remained ample room for the three of us to be quartered, as well as for our interrogatory sessions.

PFC Kasabian sauntered up to the two chairs I had set by the hearth, a matched pair of deep-cushioned affairs left over from the previous tenants. "You steal those from a whorehouse?" he asked.

"From downstairs, actually. Are they sending you lads up in any kind of order?"

He lowered himself into the chair opposite me. "One nearest the door goes next."

Avram Kasabian had been the Radio Telephone Operator for the platoon commander assigned to reinforce the men led by Sisto detailed to break through to the crest of Hill 399. I considered his lean frame and thought the burden of a 40-pound SCR-300 pack wireless must have come close to bending him double.

I recapitulated to him what I'd heard in the previous interviews thus far, most of which concerned the actual attack on the hill. "Then, at some point, your executive officer—Captain Joyce—came up to the forward observation post where your platoon leader—Lieutenant Tully—was holding. What then, Private?"

"What then is they started goin' at it."

"You mean Captain Joyce and Lieutenant Tully?"

A look of impatience from Kasabian. "I didn't think I was invited to contribute to the discussion, so yeah, Captain Joyce and Lieutenant Tully."

"According to the report produced from the hearing, I see Lieutenant Tully still refused to comply with the captain's order to advance."

"Tully said he wasn't goin'. Said he hadn't gotten the major's signal so fuck you."

"Those were his exact words?"

"I wasn't writin' it down as quote-o'-the-day, but that was kinda the feelin'."

"If you could remember his exact words—"

"Listen, pal, I wasn't payin' all that much attention. I was still tryin' to get Rainbow Six on the horn—that was Major Porter—and there was an ass-load of noise. Seems the whole kraut army was tryin' to blow us into a million pieces at the time. So I was a little distracted."

"As well as you can remember, then."

An annoyed sigh. "I remember him sayin' no. The lieutenant—"

"Tully."

"—yeah, he was goin' on 'bout how the plan was he wasn't supposed to move up without the signal, which, I think, was a green flare. 'N' the captain—"

"Joyce."

"—yeah, he said somethin' like 'Let's not argue 'bout it now, no sense goin' into it now.' Somethin' like that. He—"

"Captain Joyce?"

"—right, Captain Joyce, he said, 'Dammit, they're up there *now!*' He was talkin' 'bout the assault detail at the top o' the hill. 'They're up there *now!*' 'N' Lieutenant Tully said he didn't give a shit—"

"His words?"

"Oh, yeah! *That* I remember! 'I don't give a shit if they're halfway to Berlin!' He—the lieutenant—wasn't goin' up without the go signal from the major, 'n' that was that."

"I have to ask, Private Kasabian, as to the reason for Lieutenant Tully's refusal."

Kasabian's smile twisted into cruel amusement. "You're dancin' around askin' me if the lieutenant went yellow."

"I'm just wondering as to the grounds for Lieutenant Tully's—"

"Pal, you ever been in somethin' like that? Find me somebody there who wasn't pissin' into his boot 'n' I'll find you a candidate for a Section 8."

"I understand that."

"I'll bet," he pronounced caustically. "It was like this. Lieutenant Tully told Joyce he'd probably lose half of us just gettin' up to the jump-off line on the hill where the trenches were. Hell, we were gettin' the crap knocked outta us just holdin' there at the trees! Tully said he didn't want to move us out 'n' have us get all chopped up just to get there 'n' find Rainbow Six comin' down!"

"The lieutenant's refusal made the captain angry?"

"Well, Joyce was pissed."

"Meaning angry."

"Angry is 'Who took my matches?' Pissed is 'I'm gonna grab your ear and peel you like a fuckin' banana.'"

"Did Captain Joyce threaten Lieutenant Tully?"

"You mean like 'Move out or I'll blow your head off'?"

"*Any* threatening exercise of authority should be noted. Did Captain Joyce threaten the lieutenant with anything?"

"Told Tully he'd relieve 'im right then 'n' there 'n' bring 'im up on charges."

"And still Tully refused?"

"Lieutenant told Joyce to kiss his ass."

"Again, Private, were those his words?"

"He said somethin' like 'On whose authority?' 'N' then right after that, 'fore it got any further, I got Blue Six—that was

Lieutenant Sisto—he's on the horn tellin' me him 'n' Rainbow Six and what was left of the assault detail on top o' the hill were comin' down. See? The lieutenant knew what he was talkin' 'bout. If that fuckin' Joyce—"

"Is that why Joyce didn't prefer charges? Against Lieutenant Tully?"

Avram Kasabian went blank-faced. He blinked a few times, puzzled. "You don't know?"

"Know what? I'm afraid—"

"Lieutenant Tully didn't make it."

"No, I didn't know. I'm sorry."

"So am I, pal. The battalion was comin' off the hill 'n' then they were comin' 'cross the firebreak and the krauts were just pouring all kindsa shit down on 'em. Whatever they had: mortars, artillery, the machine gunners up on the hill were rakin' all that open ground. They were already in pretty bad shape, the companies comin' off the hill. Christ, you kept lookin' for more of 'em to come outta the trees on the other side of the break, but they didn't come. Just this little bunch, Lieutenant Sisto's guys. They got maybe halfway 'cross 'n' Lieutenant Tully sent us out to help bring 'em in, help 'em with the wounded, whatever we could do. 'N' he was out there with us, the lieutenant. That's how they got 'im." A pause. "He was all right, the lieutenant."

I let a respectful moment pass. "Major Porter's wireless designation—his radio designation—you said that was Rainbow Six, correct?"

"Headquarters was Rainbow, Major Porter was Rainbow Six."

"And Lieutenant Sisto was—"

"Sisto's company was tagged Blue, so he was Blue Six."

"And you said it was Blue Six—Lieutenant Sisto—who notified you that the men who had gone up the crest of the hill were coming down?"

"Yeah."

"It was Sisto himself on the radio?"

"Some guy came on, identified himself as Blue Six. You wanna know I could reckanize his voice? Joyce and the lieutenant are screamin' at each other, the kraut arty is comin' in—"

"I understand."

"—ya had to scream at the top o' your lungs just to talk to the guy next to you—"

"All right, then. You received a message from Blue Six—Lieutenant Sisto—notifying you that the lieutenant's men were withdrawing from the top of the hill. You relayed this message to Captain Joyce—"

"Who went bananas! I thought he was hot before with Lieutenant Tully? Joyce had a fuckin' fit! He took the handset away from me—I thought he was gonna take my ear with it—told Sisto to repeat, then he ordered 'im to hold his position on top of the hill. I don't know what Sisto said, but I guess it was kinda like another 'Fuck you' 'cause Captain Joyce got even more hot, which I didn't think was possible! The captain started yellin' into the phone: 'Goddammit, Sisto, I told you to hold!' He said he wanted to talk to Rainbow Six—Major Porter—'n' then nothin'. Looked like he lost contact or Blue Six broke it off."

We were finished. I thanked Kasabian, but he remained in the chair, a dark thought clouding his face.

"Something else, Private?"

"I don't know if this is somethin' for you to put down, but..."

"Go ahead, please."

"It's just how fucked up all this is."

"I'm not sure I—"

"If Lieutenant Tully had listened to Captain Joyce—if he'd o' taken us up that hill—most of us'd be dead. But that'd be OK. That nobody woulda got in a sweat about. I mean, we wouldn't be doin' all . . . this. Doesn't that sound fucked up to you?"

"Surprised me no end he knew I had a law degree. Hell"— Andy Thom shook his head with a dumbfounded smile—"I thought the lootenant hated me."

We were sitting in a salon now being used as the hospital canteen. Makeshift counters provided coffee, sandwiches, and even hot food for the hospital staff and the ambulatory patients. We picked a plate of something called "processed turkey loaf" laid under a plasticine substance passing for gravy.

"What made you think Lieutenant Sisto hated you?" I asked.

"Well, I guess I mean I didn't think he cared all that much for any of us. I didn't think he even knew any of our names."

"You're talking about the time you were in England."

Thom nodded. "Lootenant Sisto was a real ball-buster. Out on the trainin' field you'da thought his boot wasn't happy lessen it was planted on yer ass! Then ya'd drag on back to camp 'n' if you tried to find 'im then? Like a ghost. Invisible. Only time he talked to you was when he was workin' you 'n' that was just to scream at ya. But then . . ."

"Eh?"

"He was all different when we came over."

"How so?"

"Then he was *always* there. You were on the march, Lootenant Sisto was up 'n' down the column, talkin' to you calm-like, askin' what you needed. Sometimes, well, it was like he knew you just needed to hear somebody say you were doin' fine. On the line, that's when you found he did know yer name. Anyway, after they pulled us back from the hill, we were camped for a coupla days at the division assembly area outside Rott. That was when they had the hearin' 'n' then he came to my tent. 'Andy, would ya mind helpin' me out with this?' Coulda knocked me over with a feather, Mr. Owen."

Peter Ricks joined us then, and we spent the rest of the evening comparing notes from the interviews each of us had conducted that day. As we pored over our notes and commented on our material, I caught Peter Ricks's eye and nodded at young Thom. The hardship of the rehashing was easily apparent in the tightness in the lad's voice, the pained look in his eyes, the beginning of a tremble in his hands. He'd been through it with them.

"I'm beat," Ricks said at last. "I don't know about you guys, but I need some sack time."

I agreed, saying something gratuitous about needing to be fresh for the morrow's interviews.

I don't know if Thom saw through our wee sham. In any case, he said he still had some notations to make and we started off to bed, leaving him in the canteen. In the archway leading to the corridor, I stopped and looked back. Andy Thom was not sitting with his interrogation notes and pad pencil. He stood on the other side of the blackout curtains draped across the high salon windows, losing himself in the night.

"OK, here's the hill." Technical Sergeant Juan Bonilla didn't wait for a response. He grabbed my pad of foolscap in those massive hands of his, flipped it over, yanked my pencil away, and began to sketch on the cardboard back a shape not quite sharp enough to be described as a chevron, not blunt enough to be called a crescent. "'Bout halfway up, you got these trenches alla way 'crosst a front a the hill. Now, see, the hill is got like two tops—"

"Two tops?"

"Like is high over here, 'n' high over here, 'n' in here inna middle is low." In translation: there were two crests to the hill, one on either "wing" of the chevron, with a low saddle between them.

Dominick Sisto's platoon sergeant was short, but when seated this mild deficiency disappeared and Juan Bonilla seemed massive, with an enormous barrel chest and inflated biceps that threatened to burst his olive drab blouse along the buttons and seams. His features seemed lost on the broad face of his large, squarish head. His hands, when closed, looked like ten-pound sledges and some of my previous interviewees had warned me that a poke from those thick fingers was like being prodded with a stone rod.

"So, firs' time up, is King Company onna lef', Item onna righ'?" he said, continuing his sketching. "We can't break into the trenches. They got ten yards o' wire and mines. We pull back, Porter has the Weapons Company bring the mortars in to blow holes through the wire. We try it again, make it as far as these trenches, but can't get past that. So, the way it was that last time, Porter, he gonna shoot the works, all three companies. You got King Company 'n' Love Company together onna left, Item onna right?

"Here where it's low, between the two tops, this is all rock-like, almost alla way down to the trench, so the krauts can't put no bunker or nothin' in there. So up this way, that's the only way up."

"So, the special assault detail, they were to jump off from the trenches, charge up this rocky part up into this saddle, this low part."

"Yeah."

"There were twenty of you in the detail?"

"We scrounge up twenty o' the old crowd, just 'bout the only veterans left, 'n' then me, the lieutenant 'n' his RTO, 'n' we had the major with us, Porter. So, what's that? Two dozen, right? You gotta unnerstand, it wasn't no two dozen made the run to the top. That's what we started with comin' up the hill, but we lost one onna way up, three more got wounded just from us hole up in the trench waitin' 'n' waitin' 'n' waitin' to go."

"What was the hold-up?"

Bonilla sighed in frustration. "We hadda wait for this guy from King, he was supposed to take out a machine gun closin' the door on this way up. But he's late, so we're sittin' there gettin' the shit kicked outta us. Then it's time to go.

"Ain't no place to dig in 'n' cover up once you move 'cause it's all rock." Like someone resigned to an unpleasant obligation, Bonilla sighed again, and continued: "This Major Porter, I wouldn't cross the road to piss on 'im if he was on fire. I don't 'member no time he wasn't always hangin' back at HQ. We're up in the shit, we're takin' fire, we're livin' up to our ass in mud, Porter's always someplace where it's dry 'n' he's got hot coffee. But this time, I gotta say it, he was right there. Time to go 'n' Porter gets right out in front, goes chargin' right up the hill. 'Course, once you're outta the trench, you got no place to go but back inna trench or run for the top or they gonna chop you up. Still . . .

"Lieutenant Sisto was right there with Porter, up at the front. He tells me to pick up the back end, keep 'em movin'.

We ain't that far outta the trench when the kraut mortars come down. Like I said, you out there fuckin' naked. So you just run."

"How many of you made it to the top of the hill?"

"I was too busy tryin' not to get my nuts shot off to count noses. I thought we were in better shape 'n we really was 'cause I see these other heads, only I didn't know they come up from the Item side of the hill. Ya know"—he held up one of his granite-like fingers—"Item was only supposed to fix the krauts on their side o' the hill. But these guys, they saw a hole 'n' pushed to the top. They didn't have to do that. All they gotta do is stay in that trench 'n' keep their heads down but they made the move. They oughta get wrote up nice or somethin' for that."

"I'll pass it along. How were you disposed at the top?"

"Dis-*what*?"

"Where was everybody? How were you positioned?"

"We were kinda all spread out. Like this." He flipped the pad open, tore a sheet free, and began to sketch again. He outlined the saddle: the two overlooking crests, the drop-offs to the forward and rear flanks of the hill. "OK, now all in here"—his pencil hovered above the area of the saddle—"is all holes. Mortars, artillery, it's been droppin' all day, it's nothin' up there but holes, like that hill got chicken pox. I'm last up, me 'n' some other guys we jump inna hole, first one we see, about here." He drew a small circle immediately inside the line demarcating the fall-off to the face of the hill, to the left of the median of the saddle. "Now in here, inna middle, is a bunch o' holes all together, one after another inna line almost like a trench." He sketched a series of overlapping circles from the center of the front of the saddle in a small arc almost to the middle of it. "Lieutenant Sisto and Porter, they was first up so they jump inna first hole 'n' they crawl up as far as they can go. The rest of 'em just drop inna firs' hole. Lessee, that was Makris, he was the lieutenant's RTO. Ronnie Byrd, Don Lauffer, they was in with me. 'N' Li'l Petie Wardell, 'n' Skitch Beaudrie, they was over here."

"These other two men, Wardell and Beaudrie... They were in the same position with the radio operator? With Makris? How come they didn't testify at the inquiry?"

"'Cause they never come off the hill," Bonilla answered baldly. "A guy with me, Ronnie Byrd, he never come down, 'n' some o' those Item guys. I don't know who most o' 'em were; it was a whole other company. I think mebbe one was an officer."

"Why do you think that?"

"They had a radioman with 'em. I saw his antenna. I didn't even know they were there at first, the guys from Item, or they had an officer or nothin'. See, we get up there, we all flop inna first hole we see. We was hardly up there 'n' the lieutenant calls for the radio. That's when I see the guys from Item. Lieutenant Sisto was callin' over that way, I guess, 'cause he seen the antenna and he thought that was Makris. Then Makris pipes up 'n' that's a good thing."

"Why?"

"'Cause that Item RTO, either him or the lieutenant gotta go over the top 'n' wasn't no way to do that without gettin' a kraut pill inna head. See, the kraut, he got positions awready dug here 'n' here." He indicated the two crests. "We hit the top o' the hill 'n' the krauts come into these holes 'n' then they're just pourin' shit on our heads. Thank God Makris pipes up, 'cause the lieutenant just gotta crawl along all these holes making a trench. He musta scooted along the bottom, 'cause I didn't see 'im move but next I hear him yellin' onna radio."

"Could you hear what he said?"

Bonilla gave me that same condescending grin Kasabian had. "Eh, there was a lot of fuckin' noise up there. Then Lieutenant Sisto is yellin' to us, he blows his whistle, he says, 'OK, we're buggin' out, everybody haul ass down a hill.'"

"Where was Major Porter at this time?"

"I guess he was still back the other end alla way up here. I didn't see him, but, ya know, that guy never did give many orders to us himself."

"So. You start back down the hill."

"Like I said, Lieutenant Sisto blows his whistle and we haul ass. We get back out on the rock 'n' all that kraut mortar shit come back down. I didn't stop runnin' till we hit the trenches. Then I hear the lieutenant goin', 'Where's Porter? Where is he? Where's Porter?' He says Porter was gonna cover our rear, he was supposed to be right behind the lieutenant. So . . ." A dismissing shrug. "We figger Porter just didn't make it."

"How many of you made it down?"

"I didn't get no count then. We were takin' shit that whole time. There was the guys at the hearin'—"

"You mentioned Makris."

"Yeah, 'n' some o' the guys who were with me, a coupla other guys from Item. Eleven. Three of 'em in this hospital."

He saw me ready to dismiss him.

"Ya know, this Joyce, he tries to make it sound like Lieutenant Sisto went yellow or somethin'. You put this down on your paper, huh? The lieutenant was one o' the last guys off the top 'n' I know 'cause I was the other one. 'N' when we got to the trenches, it wasn't, 'Pass the word! Everybody get your ass out!' Lieutenant Sisto, he says the kraut see us run, he comes outta his hole 'n' chew us up. So, it was a fightin' withdrawal. Slow, organized, Sisto got the squad leaders—whoever was left—Sisto got 'em checkin' for wounded. 'We ain't leavin' no-body behind,' he says. The only time we ran was when we had to cross the clearing, that firebreak, 'cause that's the only way across with all that kraut shit comin' down. 'N' even out there, the lieutenant, he looks back to see who ya need to pull back on his feet, get on somebody's ass to make sure they get across. He come inna trees on the other side carryin' a wounded man 'n' I know that for a fact 'cause he had one arm 'n' I had the other. *That* sound like a guy who just broke 'n' ran?"

The great hands flexed and I had a vision of a furious Juan Bonilla punching his way through stone walls of the Chateau d'Audran to free Dominick Sisto. "The lieutenant don't belong where they got 'im."

"Once I got up there I didn't see anything, I didn't see any-body." Paul Makris was leaning forward in his chair, elbows on knees. The nineteen-year-old had a nervous tic of running his fingers through his curly black hair, making it even more un-ruly. One of the new men picked up by the battalion during its re-fit in England, the battle of the Huertgen had been his first exposure to combat.

"So you didn't see this other sparks?"

"Other what?"

"The other radio operator."

"Other? Brother, I wasn't any kinda radio operator! The lieu-tenant's *real* operator took a pill the first time we tried to get up the hill. I don't even know I was the *second* guy to lug that thing around! The lieutenant needed a pack mule, he saw me, stuck this thing on my back, and suddenly I'm a radioman! *He* had to set all the dials and that stuff. My whole job was, like he said, stay close to him."

"But you weren't close to him on top of the hill."

"On the run up, we all got all strung out. It was a bitch and a half trying to make that run! That top part of the hill was like this"—his arm canted at a thirty-degree angle—"and I'm lugging that goddamn radio. If Big Juan—"

"Sergeant Bonilla?"

"—yeah, if he hadn't grabbed me by my belt and practically hauled me up, I never woulda made it. We got up there, Big Juan threw me in a hole, then went to herd some of the other guys up. Like I said, I got in that hole and I went right for the bottom and kissed dirt! I couldn't even tell you who else was in that hole with me! Then somebody's kicking me in the ass, telling me the lieutenant wanted me. See, there was a bunch of holes hooked up that led into where we were—"

I showed him Bonilla's sketch of the hilltop saddle.

"—yeah, like that, that's where I was."

"And Lieutenant Sisto was here at the other end of this line of adjacent holes?"

"I guess. Like I said, I don't know where *anybody* was."

"Including Major Porter."

"If he wasn't down at the bottom of that hole with me, I don't know shit from Shinola about where he was."

"So, obviously, you didn't hear what orders—if any—Major Porter might have given Lieutenant Sisto."

"The only thing I heard was a lot of shooting until I got that kick in the ass. Then somebody musta yelled out to the lieutenant I was there because then he yells back for me not to move, he'll come to me, which considering all the lead flying around I thought was awfully goddamn nice of him."

"You would've been covered if you'd moved along the line of holes, wouldn't you?"

"You'd like to think that, huh? See up here?" He turned to

Bonilla's drawing, pointing to where the Germans had dug in. "They had the high ground. They could get a lot of fire down inside a lot of those holes. That's why I was getting as deep as I could go."

"All right, then, we have Lieutenant Sisto coming back from this forward position to where you were."

"Yeah, the lieutenant grabs the handset and he's yelling at somebody on the other end."

"Do you remember what he said?"

"You're asking me like you think it was a whole conversation. All he said was 'We're coming down,' 'We're pulling out.' Something like that. I got the idea whoever he was talking to didn't agree, so then the lieutenant says that's Major Porter's orders, for us to get the hell outta there. Then the other guy said something and Sisto said he could argue about it with the major when we got down. Then we bugged out."

"How long did all this take? I mean from the time you reached the top of the hill until the time you withdrew?"

Makris drew himself erect in his chair, his dark, youthful face puzzled that he'd never considered that particular aspect of the event. "If we were up there five minutes, I'd be surprised."

"That's all? Five minutes?"

"Maybe not even. And, brother, if it'd been just five seconds, that would've been five seconds too goddamn long!"

A clatter and thump stirred me from a shallow sleep, which was all one could manage in those damnable cots. In a wedge of light through the partly open door, I saw a figure sprawled across the corridor floor where it had stumbled over our B-4 bags, packed and ready for our departure in the morning.

I knew it was Peter Ricks even before I turned and saw the

gleam of his hook, before I heard the slurred oaths directed at the offending luggage.

"What the fuck..." he grumbled, and kicked one of the nearest bags away.

Still half asleep, I rolled off the cot and was unpleasantly reminded I was not the whole creature of my dreams as I toppled off my one leg and found myself facedown on the cold parquet. I got myself onto my elbows and saw that Ricks was now sitting on the floor. He had pulled over the milk crate Thom had cadged from the mess as a means of toting about the collective mass of our query notes. He sat with the crate between his legs and began to rifle through the papers, a silly grin on his face. He extracted a fistful of scribble-covered foolscap, held it down into the light, giggled. For a moment I thought he might reach into the crate with hand and hook and toss the entire lot into the air, chortling as it fluttered down about him.

I started to pull myself across the floor, when I felt two strong hands take me by the shoulders and help me back onto my cot. "Don't worry, Mr. Owen, I got 'im."

Andy Thom padded across the wood floor clad only in his long underwear, and crouched down by Ricks. "What say we leave all that till tomorrow, Cap'n, huh? For now, let's get you into bed."

With a tired huff, Ricks let the papers drop back into the crate. Thom helped him to his feet and set him down on the cot, where the captain's head promptly dropped forward to his chest and issued a drunken snore. Thom stripped off Ricks's boots and began to disrobe him.

I wobbled to my one foot and hopped across to Ricks's cot, sitting alongside the slumped body as Thom stripped off the captain's blouse. It was at that point the corporal was confronted with the straps and buckles of Ricks's prosthetic.

"Ya think I need to take that off?" he said.

"I'll do it, Andy." I undid the straps, slipped the sleeve from Ricks's stump, and set the device softly down on the floor. I hopped back to my own cot while the corporal swung Ricks's legs onto the canvas and pulled the blankets up to his chin. He stood over the sleeping captain for a moment, looking down on him, his face invisible to me in the darkness, then he neatly rearranged our bags and quietly closed the door.

CHAPTER FIVE

Harry was waiting for us in the shelter of the arch of the chateau's main gate. "C'mon in!" he yelled over the rain, waving us toward the keep. "The MPs'll park the jeep and bring the bags in."

Andy Thom stayed behind to ensure that the paperwork made it inside intact and dry, while Ricks and I hurried through the rain after Harry. The shivery entry hall was an improvement over the outside only by virtue of being dryer. "Let's go up to my room," Harry said. "I've got a fire going."

"I see a lot more transport parked out front," Ricks noted. "Would that herald the return of Captain Courie?"

"He got back the morning you left. You probably passed him on the road."

"I wished I'd known," Ricks said. "I would've waved."

"I wished you'd known, too," Harry said. "You could've run him into a ditch."

Harry opened the door to his quarters and ushered us in.

"Grates on one's nerves, does he, eh?" I suggested.

Harry grinned wryly. "Oh, I think you'll find Courie an

absolute joy. You'll see for yourself." He closed the door behind us, beckoned us to take the seats he'd arranged by the welcoming flames in his hearth. "He's got a meet-and-greet arranged for tonight. A chance for the respectful opposition to shake hands before fighting like gentlemen."

Harry had certainly been busy in our absence. Foolscap pads covered with jotting and diagrams were scattered here and there about the room, blue-covered depositions were spread over the rumpled bed along with those damnable index cards of his.

It was an old school trick of his. He'd boil each element of a problem down to a few words jotted on a single card. He would then take his deck of cards, spread them on a tabletop, now able to see the entire issue and its component parts at a glance. Then would come the mixing and matching as he moved the cards about, hoping that—if there were enough data on the tabletop—a Gestalt moment would come, the gaps between the cards fill in, a solution present itself.

Harry had an electric ring set on a small table, warming a pot of coffee. He poured steaming mugs and distributed them before sitting with us by the fire. "How'd it go?"

"Fine," Ricks said.

Harry studied him. "You all right, Pete?"

"Sure."

"You don't look that well."

"We were all putting in long hours, Harry," I said, "and I'm afraid we've paid a price for the hospital cuisine. What was last night's offering, Peter? Some peculiarly American devising called meat loaf?"

I saw a brief flash of gratitude from Ricks. Harry grinned at the remark because he knew he was supposed to. But he looked the captain over closely again, then me, as if evaluating the validity of my story. Finally, he nodded and asked for a report on the Wiltz interviews.

"We got through everybody on the list," Ricks replied. "I don't know what the probative courtroom value of any of it is; you'll have to figure that out. But if I might offer a strategic analysis from the view of a doughfoot, let me say that if we'd fucked up like this on D-Day, I'd be boning up on my German phrasebook by now." Then he went on to explain about the curious element of the as-yet-unidentified wireless operator who'd been atop Hill 399.

"Dominick didn't say anything about a radio operator. Then again, he hasn't been saying much, period." Harry saw our quizzical looks. "It's been like pulling teeth. He doesn't want to talk about the case; he doesn't want to talk about what happened at the hill. All he *does* want to do is tell stories about the 'old days,' which, for him, is just a couple of years ago, when he was still in school." A musing pause. "I'll bring this thing about the radioman up with him, but I have a feeling Andy is heading back down to Wiltz tomorrow. I hope he doesn't mind."

"Ach, you'll not get a word of complaint out of that one, Harry," I pronounced.

"Andy's a good kid," Ricks seconded.

Harry went on to explain the program he had outlined for the coming days, ruing—as he would, many times—that Dominick Sisto had waited so long to reach out to him.

"You know, I never went into private practice," Captain Courie said. Perhaps I should say he "narrated," for even in his most innocuous conversational statements there was an air of the practiced performance to Leonard Terhune Courie. "Never interested me for some reason. Even when I was still thinking about law school...Oh, it's very necessary, don't get me wrong. I suppose on a sheer tonnage scale, most of the legal paperwork in a given year comes from that side of the fence." He sounded like a duke professing admiration of his serfs. "It's not like the district attorney's office is all glamour and headlines. Most of the work can be pretty mundane. In that respect, it's no different from Judge Advocate work. The interesting cases—like this one—that's the rarity."

Courie had laid on his gentlemen's *soiree* in the main dining hall. Joe Ryan had, naturally, been installed at the head of the table, with Courie and Lieutenant Alth seated to his right. Harry, Peter Ricks, Andy Thom, and myself sat opposite.

Despite the tone of polite conversation, the detestation between Courie and Ryan was palpable. I found this particularly ironic, as the two men had much in common. Both came from somewhat impoverished circumstances; both had pursued their profession more for the status it endowed than for the personal fulfillment it could provide; both had made rapid progress through their respective ranks as much through clever maneuvering as through accomplishment.

"Did you specialize, Colonel?" Courie asked Harry. "Family law? Contracts?"

"A little bit of everything," Harry replied.

"Good old-fashioned general practice!" Courie effused. "Good for you! You don't see much of that in the cities these days. In the cities, it's all law firms, and there's something missing in that kind of practice, some kind of *heart*. Wouldn't you agree?"

Harry shrugged. "You'd have to work in a firm to know."

"I admire that, your going it alone. I really do. Like I said, a dying breed, at least in the cities, where the serious casework goes on. Did you ever handle any criminal actions back home?"

Another shrug from Harry. "Somebody got a little too 'enthused' on the Fourth of July, had a little too much to drink, said the wrong thing, a punch got thrown . . ."

"That's the kind of business that filled my day when I was a rookie ADA. Low man on the totem pole. You know how that is, Alth." A mentor's well-meaning jibe.

"Yessir," Alth responded with dutiful good humor.

"You should know that Colonel Voss had a hell of a track record with the Judge Advocate's office," Ryan offered.

"That must have been quite a step up for you, Harry," Courie said, "from your practice to the Judge Advocate."

"I never looked at it that way."

"I wasn't aware that you'd tackled many cases, well, any as *serious* as this," Courie probed. "When you were with the Judge Advocate."

"Not many," Harry agreed. "Like you said, how often do they come by?"

Courie pushed his plate away. "There's quite a few personnel on Colonel Ryan's staff who remember you from those days."

"Fondly, I hope."

"Respectfully. And with a certain curiosity about why you left."

"Colonel Voss there is married to one of the finest ladies you could ever know," Ryan jumped in, "and he's got two little boys like something right out of an Andy Hardy movie. He was eager to get back to them. If I was as lucky as Harry is on the home front, I'd be chomping at the bit for any chance to go home."

"Is that what it was, Colonel?" Courie pressed. "Missed the family, did you?"

"Do you have a family, Captain Courie?" I asked. "Wife? Children?"

"I have a wife, Mr. Owen, and three daughters."

"And you, Lieutenant?"

"I have a girlfriend," Alth said.

"Whom, I imagine, you miss very much."

"We're going to get married when I get back."

"Then I fail to see the puzzle in Colonel Voss's return home." Now Courie turned back to Harry. "Because he came back."

"The vagaries of war, Captain," Ricks proclaimed.

"Is that what it was, Colonel Voss?" Courie demanded. "The vagaries of war?"

"Like he said," Harry replied without looking up from his plate. "Those vagaries'll get you every time."

The mess orderlies—part of the mess staff that had arrived with Courie—cleared the table and brought out servings of a freshly baked apple pie and cups of a respectable coffee.

"Mr. Owen, I want to thank you for helping out the Defense," Courie told me. "I know poor Corporal Thom must have been feeling a little overwhelmed. I think we've all had the same feeling on our first major felony case! Especially being on such a short calendar. It's a shame Lieutenant Sisto waited so long to call on you. Of course now I look at you all lined up on that side of the table and I'm feeling a bit outgunned!"

"Somehow I have the feeling you're up to the challenge, Captain," I said.

"I hate to spoil an enjoyable evening with business," Ryan announced, "but as long as we're all here..." He lit himself a cigarette and posed regally in his chair. "The jury pool and the witnesses are being transported in on the sixth—that's less than a week away—jury selection is on the seventh, and we should have this circus up and running on the eighth. While I appreciate Captain Courie's reasons for selecting this"—eyes wryly wandering about the vaulted ceiling—"'establishment' for the proceeding, putting the accused, counsel, witnesses, and jury under one roof is asking for trouble. Gentlemen, if a mistrial comes out of this, it's going to be because of a procedural error, not because of a stupid fuck-up. So, when our 'guests' arrive, this'll be the drill:

"The jury pool—and afterwards the finalized panel—will be sequestered in rooms on the top floor of the main buildings, and witnesses will have rooms over in the east wing. That should keep some distance between them. Both areas will be secured by MPs. I'll work up a schedule of separate mess calls for evening chow; breakfast and lunch they'll get in their quarters, which is where you gentlemen will be taking *all* your meals; *three* different mess calls gets to be a bit much.

"There will be no socializing with the jurors or the witnesses. No informal chats. Everything is witnessed and on the record. Everybody understand?" A pause for nods and yessirs. "Anybody else have anything?"

"Just a mention, really," Courie said. "Colonel Voss, if you haven't discussed it with your client yet, at some time you might want to consider a plea. My practice is to deal with that as early as possible. The closer we get to the trial date, the less likely I'm inclined to negotiate."

"I'll keep that in mind, Captain," Harry said placidly.

"Well, the lieutenant and I have a little work to do," Courie said, rising. Alth, still working on his apple pie, dropped his fork and stood. "I found a lovely bottle of schnapps in Wiltz. I'll have it brought out. Please feel free. Colonel Voss, if there's anything we can do to help—"

"Stationery. A good clerk-typist. Stenographer. Transcriptionist. A typewriter."

"I'll have Alth see to the stationery. I'm afraid we thought to bring only the one typist—"

"And the one typewriter?" Harry inquired, all open-faced innocence.

"He's in the middle of some documentation for me. As soon as I can, I'll make him available."

Harry nodded his thanks, there were some polite bows, then Courie exited with Alth in tow.

After the door had closed behind the two men, Andy Thom sighed. "I don't want to sound *too* disrespectful of a superior officer . . . but if that guy dished out any more horseshit, we'da needed snorkels."

When I came atop the castle wall that night, the rain had ceased but the sky was still heavily mottled with clouds.

"Watch your step," came a caution from the gloom. Dominick Sisto. "Me and Benjie, we almost busted our asses comin' up here."

Even in the fleeting moonlight, I could see the glitter of filigrees of ice where the rain had trickled down the stone battlement and frozen, and iced-over puddles on the walk.

"I wish we had more time," I mused. "Lieutenant, I must ask, why in God's name did you wait so long to bring Harry in?"

"Hell, Mr. O, if it had been up to me, I wouldn't've brought him in at all!" Even in the dark I think he could sense my consternation. "I told you before, Mr. O, the signor is like family to me. I didn't want to drag him into this. I'm embarrassed as hell he even *knows* about this! I haven't even written to anybody back home about—I wasn't going to call him in. The Irishman—"

"Colonel Ryan?"

"He pushed me to do it. He told me Andy Thom was in way over his head, wasn't really fair to the kid to throw something this heavy on his back, then he said how would I like my people back home finding out about this when it shows up in the papers—you OK, Mr. O? Something wrong?"

"Hmm? Oh, no, it's just that, naturally, I'd assumed—well, no matter, eh?"

It's never as simple as it should be: the mantra of my profession. *Never.*

On the afternoon of Wednesday, 6 December, two deuce-and-a-halves and several jeeps and staff cars arrived in convoy at the chateau to deposit the jury pool and witnesses. Harry, Peter Ricks, and I were in Dominick Sisto's room when the column of vehicles drew up to the front gate. Through the guarded oak door of Sisto's tower room we could hear the ado in the halls as the MPs led the potential jurors this way, the witnesses that way, hear them all marveling or joking over their new surroundings.

Harry and Peter Ricks were poring over the list of veniremen Courie had provided.

"What are we going for?" Ricks asked.

Harry squinted at the typed list as if he hoped to perceive some not readily apparent clue as to the perfect choices and a means of executing them. "I want to stay away from officers with too much staff time. My preference is to get as many men with combat command experience on the panel as possible. Hopefully, they'll identify more with Dominick than somebody who's spent the war at a desk. I also want to avoid somebody on Cota's staff who might think giving the general Dominick's head is the kind of thing that'll move him up the ladder. I see here where the general has been magnanimous enough to include a few possibilities from Dominick's regiment. If we could get some of them on the panel, there might be some sympathy there. Maybe. I hope. Anybody have a line on Cota?"

"I picked up a word here and there about him in Wiltz," Ricks said. "Tough . . . but fair. Fair . . . but tough. Which side of the scale getting the weight depends on who you talk to. Cota's a fighting general; maybe that gets the lieutenant something."

"How much help do you think we can expect from the Irishman?" Sisto asked Harry. If the former had seemed distracted and disinterested in the pre-trial sessions, he was now keenly attentive. He sat leaning sharply forward, attuned to every word.

"Ryan? I wish I could tell you. I know this much; Joe won't do anything overt unless he's got good legal cover."

"You hear anything from Andy?" Sisto asked.

Harry nodded. "He sent word with one of the people who came in today. He's still coming up dry. He wanted to know if I wanted him back for the trial."

"You should bring that poor kid home, Signor. He'll run himself ragged talking to everybody in Europe if you let him."

"He comes home when there's no place left to look."

"What about a plea?" Ricks asked. "Alth buttonholed me coming out of the can this morning and said Courie told him to remind us the clock's ticking down on a plea."

Harry didn't reply; he just shook his head noncommittally. "Dominick, a note on wardrobe. Do you have a set of Class A's?"

"Lost half my gear up in the Huertgen. All I've got is my field dress."

"Do you have a tie? Spruce it up a bit, but go in there looking like a GI. I don't ever want them to forget who you are." Harry tossed the jury pool roster on the floor, slipped off his reading spectacles, and rubbed his eyes, then turned to me. "One last thing, and this is for you, Eddie: When we go in there, I don't want you sitting at the defense table."

"Oh?" I tried not to sound offended.

"I know everybody knows you've been working for us, but tomorrow I need for you to be off in the bleachers. Strictly a spectator. It'll be better for you."

I did a fairly good job of maintaining my usual aplomb. "As you wish, m'luhd."

At that, Harry scooped up his materials, pulled himself out of his chair with a grunt. "That's it, then. I've got some stuff to noodle through, but I want all of you to get some rest. Everybody needs to be on their toes tomorrow; that's when the knives come out."

The chapel was one of the smaller chambers of the chateau, yet with its bare stone walls and floor, and lofty, steeply peaked roof, hardly intimate. Like the rest of the chateau, it had been thoroughly scavenged, left denuded but for the marble-topped altar. Three folding tables had been laid end to end across the raised altar dais with seats along the far side for seven. At a small table to the left of the jury panel, on the main floor of the chapel, would sit the legal member of the court—the judge. Between the judge's bench and the jury panel, angled toward what would be the "well" of the court, was the chair for testifying witnesses. To the right of the judge was a table at which were positioned one Military Policeman to act as bailiff, and another as court clerk and evidence custodian. On the other side of the room, near the far end of the jury panel's table, the court recorder would sit. Opposite the judge's bench was a table for the Trial Judge Advocate and another table sat across from the panel for the Defense. A row of chairs was set along the rear wall of the chapel. Two Military Policemen were posted outside the double doors of the chapel, two more stationed inside, and two more by the fireplace along one wall. The last's role was to periodically stoke the blaze from a stack of firewood providing the only heat to mitigate the bone-aching damp chill.

I entered the chapel just before nine on the morning of 7 December. The jury panel tables stood empty. Harry and Peter Ricks sat next to each other in their Class A dress uniforms, while Dominick Sisto sat at the end, field trousers tucked into leggings and combat boots, his windcheater drawn over his field blouse, the only token of formality being the olive drab tie Harry had loaned him. Arrayed before Harry were those annoying little index cards of his. Courie and Alth, also in their Class A's, sat at the other table. I looked about for a place to sit, saw only the chairs along the rear of the chapel, and parked myself in one of them.

I had just settled in the chair when the doors swung open and one of the Military Policemen barked: "Ten-hut!"

The uniformed men at both tables rose as Joe Ryan entered. He was followed by a staff sergeant toting his stenographer's recorder and its flimsy little stand.

"Have a seat, everybody," Ryan called out. He tossed his briefcase on his chair before parking himself rather informally atop the table serving as his judge's bench. Ryan was a showman, and here he was in his element.

To the stenographer: "Sergeant, you let me know when you're ready." Then to the men at the tables: "As soon as Sergeant Barham has his magic box set up, we'll get started, but before we do, I want to set a few ground rules. Once the jury pool is brought in, everything is by the book. You all know the protocols, and that's when you'll have the opportunity to beat your drums. But for this morning, I want to expedite through this pre-trial stuff, so let's leave the Clarence Darrow songs and dances at the door. I'll live with a certain amount of informality to keep things moving as long as you keep all the punches above the waist and don't take too much of the Court's time blowing hot air. Are we all together on this? Fine. Jesus . . . does it get any warmer than this? Why don't you guys throw another stump in the furnace before we all freeze to death." Addressing the members of the Court: "Considering we're a little short on creature comforts here, I'll tell you what I'm going to tell the jury: If you feel the need to alter the proper wardrobe for the sake of preventing frostbite, feel free. I see that Lieutenant Sisto already has a head start on the rest of us in that regard, so bully for him. How're you doing, Sarge? All set?" Ryan leaned back, reached into his briefcase, and produced a trial gavel. When he brought it down on the table, it produced a sharp, high-court-sounding *crack!* "Captain Courie, want to start the ball rolling?"

The captain rose and, in a loud, declarative voice, announced: "This general court-martial is convened by order of Major General Norman Cota, commanding general, 28th Division, on this date, 7 December 1944, to hear evidence in the matter of the U.S. Army vs. Second Lieutenant Dominick V. Sisto, 3rd Battalion, 103rd Regiment, temporarily attached to the 28th Division. A copy of the convening order has been furnished to the legal member, both counsel, the accused, and the court reporter for inclusion in the trial record. The charges have been properly referred to this court-martial for trial and were served on the accused 15 November 1944.

"Sitting as legal member for this proceeding is Colonel Joseph P. Ryan, Judge Advocate General's Bureau, Liège. Acting as Trial Judge Advocate is Captain Leonard T. Courie, Judge Advocate's etc. Sitting as Assistant Trial Judge Advocate is First Lieutenant Wilson R. Alth etc. For the Defense, Lieutenant Colonel Harold J. Voss and Assistant Counsel Captain Peter T. Ricks."

"Let us not forget Staff Sergeant Lyle Barham, court recorder." Ryan nodded graciously in the stenographer's direction. "Captain Courie, would you mind swearing the good sergeant in?"

Barham rose at his station as Courie approached him with a Bible. Knowing the program, Barham placed his right hand on the Bible and raised his left without any instruction from Courie.

"Sergeant, do you swear that you will faithfully perform the duties of reporter to this Court? So help you God?"

"I do."

"Nicely done!" Ryan applauded broadly as Courie hurried back to his station. "Captain, I can't help but notice that pensive look on your face. Is there some grave, serious, or absolutely necessary reason you want to interrupt the nice, smooth flow of these proceedings so soon?"

Courie cleared his throat as he rose. "Sir, the Trial Judge Advocate notes there is a spectator in the room."

"And it is that keen eye for detail that makes for an effective Trial Judge Advocate," Ryan quipped. "I presume that's a lead-up to asking for a closed court?"

"Yes, Sir."

Ah, I thought, *he only wants people to know he's won, not how he's won.*

"To which I'm sure Colonel Voss is about to raise an objection," Ryan was saying.

Harry slipped on his reading spectacles, scooped up his notepad, and rose. He cut a very unimpressive figure in the well of the court. He looked up only occasionally from his notes, whether they were on his pad or in the deck of cards he shuffled through in an almost confused fashion. His stubby form moved about the well in an idle, aimless way, as if not quite sure where he wanted to stand.

I could not see much of his face, but I caught a glimpse of lips pursed in thought, saw one of his stubby fingers moving down the foolscap page, searching out a particular item. "I'd be curious as to the captain's offered grounds," he now said quietly. "The accused has a right to a public trial under the Sixth Amendment, and the public has a right to access under the First Amendment." He seemed to sense—without looking up from his page—Courie's rising to his feet again to declare his grounds. Harry held up his free hand.

"Acceptable reasons for exclusion include overcrowding or unruliness among the spectators." Harry flicked his eyes away from his notes to scan the near-empty vault of the chapel. "I don't anticipate that as a problem."

"Spectators may be excluded for security reasons," Courie countered. "Testimony will involve description of military operations in the Huertgen, including losses. Besides the intelligence value of such information, a public revelation of high casualty counts could provide aid and comfort to the enemy, and maybe even propaganda fodder. In case Colonel Voss has forgotten, one of his own defense team—Mr. Owen back there—is a professional journalist, which virtually guarantees just such a public revelation."

"Mr. Owen is not here in a professional capacity," Harry

replied. "He was generous enough to help out the Defense on some routine Q & A's. As the Trial Judge Advocate knows, there was a time problem in preparing for this case, and the only reason the Defense is ready to proceed at this time is because of Mr. Owen's assistance. That said, it should also be pointed out that Mr. Owen is not part of the defense team. He has never participated in—or even sat in on—any session involving confidential communication between attorney and client. Captain Ricks and Lieutenant Sisto can attest to this. Mr. Owen's knowledge of the case is, to date, not much more than a layman could have picked up from the public record."

I suddenly felt ashamed at bridling at having been shut out of the meetings. Harry'd expected this all along.

"Mr. Owen is still a newspaperman," Courie parried stubbornly. "What's to say something won't arise during the course of the trial that professionally compels him to file a story?"

"Nothing," Harry responded. "That's what he does. However, in the matter of security, Lieutenant Sisto's unit has been out of the Huertgen for over a month. I don't foresee any testimony that will deal with the current disposition of any other unit in the Huertgen, or even with the current disposition of any element of the 28th Division. And I'm pretty sure the Germans are well aware of the bloody nose they gave the 28th. However, if we reach a point in the trial where testimony is presented that might be considered militarily sensitive, the court can always be cleared at that time.

"I would add that Mr. Owen has assured me that should he feel some professional obligation to file a story on some aspect of this trial, he will abide by the rules of the press pool and have the story vetted by the military censor before sending it on. He has even promised to go one step further and have the story vetted by the Judge Advocate's office *before* submitting it to the censor." Harry looked up at me over the tops of his half-moon glasses. "I'm correct in my understanding, Mr. Owen?"

I pushed myself upright on my one good leg and held up my right hand. "I do so swear!" I proclaimed.

"Captain," Ryan said, turning to Courie, "Colonel Voss seems to have thrown a pretty heavy blanket over your call for a closed court. Unless you can find some holes in it...Good," he declared, ending the round before Courie could reply. "Captain, as long as you're up, I believe that, according to the manual, you have a question for me at this time?"

"Yes, Sir. Are you aware of any matter that may be a ground for challenge against you to sit as the legal member of this court?"

"Can't think of one, Captain, thank you for asking."

"The government has no challenge for cause against the legal member," Courie said, clearly uncomfortable with Ryan's flippancy.

"Defense has no challenge for cause," Harry declared.

"For the record," Ryan said, "I would like to remind the accused of what I'm sure his counsel have already told him regarding his rights. Along with whatever protections normally afforded in a civilian criminal court, you have the right, Lieutenant, to make an unsworn statement before this court without subjecting yourself to cross-examination; you will be provided with a typed record of these proceedings; in the event of a conviction, your case will automatically be appealed. Do you understand these rights?"

"Yessir," Sisto acknowledged.

"Captain Courie, would you be so kind as to arraign the accused?"

When Courie had concluded reviewing the charges, Ryan turned back to Sisto. This time, the flighty attitude was gone.

"All right, Lieutenant. How do you plead? Before you make your plea, I advise you and your counsel that any motions to dismiss or for some kind of relief should be made at this time. And I see from those neat blue-bound papers your counsel is waving at me that Colonel Voss is ready to do just that. Give it a whack, Colonel."

Harry rose. "I ask the Court to pardon the appearance of these documents. As the Court knows, we've been a little short on logistics and we've had to make do."

"I think you should've taken typing as an elective instead of woodshop." Ryan was squinting at the pages spurtled with erasures and typeovers.

Courie seemed less offended by the bad typing than the content. "Motion to *dismiss?*"

"Lieutenant Sisto has been improperly charged," Harry said.

"It would be an understatement to say you have our rapt attention," Ryan told Harry. "Aren't *you* rapt, Captain Courie? Go ahead, Colonel Voss. While I peruse this, would you mind giving the *Reader's Digest* condensed version of this for the sake of getting the brawling started?"

"Sir, I grant Captain Courie has a whole lot more experience in civilian criminal court than I do. I don't know what the statutes in his particular jurisdiction back home may be regarding duplicative charges and multiplicity—"

"Colonel Voss," Ryan interrupted, "would you mind skipping on down to the good stuff?"

"Sorry, Sir. The *Manual of Courts-Martial* specifically prohibits using one transaction as the basis for multiple charges. A given specification cannot allege more than one offense, nor can multiple specifications be used to justify a multiplication of charges when there is only one transaction at issue. Nor can a lesser component of a charge be broken out for a separate charge. For example, if you charge a man for disobeying an order, the offense of disrespect for a superior officer, or conduct unbecoming, would be considered lesser included offenses and not separate transactions. You either charge a man with disobedience, or you charge him with disrespect. The Judge Advocate's charge sheet is just a half-dozen different ways of rearranging the same specifications to say the same thing. On certain charges presented by the Trial Judge Advocate, the specification doesn't even meet the standard for supporting the charge."

"Dare I guess you have something specific in mind?" Ryan queried.

"Pending your decision on my motion to dismiss, I submit a motion to dismiss the first charge of the indictment: desertion in the face of the enemy." Harry produced another set of papers.

Courie shot to his feet. "Sir, can I get in a word? My door has been open all week to hear a negotiated plea from the Defense—"

"I'm not negotiating anything, Captain," Harry interrupted. "You don't even have a *prima facie* case to be made for desertion. I know you haven't been in uniform very long, so let me help you out:

"The standard for Article 58 defines desertion as"—Harry fumbled his way to the appropriate index card—"as 'an officer or enlisted man who absents himself, without authority, from the military service with *intent not to return thereto*.' I'd also like to call your attention to"—another card—"Article 28—Certain Acts to Constitute Desertion—which also defines desertion as quitting of one's post or proper duties without leave and with 'intent to absent himself *permanently* therefrom.'

"Being new to the war, the Trial Judge Advocate may not be

aware that to lose a position to the enemy *does not constitute desertion of a post.*" No acidic tongue could have twisted the blade of irony as deftly as Harry's flat dissertation. "In no way did Lieutenant Sisto abandon his proper duty, which was responsibility for his men, not even temporarily. The withdrawal from the hilltop was as organized as circumstances allowed, and Lieutenant Sisto was among the last to leave. Once he returned to the trench line, he organized the battalion's withdrawal from the hill. I emphasize, again, the word '*organized.*' It was a fighting withdrawal which, by definition, means the lieutenant and his men remained engaged with the enemy until contact was broken. The few officers and non-coms left—including Lieutenant Sisto—not only helped shepherd the men off Hill 399 but led trailing details to search for wounded so none would be left behind.

"The Defense concedes that what is at issue is whether or not the lieutenant had the authority to order the withdrawals, but there is not one element of the act that can justify a charge of desertion."

"I have news for both of you," Ryan said. "Since nobody has yet sat in the witness chair to tell us what Lieutenant Sisto may have done or not done, you're both arguing facts not yet in evidence. Still . . . How about it, Captain? Future testimony aside, the indication is . . ." He shook his head.

Captain Courie was frustrated. He was puzzled. He was curious. And he was respectfully appreciative. He was just then realizing how seriously he'd underestimated this "good old-fashioned general practice" barrister. Yet, he was not one to simply step back and cede a fight. "The Trial Judge Advocate would prefer to err on the side of caution on such a serious charge and let a jury decide the merits."

"By that reasoning, Captain, you could charge Lieutenant

Sisto with contributing to the delinquency of a minor and wait for the jury to figure it out, but that's not how it works," Ryan said. "I'm going to err on the side of caution, too, unless you have a more substantive point to make. Ah, I see that Colonel Voss isn't quite done with us. Another motion, Colonel? I can't wait to see what's in this one!"

"Again," Harry began, "pending your decision on my first motion, this is a motion to dismiss the fourth charge of the indictment: Making a mutiny."

"Same grounds?" Ryan asked. "Doesn't make the standard?"

I watched Ryan's face. *He's enjoying himself.* It was more than simply glorying in his central role. Then I understood.

You cunning old bastard. You cunning cunning old bastard!

Harry held out a hand to Peter Ricks, who handed him a thick-set volume. Harry flipped the book open. "If I might quote from the annotation from the most recent revision of *The Articles of War*—'Mutiny may be defined as concerted insubordination, or concerted opposition, defiance of, or resistance to, lawful military authority by two or more persons subject to such authority, with the intent to usurp, subvert, or override such authority or neutralize it for the time being—'"

"He took over the battalion!" Courie declared.

Harry held up a finger for patience, his eyes never leaving his text as he continued reading: "'*Concerted refusal to obey an unlawful order is not mutiny.*'" He closed the book. "Lieutenant Sisto did not usurp Captain Joyce's command. As the officer in tactical command—"

"He wasn't even senior on the hill!" Courie jumped in.

"True. But the only officer on the hill at that time senior to Lieutenant Sisto was Lieutenant DeCrane commanding Item Company on the eastern slope of the hill. Lieutenant DeCrane recognized that it was on Lieutenant Sisto's side of the hill where the main assault was taking place, and where the bulk of the battalion's combat personnel were committed. Consequently, DeCrane willingly ceded tactical command to Sisto. There's a statement from Lieutenant DeCrane to that effect attached to the motion papers. My understanding is that under Army doctrine this represented an acceptable exercise of initiative under the demands of a battlefield situation.

"Lieutenant Sisto issued no orders or statements indicating he'd assumed command of the battalion from Captain Joyce. His orders dealt only with the immediate tactical situation of the battalion. When Lieutenant Sisto returned to the woods where Captain Joyce had moved his CP, Lieutenant Sisto was already on his way to report to Captain Joyce, when he was informed he was to be brought to the captain. Lieutenant Sisto obeyed that instruction, reported to Captain Joyce, and though he initially argued with Captain Joyce for placing him under arrest, the lieutenant subordinated himself to the captain's command.

"It is the Defense's contention that Lieutenant Sisto's actions concerning the withdrawal of the battalion from Hill 399 constituted a momentary exercise of the on-scene field commander's discretion. The Trial Judge Advocate is certainly free to contest that judgment, but the alleged disobedience therein does not constitute an act of mutiny."

"Think, perhaps, you were a bit overzealous applying the article?" Ryan asked Courie.

"Is there *any* charge in the indictment the Defense Counsel thinks is justified?" Courie asked Harry.

There came, again, the look over the top of Harry's spectacles. "Well, Captain, as the Defense Counsel, I'd be obligated to respond to that with a big *Hell no!* Colonel Ryan, I request a ruling on my motion to dismiss."

Ryan was sitting slumped atop his judge's table, Harry's motions rolled up in one hand, his head bent. Joe Ryan was not one to whom I usually ascribed the sense of judicious contemplation, but he was still for a judiciously long time. Finally: "Taken on an individual basis, there's a *prima facie* case to support one or another of the charges of the indictment, so the motion to dismiss is denied, but the charges of desertion and mutiny are quashed on the basis of insufficiency of the evidence."

At least he's gotten the gallows out of the game, I appraised. With the two most serious charges eliminated.

"Captain Courie," Ryan went on, "the case goes on but not with this indictment. You're going to have to decide what *exactly* you think the accused has done, and say it *once*. Understand? Captain?"

Courie and Alth had their heads together, were flipping through their own notes.

"Oh, Captain Courie!" Ryan hailed.

Courie stood. "Two charges, Sir."

"Two?" This from an unhappy Harry.

It was now Courie's turn to show his muscle. "The withdrawal from the top of the hill, and withdrawing the battalion from the hill, are two separate transactions. The Judge Advocate will amend the indictment against Lieutenant Sisto to a charge of disobeying a direct order and a charge of threatening the good order and discipline of his unit."

"Move to sever," Harry declared. "Separate transactions, Sir. A rendering on either could prejudice judgment of the accompanying charge."

"Sir," Courie argued, "the proximity issue alone justifies joinder: two criminal transactions by the same individual separated by only minutes and a few yards. Beyond that, the second act is a compounding transaction arising directly from the first. Lieutenant Sisto had been ordered to hold the top of the hill. He disobeyed, and removed himself and the assault detail. Once he'd returned to the trenches, the lieutenant made no attempt to contact Captain Joyce. As the Defense even points out, these are two separate actions justifying separate charges, but they are both transactions of disobedience to the same order."

As I'd expected, Ryan—looking to conclude the whole affair as soon as possible—raised his head and declared, "Move to sever is denied." He glanced at his watch. "Guys, I'm proud of you. We got through this in record time. I'm going to declare a recess until eleven hundred hours. That should give the Trial Judge Advocate ample time to amend the indictment and provide it to the Court and to opposing counsel before we reconvene. If the Defense has any problem with the amended indictment, objection can be raised at that time. Otherwise, we'll go straight into jury selection. Colonel Voss, pending that amended indictment, can I get a plea from your client to the charges of disobeying a direct order from a superior officer and threatening the good order and discipline, etc.?"

"Sir, I'd like to request a continuance at this time. Defense has not been given adequate time—"

"Denied."

The request was strictly pro forma. No one—including, as far as I could tell, Harry—expected anything but the summary denial.

"Now," said Ryan cheerfully, "how about a plea?"

Harry and Ricks stood with Dominick Sisto. "Not guilty, Sir," Sisto announced.

"Very little suspense there," Ryan observed. "Before we wrap this up, is there anything else?"

"Approach, Sir," Courie requested. Ryan waved Harry and Courie to the judge's bench.

At Ryan's table, the three officers bowed their heads together; there were some low mumbles that quickly grew louder and more heated. Sitting at the back of the chapel, the mumblings remained indistinct to me, but I could see Peter Ricks and Dominick Sisto twitch, then Ricks's head swinging vehemently in the negative. He removed his hook from the table, self-consciously laying it in his lap and covering it with his good hand. Sisto set a hand on Ricks's shoulder: in support, in comfort.

Ryan was forced to raise his voice to quiet the overlapping arguing going on before him, and at last I heard something clearly: "Hold on a second, both of you! Colonel Voss, I take it you're making an objection?"

"To hell with an objection!" Harry made no attempt to lower his voice. "That's the most offensive thing I've ever heard! Would it be acceptable to the Trial Judge Advocate if the captain hid it under the table? Maybe we should have him strip off his decorations, too, because maybe that'll 'elicit unfair sympathy,' too!"

"Now he's being ridiculous!" Courie retorted.

"Maybe," Ryan said with a shrug, "but you were there first."

"I could always throw a blanket over myself," deadpanned Ricks.

"That's enough, Captain," Ryan warned.

"Or maybe we could have a continuance while the captain puts in some time on the line and gets his share of battle souvenirs to even out—"

"Enough!" Ryan snapped. "No brawls!"

Harry walked slowly to the defense table and stood over Peter Ricks. I couldn't hear what he said, saw only the cold glare on his face, one of his stubby fingers jabbing the tabletop for emphasis as Ricks's head began to sink. Then, when Harry was finished, he stepped back and Peter Ricks stood. "My apologies to the Court, and to you, Captain Courie. My remarks were uncalled-for."

Ryan nodded, satisfied, then turned balefully to Courie. "Anything else, Captain? And before you open your mouth this time, you better be damned sure it's an issue of honest-to-God due process! Nothing? Good. Gentlemen, we're back at eleven hundred." He brought the gavel down with finality, extracted a bundle of papers from his briefcase, and strode off down the aisle and out the chapel doors.

I hurried after him. "Colonel! A moment, please! Just a quick question if you—"

"Christ, can't this wait ten minutes? Can't you see I am moving with great urgency? Oh, no! Don't tell me you *already* want to break the peace? If you *have* to file a story, Owen—"

"Just an observation, Colonel. Or, rather, an analysis."

"Owen, I'm on my way to the little boys' room, OK? The last few minutes I was in that icebox I've been trying not to bust a gut! So I'd appreciate it if you got to the point posthaste."

I noticed the "documents" he'd taken with him. It was a copy of *Photoplay* magazine. "What better way to dispatch a troublesome heir presumptive than with the cruel story of his failure? And what better way to spread that story than through seven respected witnesses, a jury panel selected by an equally respected divisional commander. A publicly attested-to defeat!"

"I think I overdid it at breakfast," Ryan grumbled. "You're either going to have to talk faster or shorter."

"Colonel, I've never seen a better navigator of the shoals and reefs in what are commonly referred to as 'the halls of power.' You've developed self-interest to a fine art."

"Your idea of a compliment needs a little work, buster."

"So I could never understand how someone so adept let

Courie get his head on this case. All his sneaking off to discuss the matter with the general, the change of venue and so forth . . . without tipping you to it?"

"I'm getting old, Owen. Reflexes aren't what they used to be. Neither is bowel control. Do you mind?"

He tried to push by, but I kept in front of him. "Someone with Courie's naked ambition, and you the perceptive sly boots you are . . . you must have been on your guard against this blighter from the day he appeared on your doorstep. One sniff of him and you must've known he was after your job."

"It's not like I'm looking forward to putting my delicate cheeks on one of these freezing toilet seats, but I've *really* got to take a crap—"

"Dominick Sisto didn't call for Harry until *you* coaxed him into it. Sisto didn't want Harry here; *you* did. Harry is what they call in your Western films 'a hired gun,' eh? You brought him in to slap Courie down for you. Courie suffers a public professional debasement, but *your* hands stay clean. You knew Harry wouldn't come for a dirty business like that if you asked him, so you held up the plight of poor Dominick Sisto—"

Ryan held up a finger to stop me. "Harry is always telling me how smart you are! But I'll be damned if I see it. Don't convince yourself I don't care about Dominick. And Harry—it would've broken your heart to see the way he'd buried himself in some outhouse in Scotland. But, yes, I *do* want to see that little prick Courie get slapped down. A good deed, Owen"—a flash of his perfect white teeth—"can serve many masters. And you're wrong if you've got the idea Harry doesn't know what's going on. You're *not* very bright, are you? Don't you think Dominick told him what the scoop was the first time he sat with Harry?"

"If that's true, why in God's name he didn't turn on his heel and tell you to piss off I'll never know."

"Because Harry's better than you. And he's better than me. Look, Owen. I haven't always been a good friend to that fat little s.o.b., but I'm still his *best* friend. He came for Dominick. He stayed for *both* of us. Now, if you'll excuse me"—he waved the *Photoplay*—"there are matters of great import that require my attention," and the loo door slammed in my face.

When the trial reconvened, fifteen officers ranging in rank from second lieutenant to lieutenant colonel were seated in the row of chairs along the rear of the chapel.

There was one other change to the scene. Harry and Peter Ricks were no longer in their dress uniforms, but were clad—as was Dominick Sisto—in field kit.

I don't know how the distinction played to the jury panel, but evidently Leonard Courie and his tag-along Alth seemed to give it some credence. At least I assumed so from the glares they focused at the defense table. I'm sure it did nothing to alleviate their concern to see that many of the officers in the jury pool—particularly the junior ranks—were similarly attired.

For this session, Ryan was properly seated behind his little table, wearing an appropriately dignified mien. He rapped his gavel, and Courie arose to address the veniremen. After some introductory remarks, he read the new, abbreviated charge sheet. "The accused and the following persons named in the convening orders are present," he said, then listed the names of the members of the jury pool, ending with "The Trial Judge Advocate is ready to proceed with the trial in the case of the U.S. vs. Second Lieutenant Dominick V. Sisto, U.S. Army, who is present."

"The members will now be sworn," Ryan ordered.

"All rise!" the MP/bailiff snapped, and the row of officers stood to attention.

"Do each of you swear," Courie addressed them, "that you will answer truthfully the questions concerning whether you should serve as a member of this court-martial?"

There was a chorus of "I do"s in response, and Ryan ordered them seated once more. "The court-martial is now assembled." Ryan had the bailiff read seven names from a clipboard and requested each man take a seat at the jury tables. "Gentlemen, I will ask you some general questions before letting the lawyers loose on you. I would like the officers who have not yet been called to pay attention as well in case any of them end up being called to sit. That'll save us a lot of repetition." He repeated the charges and specifications of the indictment. He asked if, prior to being assigned to the case, any of them was acquainted with any member of the Court or any of the witnesses scheduled to testify. He ended by asking if any of the potential jurors were acquainted with Dominick Sisto. Two lieutenants raised their hands. Both served in the 103rd Regiment, they explained, the same regiment that contained Sisto's battalion. Neither was personally acquainted with the lieutenant but both knew of him.

"Do either of you gentlemen think this would prejudice your ability to render a fair and impartial judgment in this case?"

Both said no.

"Can any member of the panel think of any reason he would be unable to render a fair and impartial judgment in this case?"

To a man, they shook their heads.

"Well, then, gentlemen, gird your loins, because I am releasing the hounds! Captain Courie, commence firing."

Courie took a stand in front of one of the lieutenants. "Lieutenant Mills—"

"Millis, Sir," the freckle-faced lad said shyly.

"Sorry, Lieutenant. Lieutenant Millis, you say you're in the same regiment as the accused?"

"Yes, Sir, I'm in the 1st Battalion of the 103. The lieutenant, he's with the 3rd Battalion."

"You told Colonel Ryan that you had no personal acquaintance with the lieutenant?"

"No, Sir. I just know of him by name."

"In what context?"

"What, Sir?"

"Why would a lieutenant in the 1st Battalion hear anybody discussing a lieutenant in the 3rd Battalion? How many other people in the 3rd did you hear about?"

"I dunno offhand. I just remember hearing about Sisto, Lieutenant Sisto."

"Again, Lieutenant Millis: how did you come to hear about the lieutenant?"

"I think a lot of fellas in the regiment heard about him."

"Why was that?"

"Well, you know, we heard about him getting decorated back in Italy, and then him getting his bars on a battlefield commission. I mean, that's the hard way, right? You'd hear about that."

"So, before you were even called to be a member of the jury pool, you had a highly favorable opinion of the lieutenant."

Ryan held up a hand for Millis not to answer. "Colonel Voss, an objection?"

Harry had busied himself with his index cards. "Hmm? Oh, no, Sir, thank you."

Ryan looked disappointed. "You heard the question?"

"Hmm? Oh, yes, Sir, I think the Trial Judge Advocate is doing a hell of a job. No objection."

From the knitted brows on Courie's face I could see he shared Ryan's puzzlement, if not his disappointment. "In that case, Colonel Ryan, the Trial Judge Advocate challenges Lieutenant Millis for cause."

"It's a little thin, Captain," Ryan cautioned.

"As Defense Counsel keeps reminding me, I haven't been in the military very long. But I have been in long enough to understand the idea of unit *esprit*. I believe I have a reasonable cause to suspect bias."

"Colonel Voss?"

"No objection, Sir." Harry sounded a little snappish at Ryan's constant pestering.

Ryan thanked Lieutenant Millis for his service to the Court, warned him against discussing the case with anyone until the issue was resolved, then had the bailiff call a replacement.

Courie took the floor again. "Sir, at this time the Trial Judge Advocate would like to exercise its peremptory challenge." The target this time was the other lieutenant from the 103rd Regiment.

"Anything from you, Colonel Voss?" Ryan called.

Harry spent a moment studying his index cards, selected one from the table, and rose from his chair with a grunt. "Lieutenant Colonel Stanislas Pietrowski," he read from the card.

"Right here, Colonel." Pietrowski was a bull-necked, gruff-voiced bloke, thick about the middle in a way that served to give him an intimidating bulk.

"Colonel Pietrowski, you said you were on General Cota's staff?"

"That's my boss, yep." Pietrowski's small, hard eyes peered out of the broad, fleshy face, wary of the lawyerly trick.

"Have you been with the general's staff long?"

"Ever since he was given command of the division."

"That would be the 28th Division."

"Yep."

"So you were not on the staff of the 28th before General Cota took command?"

"We came into the division together."

"Were you assigned to the 28th?"

"Nope. The general requested me."

"Why was that?"

A pause. "We knew each other before."

"From where?"

Reluctantly. "I'd been with the old Blue and Gray."

"The Blue and Gray?"

"The 29th Division. General Cota had been the assistant division commander of the 29th. I was a major on the divisional staff then."

"So you two know each other quite a while?"

"We came overseas with the 29th."

"Then, when General Cota was given his own division, he requested your assignment to his staff, promoted you to lieutenant colonel . . . The general obviously thinks quite highly of you, Colonel Pietrowski. Do you return his regard?"

"I think General Cota is a helluva commander, if that's what you're asking."

"That's what I was asking. Colonel, when General Cota assigned you to the jury pool for this proceeding, did he give you any instructions?"

"The general said there'd probably be a lot of lawyer crap getting thrown around."

"Right on the money, I'd say. The general say anything else?"

"He said, 'Get up there and get it done!'"

"That's all?"

"Well, he used a lot of descriptive language I'm leaving out."

"He expressed no opinion on the charges? Or the accused? Or how he hoped the trial would come out?"

Firm: "No!"

Harry nodded, moved his finger to his head for a small, careful scratch.

He paused so long, Ryan was compelled to speak up: "Colonel Voss! Are you done?"

"Hmm? Oh, yes, Sir." He started for his seat, then, almost as an afterthought: "Colonel, the Defense finds the jury acceptable."

I don't think there was a person whose jaw didn't drop at least a little, including Ryan's, especially Courie's, and particularly the firm mandible of Lieutenant Colonel Stanislas Pietrowski.

Ryan shook his head, as if he hadn't quite heard correctly. "I'm sorry, Colonel Voss, did you say—"

"I said the jury is acceptable." Carefully and clearly.

"You have no further questions for Colonel Pietrowski?"

"No, Sir, we find the colonel acceptable. The jury panel now sitting is acceptable to the Defense."

Ryan shook his head again, then turned to Courie, who was staring toward Harry as if he could somehow peer inside that gray-templed vessel and understand what in the bloody hell he was about. "Captain Courie," Ryan called, "you're up."

Courie stood, his mouth cocked, but then he froze. His mouth slowly closed, and there was an unhappy nod of understanding that dawned on me nearly at the same instant.

Tough but fair; fair but tough. That was how Ricks had described Norm Cota.

For those of you unacquainted with the finer points of the American Army's court-martial system, allow me to point out that jurors are not selected at random, as is the case with civilian trials; they are selected by the convening authority—in this case General Cota. Harry was reasoning that a panel picked by Cota would reflect the general's own sentiments, more or less. Fiddling about with the membership of the panel might inch the jury in one direction or another, but it would never change substantially. That being the case, Harry had let it fall to Courie to appear to be the conniving legal manipulator, to show himself distrustful of Cota's choices, to doubt the honesty and fairness of good fighting men.

And now Courie, seeing he'd been outmaneuvered, could only refrain from making a bad situation worse: "Colonel Ryan, the Trial Judge Advocate finds the panel acceptable."

"Gentlemen, it looks like we're closing early today. The members of the jury pool who have not been called, you are dismissed with the Court's thanks. You are reminded not to discuss the affairs of this proceeding with anyone when you return to your units. The panel will stand, the members will raise their right hands. Captain Courie, would you please administer the oath to the members of the panel?"

Courie held up his own right hand, announced the names of the seven panel members, then stated: "You do swear that you will well and truly try and determine, according to the evidence, the matter now before you, between the United States of America and the person to be tried, and that you will duly administer justice without partiality, favor, or affection, according to the provisions of the rules and articles for the government of the armies of the United States, and if any doubt should arise, not explained by said Articles then, accustom of war in like cases; and you do further swear that you will not divulge the findings or sentence of the Court until they shall be published by the proper authority or duly announced by the Court, except to the Trial Judge Advocate and Assistant Trial Judge Advocate; neither will you disclose or discover the vote or opinion of any particular member of the court-martial upon a challenge or upon the findings or sentence, unless required to give evidence thereof as a witness by a court of justice in due course of law. So help you God."

All seven so swore. Ryan then informed Lieutenant Colonel Pietrowski that as senior ranking member of the panel he would hold the post of President of the Court. Courie then provided Pietrowski with a typed sheet containing the oath he was to administer to the prosecutors:

"You, Captain Leonard Courie, and Lieutenant Wilson Alth, do so swear that you will faithfully and impartially perform the duties of a trial judge advocate, and will not divulge the findings or sentence of the Court to any but the proper authority until they shall be duly disclosed. So help you God."

From each: "I do."

Thus ended the first day.

CHAPTER SIX

★

Leonard Courie took his moment. He stood at his table, straightened the bottom of his jacket, moved to the center of the well of the makeshift courtroom. He stood with his feet slightly apart, his hands clasped behind his back, and then he bowed his head, as if to gather his thoughts.

A log popped amidst the crackling in the fireplace. The stained glass of the chapel windows carried the fluttering shadows of the falling snow, grown heavy since the previous night. One might have thought Courie was taking a moment of prayer before beginning.

"Sirs,"—his head rose—"this is actually a rather simple case. Simple, because the facts are clear. Captain Whitcomb Joyce, in his role as acting commanding officer of the 3rd Battalion, 103rd Infantry Regiment, gave a clear and direct order to one of his subordinates: Lieutenant Dominick Sisto. And the lieutenant refused. He *disobeyed* that order. And then he compounded his disobedience by assuming command of elements of the 3rd Battalion engaged with the enemy and withdrawing them from battle against the known intent of his commander. Simple. An order was given. The lieutenant said, 'No. I will not obey.'

"You will hear testimony as to how the 3rd Battalion was engaged in a bitter fight for a vital objective: a German-held hill serving as a key observation post in the Huertgen Forest. You will hear how, as the battalion had finally begun to penetrate the German defenses, Lieutenant Sisto's refusal to follow Captain Joyce's order to hold his position forfeited the battle to the enemy."

He took another pause, again bowing his head. Then he shook it, as if some unexpected thought had taken hold and amazed him. "To truly appreciate the gravity of the lieutenant's offense, you must understand that the orders to take this objective originated not with the command of the 103rd Regiment; not with General Norman Cota's headquarters of the 28th Division to which the 103rd was attached. The order had come directly from Major General Leonard Gerow's V Corps headquarters in Eupen. It was not just Captain Joyce's authority that was refused, but Lieutenant Sisto's act was a de facto flaunting of the authority of each layer of command up to V Corps."

Ryan harrumphed. "Captain Courie, whatever moral underpinnings you may want the panel to take into account is an issue for closing argument. You know what an opening statement is for, and that's not it. The issue of law concerns only the officer making the charge and the defendant."

"I hear no objection from opposing counsel," Courie noted.

"Colonel Voss?" Ryan turned to the defense table. "Any objection to the Trial Judge Advocate's opening remarks?"

"Hmm? No, Sir. None."

Ryan sighed resignedly and nodded for Courie to continue. The captain began to pace, enhancing the drama as he inch-by-inch closed with the opposition, his voice growing slightly louder, slightly harder.

"Like you, I am interested to hear how Lieutenant Sisto's actions will be explained. I can give you some insight. His counsel will attempt to confuse the case with side issues. How do I know this? Because, as I said to you earlier, this case is simple...and undisputed. On November seventh, at a critical point in the battle for Hill 399, Captain Joyce issued an order in the execution of a command from Corps headquarters: this the Defense cannot dispute because this is a fact! And Lieutenant Sisto heard that order and refused to obey it: this, too, they cannot dispute because *this is a fact!*"

I must say, it was so deftly done—no broad emoting, no heavy-handed crescendos—that it took great will on my part not to rise and render up a wry but appropriate round of applause.

To Dominick Sisto's credit, it should be noted that his eyes held Courie's; the young lieutenant never flinched or looked away.

And Harry?

One would have thought him deaf. From the beginning of Courie's statement, he had busied himself with his note cards. Occasionally, he would lean rearward to confer with Peter Ricks behind the attentive Sisto's back. He seemed so oblivious to Courie's performance that he actually appeared taken by surprise when Joe Ryan called for his opening statement.

"Waive opening statement, Sir."

Joe Ryan frowned. "Do you intend to make your statement at a later time?"

This time Harry said it slowly, as if to a confused child. "Defense—waives—opening—statement, Sir."

Ryan topped his shrug with an I-hope-you-know-what-you're-doing look. "Captain Courie, please call your first witness."

"The Prosecution calls Brigadier General Thomas Kerry."

Thomas Boyington Kerry so perfectly fit his rank and station, one would have thought him imagined into existence by Army chieftains. He wore his forty-seven years lightly, had managed to keep his rough good looks, his lithe figure, and firm, determined stride. His full head of black hair was regally colored with gray at the temples. His Class A's hung on him as naturally as a bowler and pin-striped pants on a Parliamentarian.

Kerry's record was equally well kempt. Freshly graduated from West Point, he'd served with "Black Jack" Pershing in Mexico, as respectable a measure of distinction as was possible on the high-spirited if fruitless pursuit of Pancho Villa, then earned his captaincy with the AEF in France during the First Great War. He'd come into the Second Great War a member of that elite cadre who was therefore blooded and proven, and thus carried himself with enviable assurance.

He stood before the witness chair as Courie approached him with a Bible. "General, would you please raise your right hand and place your left on the Bible. Do you affirm that the evidence you shall give in the case now in hearing shall be the truth, the whole truth, and nothing but the truth, so help you God?"

"I do."

"Sir, please be seated and state your name, rank, and current post or assignment."

Kerry sat, crossed his legs neatly at the knees, his peaked cap tucked in his lap. "General Thomas Kerry, assistant division commander for the 37th Infantry Division." The voice: deep, sonorous, aristocratic Virginia still tingeing the syllables.

Courie returned the Bible to his table, took a manila folder proffered by Lieutenant Alth, and positioned himself to Kerry's outside so as not to obstruct the panel's view.

"General Kerry, the 103rd Regiment is normally a component of the 37th Division?"

"Yes."

"How did it come to be in the Huertgen attached to General Cota's 28th Division?"

"We had been in England for a rest and re-fit, had been since the end of August. In October, General Breen—"

"The commanding general of the 37th?"

"Yes, General Breen informed me that the division had been alerted for a partial deployment to the Continent. The general explained that even though the division had yet to reach its authorized strength, the manpower needs at the front had grown to the point that we had been ordered to transport whatever elements of the division had filled out their Table of Organization. The idea was to commit to getting the rifle companies up to strength as our priority—that was what was needed most over here—and then as each regiment filled in, ship that regiment over and deploy it where needed. The headquarters, artillery, and other support elements would fill in last. When they were ready and shipped over, the division would be reintegrated. Our first regiment came over in October and was attached to XIX Corps in their northeastward push toward the Rhine. The 103 shipped over the following month and was attached to General Cota's division."

"And your role in all this, Sir?"

"Essentially, my job was to keep tabs on the deployment and condition of the regiments, and do whatever was necessary on this end to ease the final reintegration of the division."

"As the assistant division commander, I imagine you had a

working relationship with the commanding officer of the 103rd?"

"Henry Bright, Colonel Bright, naturally."

"And the battalion commanders?"

"I had actually been the regimental commander of the 103rd before I was promoted to assistant division commander last August, so yes, I knew the three battalion commanders quite well."

"Based on what you knew of Colonel Bright and the three battalion commanders, even though the regiment was no longer under your auspices, so to speak, you were confident in the ability of the regiment's senior officers?"

"Very, yes."

"And in your dealings with General Cota—"

"An admirable officer."

"So, then, all told, the regiment was in capable hands."

"Yes."

"Thank you, General. No further questions." Courie gave a slight, polite nod to the general and withdrew to his table. Evidently, he expected little from the cross-examination of an officer whose testimony was simply to fulfill a legal formality: put the 103rd at the place specified in the indictment.

Harry took some time shuffling his damnable note cards into some sort of order—enough time that Ryan needed to call him twice to take to his feet—before he rose and shambled toward the general. He never looked at the general or the jury panel. As he had in the earlier session, he seemed to wander restlessly about the well as he scrutinized his cards.

"General Kerry. You said the 37th Division was in England for a rest and re-fit?"

"Yes."

"What was it the division needed to rest and re-fit from?"

Courie was so engrossed in his next folder that it had almost got by him, and would have had not Alth elbowed him and quickly whispered an alert in his ear. "Objection, Sir. Irrelevant."

Harry looked up over his reading spectacles, and I could swear his look of surprise at Courie's objection was a bit of performance of his own. He turned about to bring that same look to bear on Ryan. "I don't know what the Judge Advocate is objecting to, Sir. He brought up the re-fit on direct."

"Indeed he did," Ryan agreed. "Overruled. Proceed, Colonel Voss."

"Thank you, Sir. General, this re-fit—"

Kerry required no further prompting. "The division was pretty well worn down."

"From?"

"Combat, of course."

"Where had the division been engaged, Sir?"

"Italy."

"How long had the 37th been in Italy, Sir?"

"From the beginning. We had participated in the landings at Salerno."

Harry closed his eyes in thought. "OK, let's see. Pardon me, General, but math's not my strong point. That would've been September last year, then you said up until August . . ."

Kerry smiled tolerantly. "Eleven months, Colonel."

"Thank you. So, eleven months in action?"

"Not constantly, of course. There were times when we rotated into a reserve position, or were even brought off the line for a time—"

"But the division *was* deployed in Italy for eleven months."

"Yes."

"Objection," said Courie. "Granting the re-fit was mentioned in direct, I still fail to see the relevance of any of this."

Harry's responding recitation sounded matter-of-fact: "The Judge Advocate is obligated to place the unit at the scene. In doing so, he backtracked the unit to England. I'm just following that same line a little further along."

Ryan considered a moment, and then said, "Not too much further, I trust." It was a nudge to move on quickly. "Overruled."

Harry shuffled his cards. "So, General, the division would come off the line at times, periodically take on reinforcements, I would guess, then go back into action."

"Like any other outfit."

"Sure. So why was the 37th finally pulled out of Italy?"

"Considering the condition the division was in at that time, none of us were looking a gift horse in the mouth, as they say."

"Understandable. Sir, did you have any sense of why—"

"Objection." Not wary: firmly obstructive now. "Calls for speculation."

Harry never looked up from his cards. "Does the Prosecution doubt an assistant division commander's competence to provide an informed response?"

Courie's reaction was a demanding look toward Ryan.

Ryan shrugged with feigned helplessness. "Sorry, Captain, but I would think General Kerry's position ample qualification. Overruled. General, you may answer."

"General Breen and I both felt that considering how deep our needs were in the way of both personnel and matériel, the powers-that-be were not going to make that kind of investment in a division on 'The Boot.' The Continent had become the priority by that time and the resources we required were not going to be given to a division in Italy unless—"

"It would be to put it into action on the Continent."

"Yes."

"The division was that depleted?"

"I would say the average replacement percentage in the rifle companies at that time was about one third. That was an average, mind you. A few were in better shape, while there were a few that couldn't muster a platoon's worth of troops."

Courie now rose with undisguised impatience. "Colonel Ryan—"

Ryan held up a hand to halt him. "Colonel Voss, could we conclude this inspection tour of the Italian front?"

Harry nodded. "General, are you personally acquainted with Lieutenant Sisto?"

A nod and a smile in Sisto's direction. "Yes, I am."

"I've never served in an infantry division, Sir, so if I seem uninformed, well, you understand. Isn't it odd that an assistant division commander—or even a regimental CO for that matter—would know the name of each rifle platoon leader?"

"I don't."

"But you know Lieutenant Sisto, Sir?"

"When I was the 103's CO, I had the privilege of signing off on a recommendation from the lieutenant's battalion commander—"

"Who was?"

"At the time, Conrad Porter. Major Porter had recommended Lieutenant Sisto—he was a buck sergeant then—for a Silver Star. I recall he received a Purple Heart for the same action."

"As the 103rd's CO, would you have been well acquainted with Major Porter?"

"Yes."

"A good officer?"

"A competent officer."

For the first time, Harry looked up from his cards. "Now, see, Sir, I said 'good,' and you said 'competent.' Did you have reservations about the major?"

"Objection." Courie was beginning to sound tired from having to so regularly rouse himself. "If he'd asked the general if he had reservations about Lieutenant Sisto, that would be relevant. What do the general's feelings about Major Porter have to do with the case?"

"Colonel Ryan, from the moment Captain Joyce accused Lieutenant Sisto at the scene, through the initial inquiry, to this date, it has been the lieutenant's contention that he refused to obey Captain Joyce's order because it contravened the last order he'd been given by Major Porter." Harry's voice was hard and firm.

"An order to which there are no witnesses," Courie pointed out.

"Which doesn't mean it wasn't given."

"Or that it *was* given!"

"Fellas." Ryan held his hands up. "I'm as big a fan of Ping-Pong as the next guy, but that's enough."

"Defense should be able to introduce testimony from which the panel, as experienced Army officers, can deduce the likelihood that such an order could have been given," Harry said. "This means illustrating both the circumstances surrounding the event, as well as the competency and character of Major Porter."

"We don't need to try a dead man." Courie said it caustically. "We have a live one and *he's* the one named in the indictment."

"By the same token, the Prosecution is free to challenge that likelihood by introducing testimony substantiating the opposite point."

Ryan fondled his gavel thoughtfully. "So I understand: you

each have an allegation crucial to your respective cases that you both admit neither of you can prove. The Defense says the order was given. The Prosecution says it wasn't. Captain Courie, would you agree to a stipulation that Major Porter *could* have given such an order?"

Courie had been shaking his head even before Ryan had finished speaking. "Not a chance, Sir."

"I didn't think so. Because both the defense and prosecution cases turn on this point, and since you're both equally unable to prove it as fact, I'm going to allow both of you latitude in this regard."

"I strongly object," Courie said.

"I thought you might," Ryan replied. "Noted. You may answer, General."

Kerry had followed it all quite closely and he did not look appetized at having to answer the question. I had seen the same face on doctors and barristers asked to comment on the performance of their brother practitioners. I suppose it's the secret fear of possibly having it done to themselves someday.

"I will say this," Kerry began. "That there are all kinds of officers. A few are exceptional, a few are substandard. The majority have a . . . tolerable mix of strengths and weaknesses. Major Porter seemed to have a good handle on his battalion. He was not an exceptional officer, but his regimental commander, Colonel Bright, never reported to me any occasion that would have had me consider relieving Major Porter."

"General"—Harry flipped to another card—"I get an impression that there was a kind of reorganization when the division shipped to England. That's when you were promoted—that's what you said, right?—and then Colonel Bright was moved up to take over the 103rd. Of the three battalion commanders in the regiment, why him?"

The general smiled slyly. "I think what you're asking is why not Porter?"

Harry smiled guiltily. "Maybe."

"Let me put it this way. There are men who can handle a company with little problem, but give them a battalion and they're lost. Not every regimental commander has what it takes to command a division. I believe that battalion command was the highest level of Major Porter's competence."

I could see Harry weighing pressing the issue, but I saw his eyes flick ever so slightly toward Courie. "Let's move on to the action in the Huertgen."

I could swear I heard a sigh of relief from Courie's table.

"General," continued Harry, "you were not involved in any direct command way with the 103rd's operations in the Huertgen, correct? As you indicated, this was General Cota's show."

"Yes, that's correct. When the regiment was attached to his division, it passed under his command."

"Were you party to any of the briefings or planning sessions or even private discussions with General Cota or any member of his staff regarding the 103rd's operations?"

"Quite a few. As a courtesy, and because he was aware I needed to know the status of the regiment with the idea of the eventual reintegration of my own division, General Cota kept me apprised at each step of the way. I was actually present at his headquarters in Rott before the 103 arrived, and knew of his plans for the regiment then. I remained there through the date of the regiment's extraction."

"This attack on Hill 399 ... Who planned the operation? The regiment? Major Porter's battalion staff? General Cota's staff?"

"Tactical decisions devolved down to the lowest unit the closer one got to the front line. Regimental staff conferred on the movement from Rott into the field, and then as each battalion deployed, they generally tended to themselves. But this was only in a tactical regard. The overall plan for the operation came from Corps."

"V Corps headquarters in Eupen."

"Yes."

"Did General Cota ever express an opinion of that operational plan to you?"

"Objection!" Courie had grown peeved. "Hearsay! Colonel Ryan, he's doing it again! Where are we going with this? Now he's dragging V Corps into this!"

Harry pushed his reading glasses up his bulbous nose. "Actually, the Judge Advocate dragged them into this."

"Excuse me?" Courie said.

"Yes, Colonel," Ryan said, "you want to run that by me, too?"

Harry turned to the card and quoted: "'To truly appreciate the gravity of the lieutenant's offense, you must understand that the orders to take this objective originated not with the command of the 103rd Regiment; not with General Norman Cota's headquarters of the 28th Division to which the 103rd was attached. The order had come directly from Major General Leonard Gerow's V Corps headquarters in Eupen. It was not just Captain Joyce's authority that was refused, but Lieutenant Sisto's act was a de facto flaunting of the authority of each layer of command up to V Corps.'"

For the first time, I saw that lovely, polished poise of Leonard Courie's fall away. His jaw dropped. He hadn't quite shaken off his daze when he turned to Ryan: "Sir, opening and closing statements are not testimony."

"No," agreed Harry, cheerfully. "But the Prosecution flat-out told this jury that since the attack order came from Corps, Lieutenant Sisto's disobedience was as much an act of disobedience against Corps as against Captain Joyce. It may not be testimony, but it is the stated framework of the Judge Advocate's case. He can't announce to the jury, 'This is the heart of my case,' and then not allow the Defense to challenge it."

I have no doubt it particularly grated Courie it was his own words that had come back to haunt him, but I must also say that I thought I perceived a trace of admiration in his countenance. He held up his hands in surrender and reseated himself as Ryan nodded at Harry to proceed.

"General Cota was not happy with the plan for the attack on 399," Kerry recounted. "As he continued to receive instructions from Corps over the course of the attack, he became increasingly unhappy."

"Sir, did General Cota ever say where he felt Corps was falling short?"

"The general was quite plain—and colorful"—here a knowing grin from the President of the Court, Colonel Pietrowski "—in saying that he felt the planners at Corps had no idea at all of the specific conditions in which our men were fighting. He also made it clear to me that he'd felt similarly since before the 103 had arrived; that this had been the state of affairs since his division had been committed."

"Did you concur with his . . . assessment?"

"I'm afraid I did."

"Thank you, General. No further questions."

Courie was on his feet. "Colonel Ryan, redirect?"

"Proceed, Captain."

"General Kerry, let's try something shocking and actually get back to the point of this trial: Lieutenant Sisto. Along with his award of a Silver Star, are you aware that he had, during his time in Italy, been the subject of a summary court-martial proceeding? And convicted?"

"Objection. Prior bad acts are not admissible."

Ryan sustained and bade Courie to continue.

"On this particular action, when Captain Joyce first pressed charges and the incident was referred up to divisional headquarters, did General Cota consult with you on the affair?"

"As the 103 was attached to General Cota's command, he didn't have to. But, as a courtesy, he kept me informed."

"Did the general discuss the result of the initial investigation with you?"

"As I said, this was his show. It was not a discussion in the sense that I was invited to contribute, but he did make me aware of the investigation and findings."

"Based on those findings, did you have any reason to disagree with General Cota's decision to convene a court-martial?"

"Objection," said Harry. "The Prosecution's treating an indictment as if it's an indication of guilt and he's trying to give it substance by eliciting an opinion from the witness."

"Sustained. I want to remind you gentlemen that the simple fact of an indictment is not proof in any way of guilt. It only indicates the assumption that the questions raised therein can best be resolved at trial."

There being nothing further, General Kerry was dismissed. As he passed the defense table on his way to the chapel aisle, I saw him again glance in Sisto's direction. The lieutenant shrugged as if to say "I'm sorry, too."

Colonel Henry Gareth Bright seemed the very antithesis of General Kerry. Where the general had worn his years lightly, Bright's age—some ten years short of Kerry's—weighed heavily . . . literally. Short, round, nearly bald but for a fringe of mousy-brown hair, he looked more clerk than commander with his bland, bespectacled face. Where Kerry's voice was deep and authoritative, and the general spoke with a fluid erudition, Bright's was a flat New Englander's drone. But the two men were closer than their respective forms would suggest.

Bright had been a middling student at West Point (class of '29), and in the peacetime Army had presented himself as nothing more than a "competent" and "unexceptional" officer. It would not be until the war years that his true colors came through. By the time the Americans had rolled into Rome he had earned command of a battalion, and during the division's reorganization in England he had been Kerry's handpicked successor to command the 103rd Regiment. Now he sat in the witness chair, his small eyes focused on Leonard Courie in unemotional study.

After some prerequisite preliminary questions, Courie pointed to a large map of the battle area on an easel set where both the panel and the prosecution and defense tables could have a clear view. "Sir, do you recognize this map?"

"Looks to be our operational area in the Huertgen."

"If it pleases the Court, I'd like to enter this map as Prosecution Exhibit A."

"No objection," Harry stated.

"Sir," Courie continued, "would you please explain to the Court what your instructions were once you arrived at the divisional assembly area in Rott?"

"General Kerry was already there, said the regimental staff and battalion COs were all wanted at General Cota's HQ. A briefing. General wanted one battalion at Rott, divisional reserve. Another—"

"Please show us on the map, Colonel?"

Bright tapped a spot along the western side of the map with

a knuckle. "Rott. General had elements of his 212th Regiment strung out along here holding Vossenack, Kommerscheidt, some were in a hard fight for Schmidt. He wanted a battalion to reinforce the 212th's fight for Schmidt. The last battalion was supposed to take Hill 399."

"Sir, how did you determine which battalions were to take on which assignment?"

"Second Battalion had the highest percentage of new men and officers, so they went into the reserve. Overall, 3rd Battalion had the strongest officer cadre, lot of Italy vets. Figured them a good bet for the hill."

"Colonel, do you know Lieutenant Sisto?"

"Yup."

"During the time your unit saw service in Sicily, were you not, at one time, informed that Lieutenant Sisto—then a sergeant, a squad leader—had been convicted in a summary court-martial convened by his commanding officer?"

"Objection. Once again, prior criminal acts are not relevant."

"Sir," Courie addressed Ryan, "along with other testimony that will be introduced by later witnesses, this goes to demonstrate a pattern of behavior."

An unhappy sigh from Ryan. "On that basis, I'll overrule. Colonel Bright, you may answer."

"Yup. I was informed."

"Do you recall the formal violation?"

"'Formal'? Not specifically."

Courie referred to his folder: "Dominick Sisto was charged with violation of Article 96 of *The Articles of War*, which covers—and I quote—'. . . all disorders and neglects to the prejudice of good order and military discipline, all conduct of a nature to bring discredit upon the military service.' Consequent to his conviction, he lost his stripes and was fined."

"Knew about it. I was CO of another battalion at the time. Not really my business."

"Colonel, you passed along Captain Joyce's charge to General Cota? And were consulted on the initial inquiry?"

"Yeah to both."

"You signed off on the captain's charge?"

"Based on what Joyce told me, didn't see how I couldn't."

"You had no reason to disagree with Captain Joyce?"

"Not based on what he told me."

"And when the formal inquiry recommended charges, you made no argument against them?"

"No reason to."

"Thank you, Colonel. Your witness, Colonel Voss."

Harry sat back in his seat, studying not the witness but his note cards, a finger tapping one of his front teeth. He scooped up his cards and rose.

This time Courie's attention was not elsewhere. He leaned forward in his chair, rapt at Harry's performance.

"Colonel, if you don't mind, let's work backwards here. Captain Courie likes to keep mentioning that nobody had a beef with the inquiry or Captain Joyce's charge. You said you had no reason to disagree with either. Is that the same thing as agreeing with them?"

"Nope. Man makes a charge, I only know what he says, let's go to trial and settle it."

"Well, there's that American sense of fair play in action! Good for you, Colonel! Now, let's go back to that Article 96 business. For the benefit of those on the panel new to military service, I would ask the legal officer to instruct the panel on the nature of a summary court and on Article 96."

Ryan drew himself a bit more erect for his oration: "A summary court-martial is called to hear the lowest order of military offenses. If any of you are familiar with civilian courts, a loose equivalent would be charges of a misdemeanor nature.

"As for Article 96, the article is listed in *The Articles of War* simply as 'General Article' and is normally applied against non-capital crimes not serious enough to warrant application of a specific article."

"I'm sure the younger officers on the panel appreciate this dissertation on *The Articles of War*," remarked an acerbic Courie, "but does Colonel Voss have a question?"

"Matter of fact, I do, Captain, thanks for reminding me. Colonel Bright, you couldn't recall the charge. Do you recall the action that drew the charge?"

For the first time, the flinty New Englander showed a sign of emotion, the barest flicker of an upward curl of his lips. "That I *do* recall. Understand, that Italian countryside, nearly every one of those farmhouses had a stash of wine. Drank it like milk. Lieutenant Sisto and his squad, I guess you could say they 'liberated' one of those stashes."

"They got drunk."

"As lords."

"The whole squad, Sir?"

"Don't recall any took the pledge."

"And the battalion was not in a rear area at the time, correct, Sir?"

"They were in an operational area but in reserve."

"So this was a serious breach of military discipline."

"Technically."

"I gather you didn't view it as such."

"It'd been a long crawl up from Salerno, they were just blowing off some steam. I didn't disagree with the way Porter took action on it, but I wouldn't've pressed it so hard."

"Still, Colonel, Dominick Sisto was entrusted with the well-being of a squad and then he slipped like this? How did he wind up a platoon leader?"

"You need to ask somebody from 3rd Battalion."

"But the paperwork crossed your desk, didn't it?"

"Porter nominated Sisto for a battlefield commission even before we shipped to England."

"The same man who busted Sisto from sergeant to private put him up for his lieutenancy? As Major Porter's senior, you were comfortable with this?"

"Like I said, I wouldn't've pressed that wine-cellar thing like Porter did."

"Who nominated Lieutenant Sisto for his Silver Star?"

"Porter. I added my own recommendation."

"So you know the circumstances surrounding the award?"

"January '43, we were operating in conjunction with the 36th Division, trying to make crossings of the Rapido River. Never got more than a few toeholds across. Finally, order comes down to pull back across the river. Part of Lieutenant Sisto's platoon—including the fellow who was platoon leader at the time—they were holding a position a little too far out in front and never got the pull-out order. Nobody realized they were still there until the rest of the unit was back across the Rapido. Sisto and the platoon sergeant, guy named Bonilla, put a party together, recrossed the river, fought their way through, and got as many of them back as they could."

"General Kerry mentioned a Purple Heart as well."

"Sisto got himself nicked. Refused to be evacuated. Made them treat him at the field hospital and came limping back to his unit."

"Well, now, Sir, we're back where the good captain began with you. Your regiment arrived at Rott. Where did you set your headquarters?"

"Rott. General Cota said the situation at the front was 'fluid and confused.' His words. Constant problems with communications. He recommended I headquarter in Rott until—and if—the situation stabilized and I could move up closer to where my battalions were engaged."

"Sir, you said one of your battalions was assigned to the division reserve."

"Yup. Chose the 2nd Battalion."

"Colonel, didn't your 2nd Battalion constitute the *entire* divisional reserve? There was no unit from the 28th being held back, was there?"

"By the time we got there, General Cota was even putting the division clerks into the line. The well was dry."

"And how long had the 28th been in the Huertgen by then?"

"I think a little under two weeks."

Harry nodded gravely, giving the fact time to sink in on the panel. Most of those officers had been in the Huertgen: the sinking didn't take long.

"Colonel, how much time were you given to plan operations for your battalions?" Harry asked.

"General gave us our briefing and then it was 'go!' Immediate. Went back to the assembly area and put them on the march. The first assault on 399 was scheduled for the following morning."

"By whose order? General Cota's?"

"He passed the order to us. From V Corps."

"Objection," Courie said, "unless Colonel Bright has personal knowledge of an order from V Corps."

"Sustained."

"What advance intelligence were you given regarding the objective, Colonel?"

"They told us where it was. I don't think they knew anything else."

"No estimate of enemy strength? Disposition? Defenses?"

"V Corps G-2 estimate said kraut defenses had probably already been sapped by the constant fighting in that sector. Same reasoning, figured they'd be short on munitions."

"Did you make any reconnaissance of the objective?"

"Couldn't. It was dark when the 3rd took its demarcation position. Porter communicated a request for a delay, I passed it to General Cota, the general passed it to Corps, they said no."

"Colonel Bright, besides the lack of advance information on the enemy's disposition on Hill 399, did you have any other problems with the operation? Any concerns?"

"Besides my taking an outfit straight from transport to an all-night march into unreconnoitered positions to fight against an objective we know nothing about?" Bright's pinched frown transmitted bitter anger. "For one thing, the 28th was in such bad shape, I didn't know how much longer they were going to hold. Told my battalion commanders, 'Carry out your orders, but if you get a pull-back order, you run like hell.' Didn't want any of my people left hanging. Where's the Main Line of Resistance? There isn't one. General Cota's 212th was holding Vossenack and Kommerscheidt, they had a toe in Schmidt but there was no line! Kraut infiltration patrols are wandering around these woods. Snipers. Mine the roads after the engineers clear them.

"The big problem." On the map, Bright traced a wriggling line from Rott to Schmidt. "The Main Supply Route. The only supply route: the Kall River Trail. Places where the mud was over your knees. Barely wide enough for vehicles. Take a turn a little wide and off you go. Truck sticks in the mud, tank throws a track, Germans leave some mines, the road is dammed. Trying to reinforce and supply an attack all the way up here"—his knuckle again rapped Hill 399—"from here"—a tap on Rott—"along this route? Like trying to feed an elephant through a straw."

"Thank you, Colonel. Let's talk about the Hill 399 operation. You said—let's see, I have it written down here somewhere—ah! Yes, you said you picked the 3rd Battalion for the attack on Hill 399 because 'overall' it had the best officer cadre of your three battalions."

"Lot of the officers and non-coms had experience in Italy."

"Was Major Porter the best of your three battalion commanders?"

Bright paused. I sensed—even in this forthright fellow—the same strain of hesitation I'd perceived in General Kerry, the reluctance to turn on a brother officer.

"Colonel Bright?"

"Porter had his strong points and his weak points. Like most of us."

"Indeed. The rest of the officers in the battalion aside, was Major Porter the best possible choice for leading the operation?"

Bright frowned. "Don't know that there would've been any good choice for that operation."

Harry, ever patient, still hovering about, looking for a hole in the wall: "Let me put it to you another way: What was your overall opinion of Major Porter? You said he had his strengths and weaknesses? What exactly were they?"

"Porter had the organizational end of handling the battalion down. Been assigned to Fort Benning before the war. Benning's the Army's main infantry training school; he seemed to have a good understanding of tactics and maneuver."

"You can skip to the 'but' now, Colonel."

"Two serious deficiencies. One, headquarters-bound. The foxhole grapevine had him yellow, but I didn't see that. Porter was just a headquarters officer. Thought that's where you do it from."

"And the other deficiency?"

"Knew how to dig in and hole up. Got nervous on the offensive. Best way I could put it, he was so busy trying not to *lose* a battle, he didn't do enough to *win* it."

"But you were still comfortable with him in command?"

Bright shrugged philosophically. "It's a big army. Needs a lot of officers. They're not all going to be gems. Terms of men and matériel, Italy's number two. The Continent gets first choice. Any officer looking to make a name bucks for the Continent, because you know that's the real show."

"So, you were wary of what kind of officer you'd get as a replacement for—"

"If Porter had been out-and-out bad..." A small gesture of the thumb indicating he would've been sacked. "Otherwise, better the devil you know."

"That in mind, you still felt the 3rd Battalion was a good choice for the hill?"

"My money was on the subordinate officers. Some of the best."

"Did you know Captain Joyce?"

"Knew all the battalion execs."

"Your opinion of him?"

Courie stood. "Colonel Voss, I almost hate to object and ruin your streak."

Harry smiled wickedly. "I doubt that."

"Captain Courie," Ryan said, "when you write your memoirs, you can insert all the witty repartee. If you have an objection..."

"Sir, the Defense has dragged almost everybody conceivable into this case: Major Porter, V Corps—"

"Well, we don't want the good captain to feel left out," Harry quipped.

"Colonel Voss," Ryan said, "that little reprimand I just gave Captain Courie? That goes for you, too. As for your objection, Captain, Captain Joyce pressed the charge against Lieutenant Sisto; obviously there's the issue of credibility. And as his direct senior, certainly Colonel Bright is competent to render an opinion. Overruled."

Harry again turned to Bright.

"Joyce was plainly more aggressive," the regimental commander said. "Sometimes I worried maybe too much. But they—Porter and Joyce—balanced each other out. That's why I could live with Porter's shortcomings."

"Redirect," Courie announced even before Harry had taken his seat. "Colonel Bright, I want to go back to the incident at the Rapido River that Colonel Voss brought up. The one that earned Lieutenant Sisto his Silver Star. Lieutenant Sisto's 'mission' to save the stranded part of his platoon . . . who ordered that rescue attempt?"

"As I recall, it was something the lieutenant did on his own."

"To be clear: Sisto's unit had been ordered to withdraw back across the Rapido. But Lieutenant Sisto took it upon himself to violate the withdrawal order, and risk the lives of a number of men who followed him back across the river—"

"A hell of a way to put it."

"Is it accurate?"

Yet another rare show of emotion. This one of repugnance: "To a T, Captain."

"Lieutenant Schup, you are the 3rd Battalion's S-3 officer? Planning and operations?"

"Yes, Sir."

Courie gestured to the easel. It now held a sizable schematic overview of Hill 399. After Courie asked Schup to identify the schematic and entered it into evidence, he asked, "Would you please use this diagram to explain how the battalion was deployed on the day in question?"

Schup waved a hand over a shaded area along the bottom of the diagram. "This is where the rifle companies were dug in. As they neared jump-off time, they'd move up to the woods line. Between the woods and the hill is this open area—a firebreak—about one hundred fifty yards wide. The order was for all three companies forward. Item was on the far right: they were really just a fix for the krauts on that part of the hill. Then there was a gap in the line right in the middle—here—then facing the left-hand slope was King and Love abreast, King on the left wing.

"The battalion debouched from the woods on Major Porter's command and advanced to and took a line of kraut trenches that runs along here. This was the jump-off point for a special detail that was supposed to make a try for the top.

"In the two previous assaults we'd discovered a 'seam' in the German defensive line that runs along the crest." Schup gestured, indicating a path up the apex of the chevron. "The underlying rock of the hill pokes through here, so the Germans couldn't dig in any kind of heavy, fortified position the way they had all along the rest of the slope. Somebody from King Company figured there was one position in the German bunker line on the left slope angled specifically to cover this approach. The way this was supposed to work, this fella from King was going to belly-crawl up to the bunker, knock it out. On his signal the special detail was going to rush this approach and try to open up the top of the hill."

"Who was to command that detail?"

"Major Porter himself led it."

"And Lieutenant Sisto was with Major Porter?"

"The detail was drawn from Sisto's company, so the lieutenant decided he'd go with the major."

"Once the assault detail 'opened up the top of the hill' . . . ?"

"We had a pick-up company waiting back at the woods line. Once a hole was opened at the top of the hill, there'd be a signal. This second group was supposed to rush up and reinforce the assault detail, then try to open up the remainder of the hilltop."

"Which never happened."

"Yes, Sir."

"Where were you through all this?"

"The battalion staff was back at the battalion CP. You can't see it on this map. It was at a clearing about here."

"Let the record show the witness indicated a point below the lower edge of the diagram. And this was where Captain Joyce was as well?"

"Yes, Sir."

"His assignment being . . . ?"

"There were always a lot of communications problems with the forward line and the units on the hill. Because of the bend of the hill, a company on one flank couldn't talk to a company on the other, and because of the trees, they couldn't communicate with either us or the forward line until they'd reached a certain height on the slopes. Our job was to monitor all communications, act as a relay point for messages between the engaged units, as well as between the assault units and local and divisional fire support. But the big job was to always try to maintain some kind of overall picture of how the assault was going."

"Because the view of the men actually fighting on the hill was so parochial—"

"Because," Schup interrupted coldly, "most soldiers can't tell what's going on more than ten, twenty yards away from them."

"Were you able to do that? Make this picture of the assault?"

"Any hard fight is chaotic. It was always pretty confusing to us in the CP about what was happening where."

"Which was why at one point, Captain Joyce—to get a more clear picture of what was going on—"

"Objection," Harry stated. "Leading."

"Sustained."

Courie nodded apologetically and took another route. "Did Captain Joyce remain at the CP throughout the assault?"

"No, Sir. We had a field phone hookup to an OP at the woods line across from the hill. We figured if we couldn't tell what was going on from what we could hear, at least we'd have observers who could see something of what was happening. But we lost the line. Captain Joyce ordered a detail up to reestablish contact with the OP, but the captain didn't want to wait for the new line, so he moved up to the forward observation post and left me to coordinate things at the command post. Sometime after that—I don't recall how long it was—we picked up a transmission from the hill, somebody'd seen the flare that signaled the bunker covering the approach to the top of the hill had been taken out. The same transmission said the assault detail had started up the hill. About fifteen minutes later, we picked up a message from Blue Six—that was Lieutenant Sisto's radio designation—that they were coming back down from the top. From the references in the transmission, it looked like we were picking up the lieutenant's side of a back-and-forth between him and Rainbow—Captain Joyce."

"You couldn't hear Captain Joyce's side of the conversation with Lieutenant Sisto?"

"Blue Six was far up the hill. Captain Joyce was at the woods line. The trees blocked our reception of his end of it."

"From what you could hear, did the lieutenant seem to be arguing—"

"Objection," Harry called. "Leading. Speculation. Calls for a conclusion."

"Sustained."

Courie proceeded unflustered. "Lieutenant Sisto seemed to be in disagreement with Rainbow?"

"The lieutenant kept repeating that he was bringing the unit down and then communication was broken off. He sounded like he was arguing the point."

"You said 'broken off'? Not lost?"

"We could still hear Blue Six—Lieutenant Sisto—transmitting to the other companies on the hill. We picked up enough of the radio traffic among the three rifle companies to tell us that the battalion was displacing from the hill."

"Was there any indication as to who ordered the withdrawal?"

"There was nothing specific. I always had the impression that the decision originated—"

"Objection," Harry cut in. "An 'impression'?"

"Sustained. Lieutenant Schup, you can testify only as to what you know for a fact."

Courie continued: "The battalion withdrew."

"As they displaced down the hill, we lost contact because of the interference from the trees, and we still hadn't reestablished our line to the forward OP. All we had was a runner from Captain Joyce with an order to our Weapons Company to cover the withdrawal with their mortars as best they could. Outside of that, we were really in the dark."

"And then?"

"I guess it must've been about an hour or so after we heard them organizing the pullback that Captain Joyce showed up. He had Lieutenant Sisto with him. Captain Joyce told me that Major Porter looked to be dead up on the hill, and that he was now in command. Then Captain Joyce said he wanted me to witness that he was placing Lieutenant Sisto under arrest for disobeying orders and gave me the nutshell version of what he said happened."

"Which was that Captain Joyce had ordered Lieutenant Sisto to hold his position. Lieutenant Sisto refused and brought the battalion off the hill."

"Objection," Harry announced. "The Trial Judge Advocate is testifying to facts not in evidence."

"My apologies, Colonel," Courie said. "I'll rephrase. Lieutenant Schup, this 'nutshell' version would be what?"

"That, like you said, Lieutenant Sisto had refused to obey the order and withdrew the battalion from the hill."

Courie nodded with satisfaction. "Thank you, Lieutenant. No further questions."

Harry entered the well in his usual unhurried manner. The stack of note cards in his stubby fingers seemed a particularly thick one. He smiled disarmingly at Schup. "You might as well get comfortable, Lieutenant. We've got a lot of ground to cover. The captain here seems to have, as they say, 'skipped to the good parts.' We're going to back up a bit to when the regiment first arrived at Rott. The battalion was deployed almost immediately?"

"The regiment and battalion COs were briefed, then they briefed their staffs and then, yes, Sir, we moved out."

"For an assault scheduled for the following morning."

"Yes, Sir."

"We heard testimony that Major Porter requested a delay for

that first attack in order to carry out a reconnaissance of the hill, but the major's request was denied. Were you ever given any reason for the urgency to attack the next day?"

"In his briefing to us, Major Porter indicated that the situation of General Cota's division was pretty poor."

"Is that how Major Porter described the situation? 'Pretty poor'?"

"The major came out of his briefing at division HQ, had an officer's call, and began by turning to me and saying, 'Ernie, they're hanging on by their fingernails.'"

"Lieutenant, the assault you described to Captain Courie . . . that was actually the battalion's third attempt to take Hill 399 that day, right?"

"Yes, Sir."

"When you filled in the positions you indicated, were the Germans aware of the battalion's arrival?"

"You bet. Sir."

"How do you know?"

"They began shelling us almost immediately."

"What was the initial plan for the assault?"

"Objection. Irrelevant."

"Colonel"—Harry turned to Ryan—"what happened on the date in question was not a spontaneous event. It was the end product of the stresses and strains of one attempt after another by the battalion to fight its way up the slopes of Hill 399. If anybody wants to understand why it is that the events occurred that this trial is concerned with, they have to know how the battalion got to that point."

"Actually, Colonel," Courie said, stepping forward, "nobody needs to understand why. It only has to be proved that Lieutenant Sisto was given an order by Captain Joyce and that Lieutenant Sisto refused to obey that order. Despite all this other material the Defense has been able to drag into this case, that instance of disobedience is the case."

Harry was already shaking his head. "That's like saying 'We have a dead man and the man who shot the gun. It's murder. The end.' No question of self-defense? Provocation? Mitigating circumstance? The law books in Cleveland must be a lot thinner than they are anywhere else."

Because it would have been a failure of courtroom etiquette to poke Harry in the eye, Courie only smiled.

"That was cute but unnecessary, Colonel," Ryan reprimanded.

"My apologies," Harry said to Courie.

"Despite having a smart mouth," Ryan went on, "the Defense also has a point. Even if for no other reason than other elements of the act need to be considered in sentencing, the Court and the jury should understand the context of the act. Overruled. Go ahead, Colonel Voss."

"We were supposed to debouch from the woods before dawn," Schup continued. "The attack was supported by our own mortars, Division had dedicated some artillery support, and there was supposed to be an air strike by some P-47s just before we moved out. But there was fog that morning both at the hill and at the airfield. The P-47s never showed."

"There was no air strike? And the attack went off anyway?"

"Major Porter tried to call for another postponement, like he had the night before, but it was another no-go."

"No reconnaissance, no air support. You were the planning officer, Lieutenant Schup. How in God's name could you come up with a plan like this?"

"It wasn't our plan, Sir."

"Then did this come from some wizard on General Cota's staff?"

"Division relayed it to us from Corps."

"You have personal knowledge of this?"

"We were shown the operational script that had been drawn up at Corps. We weren't sure it didn't go higher—"

"Objection!" Courie called. "Speculation."

"Sustained."

"At any point during the day the 3rd Battalion was engaged at Hill 399, did you see any observers from Corps?"

"No, Sir."

"To your knowledge, had any agents from any senior head-quarters reconnoitered the area before or during the time your battalion was engaged at Hill 399?"

"Not to my knowledge."

"Or had any direct intelligence information on the objective or immediate vicinity?"

"If they did, they weren't sharing."

"In terms of tactical planning, what kind of latitude was the battalion allowed?"

"Well, the tactical end, most of it was up to us. Major Porter made most of the major immediate tactical decisions."

"Such as?"

"For that first attack, he put two companies forward: Love on the left, King on the right, Item in reserve."

"How far did that attack get?"

"The krauts had cleared the top half of the slopes for obser-vation purposes. This also gave them a clear killing ground on the upper slopes. There was about a hundred yards from where the trees stopped to this line of trenches. The upper half of that open ground was covered with barbed wire and mines. Since we didn't know about it beforehand, we didn't have any hard-ware to deal with those obstacles. We were stonewalled."

"So the decision was made to regroup and give it another try?"

"Yes, Sir."

"That attack order came from Corps?"

"Yes, Sir. This time, we sighted our Weapons Company mortars on the minefield and the wire to blow paths through. We put all three rifle companies forward. We managed to get as far as the trenches."

"The losses on those first two assaults were high?"

"Extremely heavy. We were never able to get an accurate count while we were in the area because of the conditions—"

"Well, let's see if we can illustrate this somehow. You said the troops for the assault on the hilltop were from Lieutenant Sisto's company; that's why he went along with them. But Lieutenant Sisto wasn't the company commander. He was a platoon leader, right?"

"He was the acting company CO by then."

"'By then'?"

"He'd assumed command during the second attack."

"Because of losses."

"Yes, Sir."

"Was Lieutenant Sisto the company's executive officer?"

"No, Sir."

"Was he the senior platoon leader?"

"No, Sir."

"Then how was it he came to take over the company *over* the other officers in the company?"

Ernest Schup grew very still. "Because by that time there were no other commissioned officers left in his company."

"You said someone from King Company was supposed to take out a bunker guarding the approach to the top of the hill.

That person was, in fact, King's acting company commander, was he not?"

"Yes, Sir. Sergeant Sekelsky."

"The company's top sergeant?"

"Yes, Sir."

"And Sergeant Sekelsky took command because he was the highest-ranking member of King by that time?"

"Yes, Sir."

"King and Love companies, Lieutenant: how many men were left at the end of that third assault?"

"You have to keep in mind that the mortar squads from each company's Heavy Weapons platoon had been detached and conjoined with the battalion's Weapons Company to provide fire support. And then we were still taking artillery fire until we pulled out that night."

Harry, with infinite patience: "Lieutenant: what was the score when you got back to Rott?"

"Not counting the mortar squads of the 370 or so riflemen we began with, the head count when we got back to Rott was seventy-two men in Item, fifty-two in King, and thirty-seven in Love."

"Lieutenant Schup, let's move to the incident between Lieutenant Sisto and Captain Joyce that started all this. Obviously, when Captain Joyce accused Lieutenant Sisto of disobeying his order to hold the hill, Lieutenant Sisto did something more than answer with silence."

"Lieutenant Sisto told me that Major Porter had given the order to pull out from the top of the hill. He said from that vantage point, Major Porter could see we weren't going to pull it off."

"Meaning succeed in taking the hill?"

"Yes, Sir."

"If Lieutenant Sisto had held his position on top of the hill, do you think the attack could have succeeded?"

"Objection," Courie snapped. "Calls for a conclusion."

"I think a response is within the scope of knowledge of a battalion S-3," replied Harry.

"With all respect to Lieutenant Schup, a battalion S-3 does not necessarily have the expertise of some senior planning officer at a general headquarters staff."

A hand went up from the jury panel. He was a captain, an artillery battery commander.

"Yes, Captain?" Ryan asked.

"Panel members are allowed to ask questions, aren't they, Sir?"

"Yes, Captain. Usually on points of clarification."

"Well, this'd clear something up for me." Ryan nodded at him to proceed, and the captain turned toward Courie. "About what you're saying, so I understand, you're saying that a battalion S-3 isn't competent? Or that this particular officer isn't competent?"

"I'm not saying either—" Courie was cut short by another raised hand.

"Lieutenant Pomeroy?" Ryan said, calling on a rifle platoon exec from Sisto's own 103rd Regiment.

"Seems to me that those senior guys Captain Courie's talking about were the ones who planned this whole mess. I don't see where they have the corner on military smarts. Can I ask Lieutenant Schup how long he's been with the battalion as S-3?"

"I came on as an assistant S-3 in January, made senior that March."

Pomeroy looked over at Ryan with a wry do-you-really-need-anything-else look.

"Captain Courie, if you don't have anything else, I'm going to have to overrule. At least in terms of the battalion's operation on this objective, the Court sees Lieutenant Schup as qualified to offer an opinion. You may answer, Lieutenant."

"I always thought we were going to have a problem with the third phase of the attack," Schup said. "The first phase was to regain the trenches. The second was Major Porter's try for the top of the hill. The third phase was going to be reinforcing the men on top of the hill with the pick-up company we had waiting to jump off back at the woods line, Lieutenant Tully's I & R Platoon, and some other odds and ends that we scrounged from the battalion area. About sixty men. You can see the problem: once the reinforcement detail gets the go, the men on top of the hill have to hold while Tully's group has to cover all this ground, from the original jump-off line, across the firebreak, and up the whole length of the hill."

"You made your concern known to the major?"

"Yes, Sir, but, well, Major Porter had made up his mind."

"Why did the major keep these men so far back?"

"He was afraid of them getting whittled down if they moved up with the main body. He had a point: the assault detail lost three men waiting in those trenches for the go signal.

"The first group—Lieutenant Sisto's—had the element of surprise going for them. Some of the men in the assault detail were halfway to the top before the krauts could react and get fire directed at that part of the hill. After that, the krauts'd be waiting for somebody to try to reinforce the men at the top. I thought if Lieutenant Tully could keep his casualties to fifty percent, he was going to be a lucky man. But even if Lieutenant Tully could get up there with his whole group, the way the krauts had that part of the hilltop hemmed in, I can't see how

Lieutenant Sisto could've held out long enough for Tully to reach him."

"In your opinion, Lieutenant Schup, as someone who'd served on Major Porter's staff for nearly eleven months, was Major Porter an astute enough officer to have understood his predicament once he was on top of that hill?"

Ryan held up a hand. "Captain Courie, you have 'objection' in your eyes."

"I do, Sir." Courie considered a moment, then said, "No, Sir, I'll let it go."

"All I can tell you," continued Schup, "is that everybody who was still left up on that hill saw the fix they were in. At least the ones who made it down and could tell me. And the men in the trenches who saw them fighting it out up there, they knew it, too."

"Because of your long working relationship with the battalion CO, I want to turn to Major Porter for a bit. In those eleven months, you must have formulated an opinion of the major?"

"He was OK."

"Hardly a glowing endorsement, Lieutenant."

"Objection."

"Sustained," ruled Ryan. "Save the sarcasm, Colonel, please."

"Sorry, Sir. Lieutenant, let's see if we can come up with something more ... enlightening than 'OK.' How was Major Porter's relationship with the other officers? With the men?"

"I'd have to say the major didn't have the best rapport with either the officers or the men. The enlisted men? You could see he wasn't always comfortable around them."

"It's been testified that Major Porter preferred to command from his headquarters."

"He was not one to make first-person tours of the line

positions. That was usually detailed to someone like me, or the battalion S-2, or somebody else from the CP staff."

"We've heard his conduct of offensive operations described as 'tentative.' Did you find that to be the case? Was the major indecisive?"

"Indecisive, Sir? That's a strong word. He could be *cautious*—"

This time it was the blunt Lieutenant Colonel Pietrowski from General Cota's headquarters who raised his hand. "Colonel Ryan, you said we could ask for somebody to clear up a point, and I guess that's what I want. I know people get in that witness chair and get asked about Major Porter and they all want to be polite . . ." He turned toward Schup. "Son, I'd love it if just *once* somebody'd give a straight answer about the man. He's dead, Lieutenant. Being polite isn't going to do him much good now. Let's worry about the living, OK?"

Schup saw the painfully plain sense of it and nodded. "I'd say the major'd be in a sweat whenever we were on the advance. He was always worried about being far out enough in front to get nailed without being supported on his flanks or behind."

"Major Porter never refused an order to advance, did he?" Harry asked.

"No, Sir. But sometimes he could get to be a sore spot with regiment and even division HQ about how slowly he did advance. What they thought back at regiment was a crawl, Major Porter thought was a galloping charge."

"You've also worked closely with Captain Joyce. Do you have an opinion of him?"

"The captain and the major were night and day, at least in how they looked at operations. Captain Joyce was a lot more eager, a very aggressive officer . . ."

"Yes, Lieutenant?"

"It was the way they were different..."

"Go ahead."

"Well, with Hill 399, from the start Major Porter was all worries. He didn't like the set-up from the time he came out of the briefing with General Cota in Rott. That wasn't just him; none of us liked the set-up. Captain Joyce, well, he kept trying to buck up the major. 'Remember,' he'd say, 'this is the 3rd Battalion of the 103!' like this was... Well, I don't think Captain Joyce ever understood that the 3rd Battalion we took into the Huertgen wasn't the 3rd Battalion he remembered from Italy."

"Lieutenant, I know you're having trouble explaining this, but I'm having just as hard a time understanding it."

"Captain Joyce was thinking we were this battle-tough outfit. We made it through Italy; we could take whatever the krauts could dish out. But thirty to forty percent of those riflemen were replacements we picked up in England; they'd never seen combat."

"Since Captain Joyce didn't understand this, I'm assuming he didn't have any better a rapport with the men than Major Porter."

"He seemed to have an attitude that he had the rank and that was sufficient for people to jump to his order. And then..."

"Go ahead, Lieutenant."

"Well, Sir, Captain Joyce never made a secret of it that he hoped to have his own command someday. And when Major Porter wasn't around, sometimes he'd let you know he was frustrated with the way the major ran things."

"What about Lieutenant Sisto? Did you know him?"

"Yes, Sir. I knew he could rub the major and Captain Joyce the wrong way. The lieutenant—even before he was a lieutenant—he was never shy about speaking his mind. And he could be a bit . . . emphatic."

"So, if Lieutenant Sisto got an order he didn't think much of, he sounded off."

"Yes, Sir."

"But had he ever disobeyed an order prior to that day on Hill 399?"

"Never. He'd squawk if he didn't like an order, but I'd never known him not to carry it out."

"Lieutenant, there's been a lot of talk in this room about Lieutenant Sisto's conviction on a General Article summary court-martial."

"The business about the wine cellar? Actually, I think Major Porter would have preferred to pretend it never happened. I think he was more worried about having it on his battalion's record than Lieutenant Sisto was worried about having it on his! But Captain Joyce told Major Porter that something had to be done. He thought it was a big discipline breakdown and that the major couldn't let it pass."

Finished, Harry retired, but Courie rose to redirect.

"Lieutenant, much is being made of the conservative flavor of Major Porter's style of command. Yet the major himself went up with the detail that took the top of Hill 399, correct?"

"Yes, Sir."

"Whose idea was it that he do so?"

"I assumed it was his decision."

Harry raised an objection over the assumption.

"Sustained," Ryan declared. "The jury will disregard."

"Lieutenant," Courie persisted, "did anything about Major Porter personally leading that assault seem 'tentative' to you?"

"Frankly, Sir, I was surprised he did it. It did seem out of character."

"Thank you, Lieutenant. Nothing further. Colonel Ryan, Prosecution's next witness is Private First Class Timothy Rice. Private Rice was handling communications at the battalion CP on the day in question and can corroborate Lieutenant Schup's account of the communications received at the CP. If the Defense agrees to a stipulation of Lieutenant Schup's account, we can save the Court a bit of time—"

"We have no problem with the stipulation, Sir," Harry put in.

"I love it when you guys get along," Ryan said with a smile. "Call your next witness, Captain Courie."

PFC Paul Makris's testimony under Courie's questioning was a repeat of the story he'd delivered up during my interview of him in Wiltz.

But, this time, Dominick Sisto was in the room with him. The poor lad didn't seem to know whether to look at his lieutenant or away. In the end, he spent much of his time on the stand studying his knees and speaking into his chest.

Then it was Harry's turn. He neared the witness chair, beaming comfortingly over the tops of his glasses. He leaned close in to Makris, winked, and nodded at the jury panel: "You ever see so much brass in one place in your life?"

The nineteen-year-old allowed his first tentative smile. "Sure are a lot of them, Colonel."

"I'm surprised the floor doesn't buckle under all that rank." Makris chuckled.

"Do you mind if I go back to a couple of things you said to Captain Courie? Just to get a better picture of what went on?" The tone was almost informal; cozying up to a fellow GI at a pub bar. Harry positioned himself between Makris and Sisto, solving the lad's problem of where to set his gaze. "You said that from where you were dug in on top of the hill, you couldn't see Major Porter."

"That's right, Sir, yeah."

"Couldn't hear anything Major Porter might've said to Lieutenant Sisto."

"Colonel, as much noise as there was up there, if Major Porter'd been screaming his head off, I wouldn't have heard him."

"Bet you couldn't even hear yourself think."

"You'd win that bet, Sir."

"Could you see down the hill? I mean, you were up there at the top. What kind of view did you have back down the slope?"

"Well, yeah, Sir, you could see down pretty good. Where we'd come up, the rock was like a ramp, but we'd all fanned out from where it came out on top. Where we were—where I was—the hill dropped off pretty sharp right behind me."

"So you had a nice bird's-eye view of your battalion's position?"

"Oh, yeah! Well, down to where King and Love companies were, yes, Sir. You could see right down into those trenches. You could see why the krauts never had a problem kicking our arses—, oh, sorry, Sirs. I mean, from up there, you were looking right down our throats. I mean their throats. You know, the guys in the trenches."

"You could see all the way down to the bottom of the hill?"

"Yes, Sir."

"And across the firebreak, all the way to the trees where Lieutenant Tully's men were?"

"You could even see them moving around down there, Lieutenant Tully's guys."

"So, if Lieutenant Tully's men had moved out, you could see

that they'd be under fire the second they stepped into the fire-break."

"You'd have spotted them the second they came out of their holes. When I saw how far they were going to have to come, and how much fire the krauts were putting on that hill, I figured us for dead, Sir. I really did."

Makris was dismissed.

"Sir," Courie addressed Ryan, "I have two more witnesses who were in close proximity to Private Makris. Their purpose is to corroborate what he heard of the radio communication between Lieutenant Sisto and Captain Joyce. To spare the Court's time and patience, would Defense agree to stipulate the lieutenant's end of the conversation as Private Makris has testified to it?"

"I don't have a problem with that," Harry responded, "as long as the Judge Advocate agrees that those same witnesses would corroborate Private Makris's view of the battalion's situation as seen from the top of the hill, as well as the situation of the detail on the hilltop."

"Sounds like you're getting the better bargain," Courie said. "Two stipulations for one."

"How about it, Captain?" Ryan prodded.

Courie looked over to Alth. The two exchanged a shrug, then Courie turned back to Ryan. "We agree to the stipulations."

Avram Kasabian was the next witness.

Courie's examination was brief and directed at the case's jugular: Had Kasabian heard Captain Joyce order Lieutenant Sisto and his detail to hold their position on top of Hill 399?

Yes.

He then quickly took Kasabian to the finale. "And when Lieutenant Sisto was finally brought to Captain Joyce, what happened then?"

"Well, the captain asked where the major was, Lieutenant Sisto told him Major Porter'd stayed behind on top of the hill; he was either captured or dead. Then Captain Joyce turned to me, told me to transmit a message to all battalion units that he was assuming command. Then when the captain asked him— Lieutenant Sisto—why he hadn't held his position, the lieutenant told him Major Porter'd ordered them down. Captain Joyce told him he was full of—well, Captain Joyce didn't believe him, and he said for the lieutenant to consider himself under arrest. Then they headed on the trail back to the battalion area."

Harry's examination—as so many of his interrogations— focused elsewhere.

"Private Kasabian, you told Captain Courie that Captain Joyce threatened to relieve Lieutenant Tully and bring him up on charges?"

"Yessir, said he'd do it right then and there."

"But he didn't do it right then and there. He didn't do it at all."

"Well, the lieutenant..." Kasabian looked toward the floor. "Like I told the captain, Sir, Lieutenant Tully got killed."

"Yes, I know. I'm sorry, Private. But Lieutenant Tully was killed *later*. You said Captain Joyce told Lieutenant Tully he'd bust him at that moment if he didn't move out, but he didn't."

"Objection." Courie was shaking his head. "I don't see the point of this. What does what the captain said to Tully have to do with—"

"I'm trying to determine if the defendant's conduct was singled out for any reason," Harry said.

Courie smiled condescendingly. "Amongst the many side dishes you've managed to put on the table, Colonel, are you now going to try to allege bias on Captain Joyce's part? That he's got a personal grudge against Lieutenant Sisto?"

"I'm not alleging anything," Harry replied. "I'm trying to find out why one man was arrested and another one wasn't for the very same act."

Courie turned to Ryan. "Colonel, even if Captain Joyce had sworn a personal vendetta against Lieutenant Sisto, that's not why we're here. We're here because a hearing convened *not* by Captain Joyce but by General Cota determined that there were grounds for an indictment against Lieutenant Sisto. This is yet *another* side issue that doesn't change the basic fact of the case: that Captain Joyce gave an order and Lieutenant Sisto refused to follow it!"

"He's got you there, Colonel," Ryan told Harry. "Sustained. Move on to something else."

Harry turned back to Kasabian and referred to his note cards. "Check me out on this, Private, I want to be sure I've got your testimony to Captain Courie right. You told him Captain Joyce gave Lieutenant Tully the order to move out. And then you said . . . ?"

"I said Lieutenant Tully told him to go scratch. To forget it."

"Captain Joyce then threatened to relieve Lieutenant Tully and charge him."

"Right."

"And you said the lieutenant said—"

"Tully told Joyce to take a leap."

"Did Lieutenant Tully explain *why* he wouldn't move out? Even under the threat of being relieved?"

"Lieutenant Tully told Captain Joyce we'd get hammered pretty hard on the way up, so he wasn't gonna move without the go signal. He didn't want to be headin' up there on his own and find out they didn't get the signal 'cause the guys on the hill were runnin' past him the other way. Lieutenant Tully didn't think more than half of us'd make it."

On that rather grim note, the second day of the trial concluded.

"I think this guy's got an allergy to optimism," Dominick Sisto said, amiably clapping his hands on the shoulders of Harry Voss, who was standing by the window of the lieutenant's tower room. "I mean, c'mon! Did you see the ol' signor in there? Did you know he was such a tiger? It's always those quiet guys, eh, Mr. O?"

I looked to where Peter Ricks had positioned himself on Sisto's cot, a Lucky Strike in his fingers as he attempted to blow smoke rings toward the ceiling. Though not as gloomy as Harry, Ricks was hardly sharing in Sisto's exuberance.

"I told the signor, I said, you keep milking that clown Courie's witnesses like this, we won't need any of our own! I told him I even think he oughta find out what far corner of the world Andy Thom has got himself off to and drag his arse back! The way we're going, that poor kid doesn't need to be slogging off in the cold God-knows-where!"

"The patient has been brought back from the brink of the abyss," I said to Harry. "So might I ask why the doctor looks so glum?"

"Because," Ricks announced from the cot, "we've got a looooong way to go."

"Granted, but it did look to me as if you had a good innings today, laddie. Though I must admit to a concern there at the start when the crusading captain's first volley went unanswered."

"Not for lack of trying," Ricks said with a tired smile. "We were up half of last night trying to draft an opening statement."

Harry doodled on the frost of the lead-veined window-panes. "Your opening statement is supposed to tell the jury what to look for. It's like a connect-the-dots picture. Here's what the picture's supposed to look like; here's the dots we're going to present. All you have to do is connect them and you'll get the picture.

"The problem is that having made the claim, you damned well better come through with the dots. If you don't, or try to change the picture to something other than what you said you were going to make, well, that's shooting yourself in the foot. You set your own mark; you don't make it, you lose."

I shook my head, confused. "It almost sounds like you're saying you don't have a defense."

"Is that how it looked to you, Mr. O?" Sisto said. "Sure as hell didn't look that way to me!"

"Aye, Harry, you did seem to be mounting a rather spirited non-defense!" I seconded.

"Smoke," Ricks commented flatly.

"Eh, laddie?"

Harry turned self-consciously away and began to pace the room. "Courie's right about one thing: I've been throwing in everything *and* the kitchen sink to distract the jury. I keep hoping if I can get enough out there, maybe something clicks with one or another of the jurors. If I can do that and turn one or two of them..."

"I take it one avenue is all this verbiage about Porter having given the withdrawal order."

He nodded. "It's not fun digging up a dead man and tagging him as—"

"'Unexceptional,'" cited Ricks.

"Don't feel too guilty, *Signor*," Sisto said. "The only reason Porter ever gave a shit about casualties was he was afraid how it'd make him look on the daily report! So I say, fuck him!"

Harry'd seemed not to hear a word of it. "Because Courie is right—again—that there's no definite way to prove or disprove the order was given, that point's going to come down to who the jury *wants* to believe. I'm not crazy about my other route, either."

"Which is?"

"The Army may say obeying orders is up there with the Ten Commandments when it comes to laws of God, but the ugly little secret is that you do *not* have to obey every order." With a grunt, Ricks drew himself up to a seated position. "If Harry there orders Dominick to jump off a roof, Dominick can tell him to fuck off. No offense, Harry."

"But," I objected, "he *can* order him to charge into the blazing muzzles of enemy guns. It's done all the time, aye?"

"There's a place where the line between a gallant—if doomed—charge into the enemy guns and the tactical equivalent of jumping off a roof gets a little fuzzy. I don't think the jury—or any officer in the Army—wants to get into any discussion that puts command authority into question. Hell, if I was still on the line, I wouldn't want *my* subordinates second-guessing *my* orders just because *they* don't like 'em! They buck me, I bring charges, and their excuse is going to be 'Isn't this just like that case with that Sisto fella?' The Army would rather just publicly hold forth on obedience as a cardinal virtue and deal quietly with the exceptions as they come up." Ricks sighed.

"But I have to throw it out there," Harry concluded.

"You just keep throwin', *Signor*," Sisto applauded. "You're pitchin' a hell of a game!"

Sisto's insistent optimism was beginning to grate on Harry. "This isn't a quantity game, Dominick. I'll go on and on about how Porter was gun-shy, and there was no way you guys were going to take that hill, and any other thing I can think of to throw into the mix. I've got this whole mess of things to have them think about, and Courie just has one! But it's a goddamned big one, and you better respect it and you better respect the way Courie makes sure it gets hammered home because it's something else he's right about. In the end, this trial is about only one thing: Joyce gave you an order and you told him to go scratch. We can mitigate that, but we can't make it go away. And no matter how much sympathy I get for you out of that jury, they're officers: They won't ignore what you did. Even with all the breaks, kiddo, there's no way you walk away from this clean."

Go scratch. It echoed. Then I remembered: It had been Avram Kasabian's phrase.

Sisto seemed chastened. His smile, his airy bounce...all faded. "So what're we talking about?"

"My best hope is they'll let you skate by one charge, recommend leniency in sentencing on the one they stick you with."

Sisto sat heavily at the foot of the bed, forced a grim smile. "Boy, *Signor,* you really know how to bring down a party."

"I just want you to be ready, Dominick."

"So Andy Thom stays out in the cold?"

"Andy Thom stays out in the cold and keeps looking for anything we can use. Tomorrow, they bring out Big Bertha."

"Joyce," Ricks translated for me.

"Speaking of Andy, Pete, why don't you send a message to Wiltz and see what the skinny is on that kid? We haven't heard a peep out of him in a couple of days. Something on your mind, Eddie?" Harry asked me.

"Go scratch."

"Excuse me?"

"Nae, sorry, just something there caught my fancy, I guess."

"Developing an appreciation for Yankee doggerel?" Ricks commented.

"It doesn't quite have the lyrical ring of 'There once was a young man from Nantucket,' but it does have a certain *je ne sais quoi*."

A befuddled Dominick Sisto considered the exchange, looking from Ricks to me. "I gotta start readin' more books," he said.

"Quite," I said.

Perhaps it was the inclemency of the weather. Or that Dominick Sisto had much to discuss with his counsel in preparation for the morrow. In either case, I found I had the walk along the castle wall to myself that night.

The snowfall had tapered off that afternoon and three inches of untouched white stuff blanketed the walk. It seemed almost a shame to muck it up with my boots.

The clouds were clearing, leaving the sliver of sharp-edged moon to peep through and imbue the freezing, glittering snow with a blue-tinged iridescence.

"Go scratch," I said, and my voice sounded small and feeble out alone atop the chateau's walls. I could not fathom why the absurd little phrase nagged at me so.

An icy wind swept across the open ground, stinging, bringing tears to my eyes.

It was late when I came down from the wall. The chateau had gone somnolent, except for a far-off phonograph, its echoing strains of "Harbor Lights" blurred as they caromed about the maze of corridors. The new mess staff had been in the habit of keeping an urn of coffee on throughout the night, and I stopped by in the hopes of warming myself before turning in. As I passed through the main dining hall, I saw Harry slumped in a chair pulled up to one of the fireplaces, its logs now a crumbled pile of glowing embers. A coffee cup sat on one arm of his chair, and his elbow was propped on the other, his forehead cradled in his hand. I thought him asleep at first.

"Harry?"

I don't know if I woke him or simply surprised him. "There's more in the kitchen," he said, indicating his cup. "It's still hot."

I returned with my own steaming cup and pulled up a chair alongside Harry's. I nodded at the display of note cards on the dining table. "I think you should put that away for a bit and get some rest."

"The problem," he said with a sad smile, "is that I haven't been able to work on that at all."

I noticed a message form from the chateau's communications room sitting atop his notepad. "Does that have anything to do with your sense of distraction?"

"From Wiltz. Andy Thom is gone."

"Gone?"

"He left Wiltz in a jeep sometime this afternoon. Didn't leave any word about where he was going. If he was coming here, he should've been here by now."

"Worried?"

"Concerned. I'd just feel better if I knew where he was."

"I'm sure he's all right."

He agreed.

"But that's not it," I said.

He sighed. "Thirty-seven men. That's what Schup said. Thirty-seven men. Dominick went into the Huertgen Forest as part of a full company of one hundred and eighty-odd men, and he came out with thirty-seven. Dominick told me that the first time I sat down with him, and it *still*..." His voice faded. He patted at the pockets of his blouse. "You wouldn't happen to have a cigarette, would you, Eddie? I seem to be out."

"You're in luck," I said, passing over a packet. "American."

He drew one, crossed to the fireplace, poked at the embers, trying to rouse a flame. "God willing, Dominick will go home. His mom'll hug him, kiss him, be happy he's home in one piece. She'll think, 'Good, now everything can be the way it was.' But after a while, she'll"—he looked for the word—"*feel*...that things *aren't* the same. Something's going to be wrong." Harry bent over and touched the edge of the fag to one of the glowing bits until the paper curled and smoked, then quickly put it to his mouth and took a draft to stoke the cigarette. "He'll know she feels it, but he won't talk to her about it. Sooner or later, she'll come to *me*...she'll ask *me* about it. But I won't talk to her about it, either."

He was talking as much about his own past as Dominick's future. He kicked at the charred logs in the fireplace, a quietly violent thrust of his shoe that kicked up a small cloud of ash and sparks. "Thirty-seven men. That's what he'll be carrying around inside him. How the hell do you tell anybody about *that*? Where do you make room inside to carry *that*?" He noticed the smudge of ash on the toe of his shoe, tried to shake it loose with gentle taps on the flagstones of the hearth.

"Some men don't," I said, feeling out of my depth. I considered my own recurring despondency and felt hardly qualified to offer Harry helpful hints on his own. "But you should know, my friend, that it seems to me most find some way to put it away somewhere. Like a box put away in the attic. Always there but . . . away."

"How do they do that?"

"I wish I knew, mate."

He shrugged as if to say I was entitled to my wrongheaded opinion. "Sometimes I envy you, Eddie. That you never had kids."

"Why didn't you go home, Harry? What were you doing in Scotland?"

"I'm not sure. I'm really not," he said wearily. He realized he'd been ignoring the cigarette smoldering between his fingers, took a long pull, and resettled himself in his chair. "Why don't *you* go home? How come you don't quit?"

"Oh, mate, don't think I haven't considered it! Inertia, I suppose. One needs to pay one's pub bill, eh?"

"That simple?"

"No," I said grimly, "it's *this* simple: it's all I know. You see, Harry, the god-awful thing about dedicating yourself to some grand . . . thing . . . is that should it fail you, should your dedication falter, you find yourself—well, Harry, you have nothing. Nothing. It—the Job, the Trade—it has it all."

He nodded. "Maybe that's what it was for me, too," he said mordantly. "I didn't know how to do anything else. And I wasn't sure . . ."

"Sure of what, Harry?"

He shook his head.

We sat for a quiet time, then Harry said with a sudden certainty, "Hiding."

"What's that?"

"Scotland. I was hiding."

"Hiding from what?"

"Everything."

As I lay in my four-poster that night, I came to find myself envying poor old Harry. I envied him his dowdy, earnest wife, his bratty tykes, his dreary walk-up tenement flat: all those things I had spent years considering myself above, too involved in matters of import to become enmired with.

Go scratch. The ridiculous little phrase ran absurdly in my head. I lay there some time, listening to the phrase whir: *goscratchgoscratchgoscratch...*

In each young soldier, Harry saw a son. It was why he so doggedly sought to free Dominick Sisto. He had come out of hiding driven by the idea that in his absence he'd want someone to do as much for his boys.

Captain Whitcomb "Whit" Langham Joyce was the twenty-six-year-old son of a mill worker in one of those Something-bury towns in Connecticut. He had aspired to be more than the son of a mill worker and had poured great energy into doing so. But like his attempt to subdue his tightly curled hair beneath a sheen of pomade, his efforts were only half successful: the overly careful diction and modulation of tone, the heavy-handed application of high-station vocabulary. His almost frail-seeming body was lost in his uniform: the cuffs of his jacket and shirt drooped across the back sides of his hands; his collar swam about his thin, graceful throat; the shoulders of his jacket sagged past the cut of his shoulders, and its rear bunched where the belt cinched across his narrow back; his thin legs seemed lost in his billowy trouser legs. One could almost feel pity for him, his doll-like looks so out of place in that chamber of cold stone and hard-faced men.

"Captain Joyce," Courie began, flipping open the fresh folder handed him by Alth, "how long have you been the executive officer for the 3rd Battalion?"

"I shipped over in November of 1943."

"To Italy."

"Yes. Correct. Major Porter had moved up to take command of the battalion the previous month."

"Major Porter had commanded one of the rifle companies prior to assuming command of the battalion?"

"Yes."

"Having served as the man's exec for more than a year, I imagine you've formulated an opinion about Major Porter?"

"Professionally, we had a very good working relationship, though I can't say we were always in complete accordance on things."

"Such as?"

"Any, um, number of issues. I would say a variety of issues, yes."

"Such as policies on how the men should be managed?"

"For example, yes." Joyce crossed his twiggish legs, left over right, seemed unhappy with the pose, then recrossed them right over left. "Yes, that would be one area of disagreement."

"Difference of opinion in combat situations? On tactical issues?"

"Yes, that as well."

"Could you illustrate those differences for us, Captain?"

Joyce cleared his throat several times. "Yes. Illustrate them? Certainly. Well, for instance, as a rule, Major Porter tended to hesitate in a combat situation and allow a situation to develop. He was extremely uncomfortable committing the battalion into a, um, *predicament* where there was some question about what the end result might be. I, on the other hand, recognize that a commander does not always have the luxury of waiting. I'm sure the gentlemen on the jury know what I'm referring to when I say that often a combat situation can be highly, um, fluid and volatile, yes, *volatile*. Opportunities to win the day can open and close in minutes."

"Yet despite these philosophical differences, you managed a good working relationship."

"Yes, despite our differences. I also mentioned, remember, that we had a good, a *strong*, personal rapport. That allowed us to negotiate our differences and provide for effective leadership of the battalion."

"How well did you know Lieutenant Sisto?" Courie stood aside to allow Joyce a look to the defense table. From where I sat I could not see Sisto's face.

Harry sat forward, keenly studying the man still trying to find a comfortable position in the witness chair.

"I have something of an acquaintance with the lieutenant," Joyce answered.

"Captain Joyce, there are over eight hundred men in your battalion—"

"Eight hundred and thirty-six when at authorized strength."

"—eight hundred and thirty-six, thank you, and we have heard testimony that the battalion experienced a regular turnover when in Italy. For much of that time, Dominick Sisto did not rise higher than the rank of buck sergeant: a squad leader. How did you come to develop an acquaintance with him?"

"I would say, upon reflection, it begins with the incident, the *occurrence*, that came out of the Rapido River crossings."

"You mean the lieutenant's action of recrossing the river—"

"Yes, yes, precisely! *That* action! As you said, the lieutenant was a squad leader at that particular point in time. Some of the gentlemen on the jury may know that casualties among lieutenants—platoon leaders—are disproportionately high. So, as it happened, it would occur that the lieutenant—then *Sergeant* Sisto—would come to be acting platoon leader, sometimes for days at a time, until a replacement could be instituted—installed, you know. In such a position it would come about that I would, on occasion, hear reports of his actions from his company commander. He would even, at times, depending on the circumstances mind you, be included in planning briefings for certain operations."

"It sounds like, over time, you found yourself dealing more and more with Lieutenant Sisto on a direct basis."

"Yes, I would put it that way, over time, yes, correct."

"Your opinion of the lieutenant?"

"A good soldier. A fine soldier, actually, in terms of combat. An able fighting man. He also had positive qualities—*assets*—as a small-unit leader."

"I sense you had some reservations, though."

"Reservations? Yes, *qualms*, you might say. If I had to qualify what I've just said, I would say . . . um, well, I suppose you could say, *one* might say the lieutenant could appear a bit rough around the edges. You know. *Rough*." Joyce's face brightened. "Ah, but the main factor, the main point of *friction*, was his inability to obey without hesitancy or question. I often gathered the impression—and I believe Major Porter agreed with me—that Lieutenant Sisto felt his combat experiences warranted a voice in operational planning for which his rank did not provide."

I could see the concern on Courie's face. The Prosecution had evidently noted—as I had—that the captain's bent toward multisyllabic presentation was not all that welcomed by the gruff-looking members of the jury.

"Simply put," said Courie, "Sisto could be argumentative."

"Objection. Leading."

"Sustained."

From Courie, without missing a beat: "How would you characterize the lieutenant's attitude in this regard?"

"Well, yes, 'argumentative' would be the word."

"To the point where he was a discipline problem?"

"Um, well, not in a militarily criminal sense. However, it could be difficult to get him to observe all the, um, protocols."

"Yes."

"Again, I think it was a matter of his combat experience— this is in his eyes, the lieutenant's eyes—he felt this exempted him from some of the formalities."

"Captain, within the same four-week span—from the time of the Rapido River operation into the following month—then-Sergeant Sisto was recommended for a Silver Star, and also summarily court-martialed under Article 96 of *The Articles of War*. I think you'd agree that most people would find that striking: from an award for valor to being busted down within a month."

"Yes, well, it's not as paradoxical as it seems." Joyce looked eager to explain. "In fact, that very much illustrates what I've been saying. The award was a testament to his fighting abilities. The Article 96 applied to his conduct off the line, although the unit was still in an operational area."

"The particulars of the incident have been testified to. The Defense seems to be of the opinion that the incident was simply a matter of boys-will-be-boys."

"Objection." Harry rose. "That's the Judge Advocate's characterization, not mine."

"Sustained," Ryan ruled.

"Withdrawn," Courie declared. "Captain Joyce, did you and Major Porter think the incident was a serious infraction?"

"I did more than the major, but yes."

"Why? The men were not on the battle line."

"It was not—as I saw it—the issue of the act itself, which, I grant, could be perceived as minor. However, the underlying issue of discipline, that I found serious. The battalion was in an operational area. We could have been called up to the line at any time. If it had been simply a case of the lieutenant allowing himself to compromise his readiness by getting drunk, that would have been one thing. But he was responsible for other men, the men of his squad. If there had been a need to bring them up to the Main Line of Resistance, in their condition... my feeling—my stand, if you will—was that he had placed their lives along with his own in jeopardy."

"Was this the lieutenant's first breach of discipline that you noted?"

"Actually, in point of fact, I was not completely in favor of the recommendation for the Silver Star. There's no denying Lieutenant Sisto showed great personal courage when he re-crossed the river, but, again, he put the men under him in, um, at risk. It was an unauthorized act, which, being the case, he did without proper fire support."

"Sisto just ran off and did this on his own."

"Yes, a renegade operation, you might say. He was lucky to return with as many men as he did."

"So, if you'd been in command, you would not have signed off on the Silver Star recommendation?"

"I would not reward a man in a position of responsibility for putting his men unnecessarily at risk."

"Then, to you, there really was no paradox between the action that earned Lieutenant Sisto his Silver Star and the action that brought him his court-martial."

"I felt the discipline issue was the same in both cases."

"That being that the lieutenant had a tendency—"

From Harry: "Objection. Do two incidents constitute a 'tendency'?"

"Withdrawn," Courie said, then turned back to Joyce. "The lieutenant eventually earned his sergeant's stripes back."

"Had I been in command, I don't know that I would have allowed that, I don't know that it would have been *tolerated*. Major Porter—I must say this—was not a particularly confrontational person. As a result—a *consequence*—he could be soft on discipline issues. But we had a serious casualty rate in Italy, so, naturally, there was a constant shortage of experienced unit leaders. It was a matter of closing one eye and learning to live with it, with the lieutenant's, um, *deficiencies*. But let me say— this should be pointed out—that his conduct did seem to improve when he got his stripes back. My thinking had always been that the disciplining that went with the Article 96 had had its desired effect."

"At the end of the battalion's tenure in Italy, Lieutenant Sisto's company commander nominated him for a battlefield commission to second lieutenant. Major Porter signed off on the nomination."

"Again, I'd have to say that had I been in command, I'm not sure I would have done so, and I did counsel Major Porter in that regard."

"Because of your concerns about Lieutenant Sisto's discipline problems?"

"Yes, correct. But, as I said, his conduct had improved. And the re-fit in England was going to result in a substantial number of new and untried troops coming into the battalion. It, um, *behooved* us to have our more experienced men in positions of leadership. Regretfully, it seems, with the benefit of hindsight, I must say that my leeriness about putting Lieutenant Sisto in such a command position seems to have been borne out."

"Objection," announced Harry. "The witness is offering a conclusion."

"Sustained," Ryan said. "Strike that last remark. Jury will disregard."

"Let's go to the incident in question," Courie proceeded. "When did Lieutenant Sisto assume command of Love Company?"

"That would have been during the closing, um, *phase*, you might say, of the second attempt on Hill 399. The then acting company CO had been seriously wounded, and Lieutenant Sisto was the last commissioned officer in Love Company still in action."

"What was the lieutenant's first act immediately upon assuming command?"

"He requested—well, I can't honestly call it a request. He *demanded* the battalion be withdrawn from the hill."

"At that time, all three rifle companies were engaged and lodged in this trench system, yes?" Courie turned to the diagram of Hill 399 and indicated the jagged line along the upper slopes.

"Yes, in that line of trenches."

"Major Porter gave the pull-back order?"

"Yes."

"Did you agree with it?"

"Um, well, I must admit it was very difficult to get an accurate picture of the situation on the hill. I assume you've already heard about the obstacles we had maintaining communications in that area. And battle itself is, by its nature, chaotic. The major was usually, um, was *prone* to err on the side of caution, you might say, and with the scant information we had, his decision to displace from the hill is understandable."

"That still doesn't answer my question, Captain Joyce."

The captain drew himself erect. "It was the farthest up the hill we'd been able to get. We'd actually broken the Germans' first line of defense, that trench system. I would have preferred to hold, at least until we could get a better picture of the situation, to see if we could possibly exploit our gain rather than withdraw entirely from the hill and have to begin anew with a fresh attack."

"Major Porter ordered the withdrawal, the battalion pulled back from the hill, back to its original jump-off position. What happened next, Captain?"

"Major Porter conferred with General Cota's headquarters about what the next course of action should be. The general conveyed to us orders from Corps that we were to resume the attack on the objective as soon as we could regroup. Because of our, um, restricted manpower, the script also called for the commitment of all three rifle companies again. Major Porter had an officer's call for the purpose of working out the tactical, um, *issues* for the attack. Some of the company commanders had noted weaknesses in the German defenses and worked out a script to try to exploit them and make a push to the top of the hill. That detail—the push—fell to Lieutenant Sisto's company, to Love Company."

"Your opinion of the plan?"

"With the resources we had—at the risk of sounding flippant—it was as good a plan as any. I had some reservations about the reinforcement detail—"

"That was this 'pick-up' company under Lieutenant Tully that was supposed to move up once Major Porter had reached the top of the hill?"

"Yes, the saddle. The hill had two, um, crests . . . We called it 'The Camelback.' The assault detail was to try to gain this lower section between the two crests, this saddle."

"From what we've heard, Major Porter was not normally an officer who decided to 'carry the flag' himself, so to speak. At what point did the major decide he would personally lead the hilltop assault, and—if you know—could you tell us what went into his making that decision?"

"I think we—the battalion staff—we were all of the opinion, the view, that this was going to be the last opportunity for the battalion to take the hill. There were only a few hours of daylight left, and in all probability, we would not have had the resources to mount a fourth attack."

"Do or die."

"To be blunt, yes. That being the case, Major Porter indicated to me that perhaps his presence might offer some kind of, I guess you would say inspiration to the men not only in the assault detail but to the battalion as a whole. It was his attempt to rally the men."

"And your assignment?"

"Because of our communications difficulties, Major Porter wanted me at the battalion CP to try to coordinate the different, um, flows of information. I think any commander, such as these gentlemen on the jury, they can tell you that someone actually in combat on the line does not necessarily have the best view—the best overall view—of how an operation may be going. I think that was a problem we had on the hill. If one can't see any farther than the immediate ten or twenty yards around—and *that* appears to be hard going—one might be oblivious to the fact that opportunities just out of sight are presenting themselves. My job, along with the battalion HQ staff, was to attempt to piece together that overall picture as the operation developed and advise the major on the hill accordingly."

"Now, Captain, we come to that last attack."

"That third assault progressed at a much slower pace than the previous attempts. I think after what the men had already been through, they may simply have been more, um, *tentative* about advancing, but I'm just assuming. You see, again, because of the difficulties with communications, it was hard to determine, to *ascertain* exactly what the situation was on the hill, and it became harder still when we lost our hard-line connection with the forward OP at the woods line. When that happened, I decided to move up to the forward OP to make a personal estimate of the situation. When I reached the OP, Lieutenant Tully reported to me that he had seen the flare signaling that the bunker had been destroyed and that he could see the assault detail making their way to the top of the hill."

"What happened then?"

"At that point, that instant, even though the assault detail had yet to reach their objective, the hilltop, I was so concerned as to how long it would take the reinforcement company to reach them that I ordered Lieutenant Tully to move out."

"And Lieutenant Tully's response?"

"Tully refused. He said his orders had been to wait for the, um, *prescribed* signal. Even as we were arguing, I could see through my field glasses that the assault team had gained the hilltop. Still, Lieutenant Tully refused my order. I tried to explain the, um, uh, *exigencies* of the situation that mandated using our initiative, but I couldn't get him to advance his troops."

"You went as far as to threaten the lieutenant with arrest, did you not?"

"Yes. I said I would relieve him and place him under arrest. He remained adamant. While we were arguing, a runner from the battalion CP notified me that the ammo train had arrived. Even with the promise of cover fire from our Weapons Company, Lieutenant Tully refused to move his men out without the signal from the hill. I was on the verge of relieving him when we received a radio transmission from the hilltop detail that they were withdrawing."

"Who sent the radio message?"

"I took the radio from Lieutenant Tully's operator. Lieutenant Sisto was on the other end."

"Can you recall what Lieutenant Sisto said? As close to the exact words as you can, please."

At this point, Joyce turned toward the defense table. I suppose the look was intended as a steely, accusing glare, but the young man simply could not muster the prerequisite intensity. It seemed a blank and pointless gesture. "Lieutenant Sisto said, as well as I can recall, he said, 'We've had it. We're coming down.' I couldn't believe what I was hearing! I asked him to repeat the message, he did, and then I ordered him to hold his position. I even repeated the order to make sure he'd received it and understood. That was when he told me they'd been ordered out by Major Porter. I asked that he put the major on the line, he said something to the effect—I'm sorry I can't recall the precise, the *exact* words—something along the line that I could argue about it with the major when they'd returned to the woods. I naturally tried to press the issue, but Lieutenant Sisto broke contact."

"Did you receive any further contact from Lieutenant Sisto? Or any of the other commanders on the hill?"

"No direct contact. Through Lieutenant Tully's radio I could hear transmissions between the three rifle companies on the hill intermittently. That's when I heard them arranging to bring the whole battalion entirely off the hill. I again tried to contact Lieutenant Sisto, as he seemed to have taken charge up there. Since I could receive their signals, there seemed no reason he could not receive mine, so I presumed that he simply refused—he *elected*—not to respond."

"And then?"

"Since there was nothing I could do to prevent the withdrawal, I sent a runner with orders to the Weapons Company to cover the withdrawal as best they could. I also passed the word to Lieutenant Tully's people that wherever Lieutenant Sisto came into the line, he should be brought to me. Which he was."

"You confronted Lieutenant Sisto with the charge of disobeying your orders?"

"I did."

"And his response?"

"He continued to maintain that he had been operating under Major Porter's orders. I asked as to the whereabouts of the major and he indicated that he believed the major to be dead back on the hill. I asked him if anyone who'd been with him on the hill could substantiate his claim, he said no, and at that point I relieved him of his command and placed him under arrest. We then returned to the CP area, where I had the lieutenant held in custody. That night we received orders to displace behind the Kall River, and then back to Rott. At which time I initiated charges."

"Thank you very much, Captain. I have no further questions." Courie closed his reference folder with a solemn finality, took a moment to face the jury gravely, another moment to turn toward the defense table—where he seemed to flash a look of quiet satisfaction—before returning to his seat.

"All right, Colonel Voss," Ryan called, "you're up."

Harry stood. His note cards were fanned in three long columns. He scooped up each fan, consolidated them into three decks, and set them back on the table. "Good afternoon, Captain. You've been up there a long time. Can we get you anything? Would you like a glass of water? Coffee?"

The small cordiality took Joyce by surprise. He blinked, then: "Actually, I am a bit parched. Water would be fine, thank you, Sir."

Harry turned to Ryan with a questioning nod, Ryan called to one of the MPs to fetch the drink.

"It's all right, Captain," Harry soothed, "I'll wait for the water." Then, as if idly marking time, "That was a bad day."

"Yes, Sir."

"A bad fight."

"Very, Sir."

"I compliment you on how articulately you explained it all to us."

"Why, thank you, Colonel."

"Ah, here's your water. Cold enough?"

"I appreciate this, thank you, Sir."

"Good." Harry turned to the three decks of cards on his table. His hand hovered over them, hesitated, then scooped up one deck. "Make yourself comfortable, Captain, I'm afraid Captain Courie has left us with a lot of ground to cover. I'm going to jump around a bit. Hope you don't mind."

"Not a bit, Sir."

"Captain, there was a word you used earlier to describe Dominick Sisto," Harry began.

"Yes, Sir?"

"You described him as 'rough.'"

"Well—"

"As in rough around the edges? Knockabout?"

"Yes, well, along those lines. You know."

"Tough guy."

"I don't know that I'd put it in quite—"

"Vulgar? Coarse in some way? Is that how you meant it?"

"Well, Colonel, *any* line soldier, you know, it's a pretty tough life they have up there. They're not exactly drinking tea with pinkies extended."

"So it wouldn't necessarily grate on your sensibilities for someone like the lieutenant to say to you, 'Hey, Cap, how 'bout passing me the effing salt?'"

Chuckles about the room.

"I'm not even sure the word would register." Joyce grinned.

"Captain Joyce, did you like Lieutenant Sisto?"

"I didn't know him that well. I mean, on a personal basis."

"Did you dislike him?"

"As I said—"

"Captain, I'm not asking if you two had a deep and abiding friendship. You bump into somebody in the elevator, you start talking. You get a good feeling, you keep talking. Something doesn't hit you just so, you watch the floors go by instead."

"I really wasn't acquainted well enough with the lieutenant in that fashion to have a personal opinion."

"'In that fashion,'" Harry murmured. He nodded, as if impressed by the phrase.

Joyce cocked his head, uncertain whether Harry was mocking him or not.

"And, of course, he was . . . 'rough.'" A contemplative pause. "In all that time in the battalion together"—and he turned from one note card to the next—"there was the court-martial, the Silver Star business...I think you also said—didn't you?—that Sisto wound up an acting platoon leader? At least at times? Yes, you did. Then with his promotion...and I believe you also told Captain Courie that you found yourself dealing with the lieutenant more and more over time...But still you didn't know him enough to—"

"I've always tried to keep a personal distance between myself and most of the men in the outfit, Sir."

"Even the officers?"

"Especially the officers."

"A 'personal distance.'"

"I didn't see the merit in creating relationships with men who would, most probably, be ordered into critical situations at one time or another."

"'Critical situations.' Meaning situations that could result in injury or death?"

"Exactly, Sir."

I saw nods among the jury.

"A fair point," Harry said, nodding as well. "Better not to be too close to your men."

"You see what I mean, Sir."

"Yes. But still..."

"Sir?"

"After all that time, there must have been—how can I put this? Putting aside the issue of dislike and like—"

"Thank God," muttered Courie. This earned him a rap of the gavel and a reproving frown from Ryan.

"—was there anything *about* Lieutenant Sisto, a characteristic, that maybe rubbed you the wrong way?"

"I try not to let myself be distracted by the petty idiosyncrasies—"

Harry held up a halting hand. "Look, Captain, I've been in

close contact with the lieutenant for a few weeks now and—I don't know if you'd call this a petty idiosyncrasy—but I think he can be pretty lippy."

"Excuse me, Sir?"

"He has a sharp tongue."

"Oh, yes, he does that, Sir."

"If he has something on his mind . . ."

"Yes, Sir, he does not hesitate to express himself."

Again, that amused nod of Harry's: "'Hesitate to express himself.'"

This tic of repetition was beginning to abrade the captain. "Yes, well, what I mean—"

"Is that if you said 'Jump!,' Lieutenant Sisto isn't exactly the type to say, 'Yes, Sir! How high?'"

"That's a colorful way of putting it, Sir, but yes."

"You hardly ever give an order without him having a beef."

"He seems to think that his combat experience entitles him to a certain, um . . ."

"License?"

"Yes, Sir, that it allowed him to be free with his opinions on operational orders. Even blatantly disrespectful."

"I guess over time that could be pretty annoying."

"Yes, Sir. I thought Major Porter should have taken a firmer stand with the lieutenant about his attitude."

"Gets to a point where you want to say 'For God's sake, just once, Sisto, can't I give you an order without getting an argument?'"

Joyce beamed at the understanding of his predicament. "Exactly, Sir!"

"And then if the enlisted men hear him back-talking like this, well, what does that do for 'good order and discipline'?"

"That's the problem succinctly, Sir. I don't know that Major Porter quite appreciated that."

"Yes. 'Succinctly.' I imagine that kind of backtalk could be *especially* irritating in a real pressure-cooker situation. Like at Hill 399. It sounds like nobody was happy with the operation, and then here's Lieutenant Sisto *indulging* in a snit every time he's told to do something . . ."

"One doesn't need additional headaches at a time like that."

"No, 'one' doesn't." Harry tapped the 'one' with an ever-so-slight depreciative note. "During the re-fit in England, it was the same way?"

"Well, the circumstances were different. The gravity of a combat situation was, naturally, lacking."

"Naturally. But that didn't stop his squawking."

"No, Sir, I'm afraid not."

"About?"

"He didn't seem to see the value of some elements of the training program."

"Such as?"

"The usual routine items: inspections, parade formations—"

"Drills, and so forth."

"Yes, Sir. I don't think anyone disputes that inspections can be tedious, but I think the lieutenant failed to value how those kinds of activities build unit cohesion and discipline. With so many new men coming into the battalion, we needed that."

"Felt he'd fought his way through Italy, he shouldn't have to put up with all this—the men had a word for this kind of thing, didn't they?"

"Sir?"

"Isn't there a word the veterans use for activities they think are unnecessary? That they think are pointless, useless . . . ?"

Captain Joyce cleared his throat, glanced insecurely toward the jury panel, toward Pietrowski. "Well, um . . ."

Harry smiled broadly. "Come on, Captain, we're all over twenty-one here. They call that kind of thing 'chickenshit,' don't they?"

I could tell from the looks on the panel that most of the military brotherhood were acquainted with the term and its meaning.

"I believe that is the word, Sir, the phrase."

"So, does this mean Lieutenant Sisto was easy on his men?"

"I wouldn't say that, Sir, no."

"If he didn't have them doing drills, what did he have them doing?"

"Nothing unusual, Sir. Tactical problems. He'd take them out in the field, set up situations. Cross-country hikes, obstacle-course runs, live-fire exercises, infiltration-course exercises . . . aside from the more, um—"

"Tedious?"

"Yes, tedious training routines, his program included many of the usual exercises."

"His emphasis seems to have been on training that dealt with actual combat situations."

"I suppose that's how they'd be characterized."

"And he pushed his men hard, didn't he?"

"I'd like to think we were all trying to toughen up the new men."

"Of course," Harry agreed amiably. "Captain Joyce, didn't Major Porter call Lieutenant Sisto on the carpet at one point to tell him to ease up? That he thought Lieutenant Sisto was going too hard on that end of the training?"

"I recall they'd had a discussion about training, but as to the precise nature of that discussion—"

"There were some injuries, weren't there? Among Lieutenant Sisto's men?"

"I believe so, Sir, yes."

"Over the two and a half months the battalion was in England, in Lieutenant Sisto's platoon: two broken wrists, one broken ankle, a strained back, three cases of heat exhaustion, and one minor gunshot wound."

"While I was not party to the discussion you're referring to, I do recall that Major Porter wanted the lieutenant to temper the training a bit. It was the major's opinion—and I quite agreed—that we'd have enough casualties in battle without inflicting them on ourselves."

"Maybe the lieutenant's priority was: better they happen in training than in battle."

Joyce fidgeted, feeling boxed in, took a slow sip of his water. "That, I imagine, is a point worth debating."

"That court-martial, the Article 96 . . . I understand what you told the Court about the seriousness being not in the act but in the breach of discipline. If you don't mind, though, I'd like to be clear about some of the circumstances of that incident."

"Of course, Sir."

"Now, you said the battalion was not on the line at the time, correct?"

"We *were* in an operational area, Sir."

"But the lieutenant's company . . . ?"

"Was being held in reserve."

"Any imminent danger of them being called into action?"

"Well, Sir, that's the kind of thing you can never anticipate. The idea of being in reserve is that you're available for action if needed."

"Of course. But I mean there were no *obvious* signs of threat at the time?"

"No, nothing obvious. Nothing, um, *overt*."

"'Overt.' And over the course of the time the lieutenant's company was in the reserve area, was it ever called into action?"

"Fortunately, no, Sir."

At that point, Peter Ricks waved Harry over. They conferred for a brief moment, Harry nodded in agreement, then resumed his stand in the well. "The lieutenant was a sergeant—a squad leader—at the time, correct?"

"Yes, Sir."

"When the incident was discovered, his platoon leader did not call for charges, did he?"

"No, Sir, he did not. I thought that constituted a lapse—"

"And his company commander did not call for them?"

"No, Sir, he—"

"Did Major Porter make the decision to press charges on his own?"

"Major Porter was the battalion commanding officer."

"And you were his exec."

"We . . . consulted."

"In this . . . 'consultation' . . . you offered the opinion that the major should press charges?"

"Major Porter asked my opinion, and I gave it."

Infinitely patient: "That he should press charges?"

"Yes, Sir, and, as I said earlier this morning, it's obvious from the subsequent change in Lieutenant Sisto's conduct that the court-martial turned out to be a productive discipline."

"Even though it sounds like Sisto was just as lippy and insolent *after* the court-martial as he was *before*."

"Well, a little smart-mouthing hardly compares to—"

"Captain, did any other man in the battalion ever fall victim to the same indulgence as the lieutenant?"

"Indulgence, Sir?"

"We heard testimony—from Colonel Bright, no less—that every one of those Italian households had a stash of booze in the basement."

"That might be something of an exaggeration—"

"Well, let's leave it that when it came to spirits, there was no real *availability* problem."

Another set of grins about the court, including one from Joyce himself. "That would be fair to say, yes, Sir," the captain said.

"So, with that much alcohol around, did you have to deal with any other cases similar to Dominick Sisto's?"

"It's always possible other men in the battalion may have acted improperly—"

"But there's nothing you have any direct knowledge about."

"Yes, correct, Sir."

"If another such incident had come up, would you have pressed charges?"

"If the circumstances were the same . . . the same exercise of bad judgment, the same failure of responsibility, the same circumstance of it occurring in an operational area—"

"That's a lot of ifs, Captain. See, I'm getting a feeling—and please correct me if I'm wrong—that essentially Lieutenant Sisto was busted because he was the only one you caught."

"I think that's an oversimplification. We did have occasional incidences of *individual* drunkenness—"

"You caught these other men?"

"I can't recall every bit of minor misconduct—"

"'Minor misconduct'?" Harry echoed disbelievingly. "The incident cost Dominick Sisto his sergeant's stripes."

"As a squad leader, Dominick Sisto's act was considered to be of a more serious degree. These other incidents were minor enough that they were not referred for court-martial; they did not come before the battalion commander. In an individual occasion of drunkenness, Major Porter and I would have left disposition of such a case to the immediate superior. We may not even have known about it until it appeared in the daily reports."

"Captain, has any other officer in the battalion ever been court-martialed for disobedience or insubordination?"

"Court-martialed? No, Sir, I don't believe so."

"Reprimanded?"

"Yes, Sir, but every unit—"

"Yes, Captain, into each life a little rain must fall. But Dominick Sisto—first in Italy, and if you'd had your way after the Rapido River, and now here—he's the only officer—"

"That's it!" Courie stormed, rising. But before he could object—

"I'm already there, Captain," Ryan said, turning an inhospitable stare on Harry. "Colonel Voss, pardon my bluntness, but what the hell is this all about? You've had the captain under cross-examination for a good while now and not once have I heard you refer to the act that's being contested here!"

"I'm looking to establish a foundation, Sir," Harry answered with a blitheness I'm sure was calculated to get Ryan's goat as much as Courie's.

"Foundation for what?" Courie demanded.

"I want to know how come two officers committed the same act on the same day during the same battle, but only one of them wound up under arrest."

"What're you talking about?" Ryan looked almost dizzy. "What other—"

"Lieutenant Tully," Ricks explained.

"Are you accusing Captain Joyce of bias?" Courie asked, incredulous. "There hasn't been one bit of testimony that's come into this courtroom that's even *hinted* there might be something personal between these two men!"

"I'm not accusing the captain of anything," Harry maintained. "I didn't say it was personal. I didn't say there was a bias. That's why I'm trying to set a foundation: so I can explore the possibility."

"And you're wrong, Captain," Ricks put in. "There *has* been testimony that raises the question. The testimony about Lieutenant Tully."

Pietrowski raised his hand. "Colonel Ryan, don't you think we'd save a lot of time without all this waltzing around if Colonel Voss just asks the question outright?"

"I was just trying to set up a proper framework, Sir," Harry said.

"You were trying to do a hell of a lot more than that!" Courie retorted snidely. "You're practically conducting a *smear*—"

Ryan silenced them all with a bang of his gavel. "Captain Courie! You're getting on thin ice yourself with that kind of remark!"

"Colonel Ryan," Courie replied, "even if the Defense somehow substantiates this claim of bias, that doesn't mitigate the case of the defendant. If two men disobey an order and I charge only one, that may make me an unfair s.o.b., but that doesn't invalidate the charge."

"It may not invalidate the charge, Captain, but it does raise the question of ill motive. Colonel Voss, ask the question so we can move on!"

"Fine." Harry turned to Joyce. "Captain, you ordered Lieutenant Tully to take his men across the firebreak."

"Yes, Sir."

"He refused."

"Yes, Sir."

"You threatened to relieve Tully of his command and press charges."

"Yes, Sir."

"You didn't. Why?"

"Lieutenant Tully was killed."

"A bit later. Why didn't you relieve him right then and there?"

"Sir, we were in the middle of a fight, a damned nasty one, as I'm sure you're aware!"

"Captain, Lieutenant Tully's men were not in that fight. They were dug in inside the woods line. Command could have passed smoothly to the next-senior. So, why didn't you relieve Tully?"

The young captain could not hide his temper: "*I suppose I had a hell of a lot on my mind just then! Sir!*"

"The situation was crazy. Chaotic."

"Yes, Sir!"

"You'd deal with it later."

"Yes, Sir!"

"Relax, Captain, that's all I wanted. An explanation. You provided one. Thank you." Then, so innocuously asked as to be sinister: "But when Lieutenant Sisto was brought to you, once he reported that Major Porter was dead, you *did* relieve *him* on the spot, didn't you?"

"The fight was over by that time! The battalion was off the hill!"

"Yes, the battalion was off the hill. Had Tully's men been withdrawn from the woods-line position, and the battalion survivors redeployed in the woods at that time?"

"Not yet—"

"Weren't the medics and some of Lieutenant Sisto's and Lieutenant Tully's men still bringing in wounded from the firebreak?"

"There were a few stragglers—"

"Was the battalion still taking fire?"

"Artillery was *always* falling on the woods—"

"The battalion was taking fire?" Harry pressed.

"Yes, Sir."

"Had Lieutenant Sisto seen at all to his men? Did he even have a head count for you?"

Joyce fumbled for words. "I—"

"I'll answer for you, Captain. No. No, because he never had the time. You had Dominick Sisto brought to you immediately, you relieved him immediately, you dragged him off to the battalion area immediately."

"Objection!"

"Lieutenant Tully's men were safely dug in, but you didn't relieve him. There were still a lot of things Lieutenant Sisto needed to see to, but Sisto you placed under arrest."

"Objection!" Courie's anger exploded as his hand slapped down on his table. "Argumentative. The Defense is making his closing argument!"

"Sustained!" Ryan reprimanded.

Harry gave a chastised nod, then continued. "Did you inform the next-senior that Lieutenant Sisto had been relieved before you left for the battalion area?"

"I, um . . ."

"No. You were in such a hurry to get the lieutenant back to the battalion CP—"

"I felt it was a priority to report the failure of the attack to Division, and the loss of Major Porter."

"And the arrest of Lieutenant Sisto."

"Since I felt—and still feel—he'd cost us the opportunity to take the hill, yes, Sir, I did feel that was a significant priority!"

Harry took a moment to let the tension in the chamber ease. He turned away from the captain, left the younger man to recompose himself, take another drink of his water. When Harry returned to the questioning, he was shaking his head mournfully. "The shame of it is I would've thought you and Dominick Sisto would've hit it off from the start."

"Sir?"

"I mean you both have a lot in common. You're more well-spoken, better educated, but both of you—"

"Objection," Courie snapped. "I don't know where the colonel's going with all this pal-o'-mine stuff—I don't know where he's *been* going for quite some time, he's been all over the map—but wherever it is, it's hard for me to imagine this has anything to do with this case. It sounds like he's setting them up for a date!"

Which brought a few more grins on the jury panel, grins swiftly extinguished, this time, by a harrumph from Colonel Pietrowski.

"As Captain Joyce is the officer who initiated charges, he's presumed to be hostile—" Harry turned toward Joyce. "No offense, Captain. I'm afraid that's the lexicon of the trade. You know what I mean by 'lexicon,' don't you?"

The suspicious cock of the head. "Yes," Joyce replied warily, "I know what lexicon means."

Harry returned to Ryan. "As such, Defense usually enjoys a certain latitude in its examination."

"There's latitude and there's latitude!" Courie opined, red-faced. "Right about now the Defense is just west of Fiji!"

"Colonel Voss, the Judge Advocate makes the point with a certain flair, but he *is* on point," Ryan noted. "I'll let you go for a bit more, but this has been going on for a while and I'm having trouble seeing the relevance of a lot of this testimony." His look warned that Harry was getting himself into a position where Ryan not only would be unable to help him but unwilling.

Harry nodded without showing much concern. "Captain Joyce, all I was trying to point out is that you're both from working-class families. I mean, I see from your records that your father—"

Joyce brought his head up. "I'm not ashamed of it, Colonel."

"Good!" Harry smiled. "You should be proud! You've obviously done quite well for yourself!"

Courie theatrically cleared his throat, warning that another objection to the line of questioning was not far off.

"I see here," Harry continued, "where you had tried to get into West Point—"

"I couldn't manage the congressional appointment."

Harry nodded sympathetically. "University of Connecticut, degree in business, class of 'forty-one. ROTC. Yes, you've done quite well for yourself even without making The Point."

"Thank you, Sir."

"What's next? A trip back to the womb?" Courie growled. Ryan rapped his gavel for order, but Courie did not restrain himself. "I'm sorry, Colonel," he said, rising to his feet, "but enough's enough! What has any of Captain Joyce's biography—"

"Goes to credibility," Harry interrupted quietly. "Captain Joyce filed the charges. The panel should have the right to gauge the character and caliber of the officer who's responsible for us all being here."

"That sounds very nice," Ryan said skeptically, "but I'm telling you, Colonel Voss, if I don't see a more direct connection between your questions and the Judge Advocate's examination of this witness, whatever line you're following will be over! Understood?"

"Is it allowable that I ask the captain about his previous military assignments?"

"Yes, Colonel," Ryan answered with clearly fraying temper, "that is allowable. Just don't beat it to death."

"Thank you. Captain, before you came to the battalion, where were you? What did the Army have you doing?"

"I, um, was in Washington."

"Doing?"

Joyce fidgeted. "I was attached to the Quartermaster Corps. I liaised with manufacturers to arrange production schedules and shipments of goods contracted for by the Army."

"That business degree sort of damned you."

Joyce smiled sheepishly. "I'm afraid so, Sir."

"And that's when you were assigned as executive officer to the 3rd Battalion?"

"Yes, Sir."

"So, your entire military career before coming to the battalion was with the QM?"

The captain's smile faded. He took a sip of his water. "Yes, Sir."

"You had never had a combat command prior?"

"Correct, Sir."

"No experience at the platoon or company level? In the field?"

Courie stood: "Objection. Asked and answered."

Ryan: "Colonel, I warned you about—"

"Sorry, Sir. Captain Joyce, that being the case, you must have been gratified at serving under Major Porter. We heard that before coming to the battalion Major Porter had been posted to Fort Benning. I understand there's a big infantry training school there. The major must have known his business."

"Major Porter had been at Benning, but only in an administrative capacity. He didn't have much more combat experience than I did when I was assigned to the battalion."

"Didn't you ever feel out of your depth, Captain? I mean, here you were, executive officer of an *infantry battalion*—"

"Objection! Argumentative!"

Harry plodded on: "—but you yourself had never had the experience of leading men into battle?"

"Neither has Eisenhower!" Joyce quipped.

Harry smiled. "*Touché.*" He turned to Courie. "Captain Joyce did just fine without your help, Captain."

"I'm still going to sustain," Ryan said. "Strike the last question and answer. And that remark about General Eisenhower. Let's not drag *everybody* into this."

"Let's talk a little bit about Major Porter," Harry went on.

A moan from Courie, a silencing look from Ryan.

"Captain Joyce, you said you had a fairly good working relationship with Major Porter. Did you *like* him?"

"Colonel Ryan!" Courie intervened wearily. "Is the Defense going to take us through another one of these popularity contests?"

"I think we've already settled the need to discuss Major Porter's role in these events," Harry returned.

"I'm afraid we did," Ryan said glumly, and nodded for Harry to proceed.

"I was asking if you liked Major Porter, Captain," Harry said. "You two served together about a year. Did you ever have a drink together? Sit around and swap lies?"

"We were not . . . unfriendly—"

"Cordial?"

"Yes, but I wouldn't say we were good friends."

"Captain, it seems you've spent most of your time in the battalion keeping company with yourself."

"Objection!" Courie said. "We don't need that kind of remark, do we, Colonel?"

"Sustained."

"You're right, Captain Courie," Harry said with a bow. "My apologies. I didn't mean anything by it, Captain Joyce. You said you had a good working relationship, but I can't imagine you were completely happy serving under him. You seemed to have had two entirely different schools of thought on managing the battalion. On discipline, he was unwilling to confront the men, while you felt . . . 'obligated' . . . ?"

Joyce shrugged noncommittally.

" . . . to be more stern. On tactics, Major Porter was not a risk taker, am I right? And there were times when you would think it was time to take a chance, roll the dice. Am I being fair?"

"I had a good deal of respect for Major Porter. I would not want my attitudes to be construed as denigrating—"

"Please, Captain, you can't say you didn't like the way he ran his show and then say you're not being critical! I can appreciate your not wanting to speak ill of the dead. I'll put it to you another way. If you had been given command of the battalion, would you have run it the same way Major Porter had?"

A deep breath, then a commitment: "No, Sir, I would not."

"Thank you, Captain. Honesty is refreshing, isn't it? It must have been very frustrating for you to serve under him, then."

"Frustrating?"

"You did hope to get command of the battalion at some future point, didn't you?"

"Well, I, um, one goes where the Army—"

"Ambition's not a sin, Captain. You wanted your majority, didn't you? You came into the war a captain. You don't want to go out of it the same way, do you?"

From Pietrowski: "Son, we're all grown-ups here. We all know the facts of life."

"I flatter myself to think I could earn a promotion at some future time."

"Good. As I see it—and if I'm off base here, straighten me out—that wasn't going to happen as long as Major Porter remained in command. It didn't look like he'd ever get promoted out of the battalion, and as long as he kept running the show the way he was, you'd never get a chance to, let's say, 'display your wares.' Is that a reasonable picture of the situation?"

"I, um, I . . . more or less, I suppose so, Sir."

"When Major Porter approved the nomination of Dominick Sisto for a battlefield commission . . . you disagreed?"

"I was not completely comfortable with it, Sir."

"Because by then there'd already been the Article 96, and the incident at the Rapido, and Sisto did have that attitude problem you'd mentioned."

"Yes, Sir."

"And he was kind of rough around the edges."

Nothing.

Harry flipped to a fresh card. "According to the officer fitness report that Major Porter filled out on Lieutenant Sisto just before the unit shipped out of England, well, a lot of this is what you've already told us today: '*Excellent combat soldier . . . has a problem showing proper respect . . .*' Also says here, '*. . . reliable under demanding circumstances . . . despite some abrasive conduct, undeniable leadership qualities . . .*'" Harry looked up from his cards. "Do you agree with the major's assessment?"

"The major was entitled to his opinion."

"Then I take it you disagree?"

"I've said the lieutenant was a good combat soldier. But I'm not in complete agreement with that report."

"You felt he had a, um, I think the word that came up earlier was 'tendency' . . . to disobedience. Or at least insubordination, a problem with authority."

"I'll say I wasn't as sure of his reliability as the major."

"You think Major Porter's judgment was questionable on Dominick Sisto?"

"I think the major tended to be overly generous in his evaluations. I think he sometimes tried to gain the good favor of his subordinates in ways that were, ultimately, not supportive of good order and discipline."

Harry grinned. "Major Porter buttered them up."

"I guess that's a way of putting it, Sir."

Harry flipped to another card. "Says, '. . . loyal, diligent, intelligent . . . prone to take issue with orders he finds disagreeable . . .'"

"I'm not sure how diligent the lieutenant was, though he could be—"

Harry looked up, contrite. "Oh, I'm sorry, Captain. This isn't from Dominick Sisto's fitness report. This is from yours."

Red-faced: "Oh."

"Was Major Porter being overly generous with your evaluation? Or was he just trying to butter—"

"Objection!" Courie looked thoroughly peeved. "Not only is the question argumentative, but I have to keep coming back to the issues of relevance and materiality. I don't see how this relates to the question of credibility that the Defense keeps hiding behind! The Defense questions Captain Joyce's conduct! He questions Major Porter's conduct! The issue here, however, is Lieutenant Sisto's conduct, and that never seems to come up when

Defense Counsel has the floor! It doesn't matter if Major Porter was Sad Sack with oak leaves! The major was dead when the issue at trial occurred! It doesn't matter if Captain Joyce's fitness report indicates he was a prince among men or Captain Bligh! Captain Joyce gave an order *and Lieutenant Sisto refused to obey!* Why in God's name are we wasting the Court's time on all this other material?"

"All right, Colonel Voss!" Ryan said, now evidently in irate sympathy with Courie. "Let's hear it; and you'd better make it good."

Harry bowed his head, tucked his hands behind his back. When his head rose and he turned about, he seemed to be facing the jury as much as Ryan. "Every time the Judge Advocate has objected on the basis of relevancy and scope, he keeps saying the issue at trial is simple: an order was given; the order was disobeyed. And put that way, the issue at trial *is* that simple. But there's a third element to this case that the Prosecution consistently refuses to acknowledge: *that Dominick Sisto insists he was under Major Porter's orders."*

Courie stepped forward to interject, but Harry held up a hand and kept on:

"We've been over this before: the jury is entitled to make a judgment as to the likelihood that such an order may have been given, and that *does* mean examining the competence of Major Porter. As far as the Defense is concerned, this issue was settled yesterday. I apologize if that means this trial is a bit of a slog for the Judge Advocate. Perhaps if he had as much at stake as Lieutenant Sisto, the Trial Judge Advocate might not be so bored. So now the Court either has to reverse its previous ruling on the admissibility of this testimony or allow the Defense to continue along this line."

Ryan closed his eyes as if suffering a severe migraine. Harry's trump card—and I was acquainted enough with Ryan's sense of do-no-wrong *amour-propre* to know this to be so—was that Ryan would never demonstrate a *mea culpa* by reversing himself. What he *would* decide on this issue, however, was fuel for suspense.

The colonel was silent a long time before his eyes opened. He shot a bitter glance at Harry, and I could tell he was not likely to forget that he was now corralled by the ruling his friend had coaxed from him the day before. He assumed an air of judicial sagacity. "Both counsel have a point. We have established the relevance of Major Porter's conduct and the Defense can present testimony accordingly. But the Judge Advocate also has a point in that this does not allow the Defense to roam willy-nilly through the life stories of the concerned parties."

Harry's eyebrows went up at "willy-nilly," which drew a glare from Ryan I can characterize only as *Shut your trap and behave yourself!*

"So. Colonel Voss, you can continue to ask questions about Major Porter but only insomuch as they connect directly—I repeat—*directly* to the events surrounding the action at question here. Now: do you understand? Or do I have to make it plainer?"

While Harry's "I understand, Sir, and I appreciate the Court's patience" was humble enough, it was clear from his look that he was enjoying Ryan's discomfiture. After all, the shoe was—as the proverb goes—usually on the other foot.

Harry set that second deck of note cards on his table. There was yet another quick conference with Ricks before he scooped up the last deck and turned back to Joyce. The latter was looking rather fagged by this point.

"All right, Captain," Harry began, "it's time to talk about Hill 399."

I think the only thing that kept Courie from standing on his chair and shouting "Huzzah!" was anticipating Ryan's withering glare.

"Captain Joyce, we've heard testimony that Corps had commanded Hill 399 be taken, and those orders were relayed through General Cota's division to General Breen and Major Porter and yourself. But the actual tactical approach to taking the hill on that third assault—this idea of knocking out the bunker covering the approach to the top of the hill, then attacking up a seam in the German defenses—who came up with that plan?"

"Well, we were all huddled—"

"'We'?"

"Major Porter, myself, Lieutenant Schup, and the rifle company COs."

"*Acting* COs, right?"

"Well, yes, they'd all had to assume command."

"Because the regular COs were dead or wounded?"

"Yes, Sir."

"Who said 'You do this and I'll do that'? I mean, who worked out the specifics?"

"As I said, all of us sat down together—"

"Wasn't it the three acting rifle company commanders, Captain?"

"Objection," Courie said. "He asks the question, doesn't give the witness a chance to answer, then supplies his own answer."

"Sustained. Colonel Voss, I understand you may want to take issue with an answer from the witness, but you can't do that until the witness gives an answer you can take issue with."

"I'm afraid I was a little eager there, Sir, I'm sorry." Harry turned to Joyce. "I didn't mean to jump on you like that, Captain, sorry. Now: to the question."

"The, um, company commanders *were* the ones who were going to have to carry out the attack, so it's understandable they'd work out the, you know, particulars, specifics . . ."

"Among themselves."

"We were *all* there, Colonel."

"Yes, but those acting COs, they were the only ones in that huddle who had firsthand knowledge of what it was really like on the hill."

"Yes, Sir."

"So, it was not Corps, it was not Division, it was not your own battalion planning-and-operation officer, it was not you and Major Porter. You may have offered some guidance and counsel, but the three *acting* company COs worked out the plan of attack— Lieutenant Sisto, Sergeant Sekelsky, and Lieutenant DeCrane."

"You make that sound small, somehow, Colonel. I think they did a respectable job."

"You misunderstand me, Captain. I think they did a *hell* of a job! They didn't get their promised air support, their companies had suffered devastating losses, yet those three guys got the battalion its farthest advance up that hill. True?"

"True, Sir."

"Now, as you say, you were there when they were putting the plan together. You approved the plan?"

"Major Porter as the CO—"

"Didn't ask your opinion?"

"The plan seemed workable."

"So, for once, you and Major Porter agreed on something."

Courie: "Objection."

Ryan: "Sustained. Behave, Colonel Voss."

"Captain, I want to talk about Major Porter's leading the assault team that made the drive to the top of Hill 399. The words we've used so far about Major Porter's tactical 'style' have been 'conservative,' 'tentative,' and so on, and you've agreed with that characterization, correct?"

"In general, yes, Sir."

"So you didn't think Porter was a rash commander? Impetuous? Somebody who got some half-cocked idea in his head and went running off with it?"

"No, Sir. Nothing like that."

"So you must've been surprised when Major Porter decided to personally lead that push on the hill?"

"I was, yes, Sir."

"Before the major decided to personally participate in the attack, didn't he meet privately with the three company commanders?"

"There were several briefing sessions—"

"I'm thinking of one particular session. Things got a bit heated. Didn't the commanders—particularly Lieutenant Sisto—make remarks that might be considered insulting about the major's leadership?"

"I was not party to that meeting."

"Wasn't Major Porter *shamed* into leading that attack?"

"*Objection!*" howled Courie. "The witness has already testified he was not party to that meeting! And even if Major Porter went up that hill only because someone held a gun to his head, that has nothing to do with the issue the Defense has been instructed to confine itself to: the likelihood of Major Porter's having given the withdrawal order."

"Sir," countered Harry, "I don't want the Judge Advocate claiming Major Porter was a hold-to-the-last-man kind of guy because he committed *one* completely out-of-character—"

"The Judge Advocate can claim whatever he wants," Ryan snubbed, "and so can you. It's the jury's responsibility to decide what the truth of the matter is. So, let's not take their job away from them, shall we? And try to leave poor Major Porter alone if we can? Objection sustained. Strike it back to when the Defense brought up the meetings between Major Porter and the company COs."

The stenographer fiddled with his paper recording tape and began to read: "'*Before the major decided to personally*—'"

"That's it," Ryan declared, "up to there. Strike all that. OK, Colonel Voss, move on."

"Captain Joyce, earlier Captain Courie asked you about Lieutenant Sisto's conduct on the *second* assault on the hill, when the lieutenant assumed command of Love Company. You said that Dominick Sisto's first act having taken command of the company was to *demand*—that was the word you used—the battalion's withdrawal from Hill 399. Do you remember saying that?"

"I remember, Sir."

"And do you remember taking issue with the decision to withdraw at that time?"

"I don't know that I'd use the phrase 'taking issue.'"

"Let's keep it simple. Dominick Sisto wanted to pull out, Major Porter agreed, and you did not."

"As I recall, I said that it would have been my preference—"

Resolutely: "Lieutenant Sisto wanted off the hill; you wanted him to stay."

"At that point, yes, Sir."

"Did Lieutenant Sisto give any reason for his wanting the battalion pulled off the hill?"

"He said he believed the battalion couldn't hold."

"Did Lieutenant Sisto say *why* he believed the battalion couldn't hold?"

"I'm sure he did, but I'm having difficulty recalling—"

"Didn't the lieutenant say that he was short of men? And the ones who were left were low on ammunition?"

"That sounds, um, yes, I believe that was the report."

"*Were* they low on ammo? Were they short of men?"

"Obviously, we could go only by what was being reported."

"Did you have any reason to doubt that Lieutenant Sisto was being truthful?"

"The decision to withdraw was Major Porter's."

"Captain, I'm asking if *you* thought Lieutenant Sisto might have been lying—or, if you're more comfortable with the word, *exaggerating*—about his situation to get a pull-back order from Major Porter?"

"My concern was that, considering the confused situation on the hill, Lieutenant Sisto might not have been able to give an accurate report. What he could immediately witness would not necessarily have been an accurate overall picture. Do you get my meaning?"

"Yes, Captain, I do. All right, Captain Joyce, let's get down to cases. Let's talk about that last attack on Hill 399."

A gratified sigh from the captain.

And a renewed interest from Courie and Alth.

"Yes, it has been a long time coming," Harry said good-naturedly, bowing toward Courie, Ryan, the jury panel, and Joyce, "and I appreciate everyone's patience. I'm going to try and deal with a number of issues in a loose kind of chronological order. I think that'll make it easier for everybody here, including myself"—a humble shrug and smile—"to follow. Let's start with when the battalion command post lost the communication line to the forward observation post. You decided to leave the CP—your assigned post—and move up to the demarcation line."

"Objection," Courie called, though this time he seemed less sure of his ground. "The colonel's use of the phrase 'assigned post' is obviously intended to prejudice—"

"It *wasn't* his assigned post?" Harry asked Courie innocently.

Courie looked helplessly toward Joyce, then toward Ryan.

From Ryan, coolly: "Was it or was it not the captain's assigned post?"

Courie's shoulders heaved in surrender. "Objection withdrawn."

"Without that communication line we were blind," Joyce volunteered. "I only moved up—"

Harry nodded understandingly. "So you explained under direct. Did you take a radio with you when you moved up to the forward OP?"

"We had no working sets in reserve, Sir."

"How long did it take you to get from the CP to the forward line?"

"How long, Sir? I'm not quite sure. I did it at the run. Ten minutes perhaps."

"Maybe fifteen?"

"I wouldn't think so. No more than that, I'm sure. Probably less."

"Between ten and fifteen minutes, then."

"Yes, Sir."

"During which time you were out of communication with the CP, Lieutenant Tully's reinforcement company, the Weapons Company, the rifle companies on the hill, and Major Porter's assault detail."

Joyce shook his head condescendingly. "Lieutenant Schup

was quite capable of filling in for me at the CP until I reached the forward line. Remember: all I was supposed to do was co-ordinate cross-communications between—"

"Why didn't you send Lieutenant Schup forward while you remained at your assigned post?"

Joyce hesitated; he'd apparently never quite considered the point himself. "I, um, well, the phone line, communications with the OP were still out, there was no telling when they would be restored . . . If I'd sent someone else, I'd've had to wait for their report. I thought it was important that I should know, I should *personally* know what was happening on the hill as soon as possible."

Harry nodded. "So, now we have you at the forward OP. You can now personally observe the hill. You can see that the assault detail is reaching that part of the top of the hill you call the saddle."

"Yes, Sir."

"Could you tell how many men had actually made it to the saddle?"

"They were dug in, Sir. It wasn't possible to get that kind of—"

"But you knew they hadn't all made it?"

"That was a reasonable assumption."

"Did you have an inkling that the assault detail might have suffered serious casualties?"

"I had no information on which to make that sort of esti-mation."

"'Sort of estimation.'"

"Colonel Ryan!" Courie groused as he rose again. "Could you please instruct the Defense to stop this repetition tic of his? It's a thinly veiled attempt to demean the witness!"

Harry looked surprised. "Oh, I'm sorry! I wasn't even

conscious I was doing it!" He turned to Joyce. "I'm sorry, Captain. Have you felt demeaned in any way?"

Joyce put on a face of brave rebuff. "Not by you, Colonel."

Harry turned back to Courie, as if to say, *See? It's all in your head!* "I'll try to watch myself, Captain, thank you for pointing that out to me." Then, back to Joyce: "The enemy fire was heavy?"

"Yes, Sir."

"So, considering the casualties the battalion had suffered on the previous attempts to take the hill, and the heaviness of the fire on that third attack, it was a reasonable bet that the assault detail hadn't made it to the top of the hill without losses."

"Yes, but how many—"

"I know; you had no way to know. But when Lieutenant Sisto told you he was bringing the assault detail down, you thought however many of them were up there was enough to hold."

"Yes, Sir."

"Based on?"

"As I say, I could see them. I observed them through my field glasses. It looked like they had an adequate defensive position. To be honest, I couldn't be *completely* sure they'd be able to hold, but it appeared to be a chance worth taking. If Lieutenant Tully had been able to move out sooner—"

"You saw the assault detail dug in on the saddle."

"That's what I said, yes, Sir."

"Then you must also have seen the Germans filling in the positions on the high ground on either side of the saddle?"

"I could see some enemy movement, but it was difficult to make out details."

"But you *could* make out enough details about Major Porter's men to know they could hold?"

"It was, I grant, just an estimation. It was quite some distance from where I was to the top of the hill, and there was still considerable fighting going on all along the slope."

"Hard to get a clear picture."

"Yes, Sir."

"You couldn't get a clear picture. But you wouldn't believe the men who were up there when *they* said they couldn't hold?"

"As I've said several times this morning, I couldn't be sure that the men on the scene could completely appreciate their overall situation."

"How long did you study the situation on the hill? How long did you examine the position of the assault detail through your field glasses? And the German positions?"

"Objection. Compound. Would the Defense please let the witness answer one question before he asks another?"

"One at a time," Ryan advised Harry.

Harry nodded. "OK, Captain, one at a time. How long did you study the situation on the hill?"

"I really don't recall. It wasn't that long before—"

"Before you were arguing with Lieutenant Tully, and then Dominick Sisto's transmission came through on the radio. Maybe a glance or two?"

"Certainly more than that, Sir."

"A few minutes?"

"Possibly."

"So, on the one hand, you have the opinion of a man on the scene who has had front-line combat experience of over a year, and who helped plan the hilltop assault, and he says they need to pull out, and then what? From the far side of the firebreak, a few minutes' study through your binoculars—"

"Objection! Argumentative!"

"Sustained."

Ricks waved Harry over. Their conference was extensive

enough to bring a rebuke from Ryan. With a last nod to Ricks, Harry resumed his position in front of Joyce.

"Captain, the concept of 'fire superiority.' What is that?"

"Sir?"

"Fire superiority. That was part of your combat training, wasn't it?"

"Yes, Sir. Well, it means just what it says."

"That you outgun the enemy?"

"It doesn't necessarily mean you have more guns in action, but that at a given point you can lay down more fire than they can to either break up an enemy assault or penetrate an enemy defense."

"On the day of that third and final assault against Hill 399, where and when did your battalion have fire superiority? The expected air support had not come through, and by that third assault, the mortars of your own Weapons Company were running short of ammo. Where was your fire superiority?"

"In training, we learned a lot of principles. But circumstances in the field don't always allow their application."

Harry nodded. "I understand. I still haven't found the opportunity to use the geometry they taught me in high school. Let me ask you about another, oh, I don't know what you'd call it. Doctrine? Formula? Philosophy? Isn't the rule of thumb that when attacking a fixed enemy line, the attack force is supposed to have a numerical superiority?"

"They preach a minimum of three-to-one advantage to the attack force, preferably more."

"Because, obviously, the attack force is going to be exposed to fire and suffer losses on the assault."

"And one has to be sure of enough remaining troops to make the penetration and secure a lodgment."

"Did you have numerical superiority against the Germans

on Hill 399 on that third assault? On *any* of the three assaults on the enemy position?"

"That's impossible to determine, Sir. We had no intelligence on the enemy strength."

"Obviously Major Porter's assault detail couldn't have had a numerical advantage. Even if the detail made it to the top of the hill intact, that was less than two dozen men. From what you saw in your 'study' of the saddle, did the Germans have only eight men on the high ground around the major and his men?"

"I said to you earlier, it wasn't possible to determine—"

"Captain, I'm sure even from your distant vantage point you could tell if there was something more than a squad firing down on Major Porter and his men?"

"I was sure our men could hold," Joyce sidestepped.

"Captain, were you aware that by the time the battalion undertook that third attack, the Germans had retaken Schmidt and were threatening Kommerscheidt?"

"I didn't know about Kommerscheidt."

"But you did know that the 28th Division had been pushed out of Schmidt."

"Yes, Sir."

"And on Hill 399, according to the after-action reports of your rifle companies that had taken the trench line on the hill, on both the second and third attempts on the hill, the Germans regularly sent at least platoon-sized counterattacks around the sides of the hill in attempts to take back the trenches. True?"

"The strength of those counterattacks was only a rough estimate."

"Did you at any time over the course of the battalion's engagement on the hill—and particularly during the final assault—notice any weakening of the German fire on the hill?"

"That's a difficult judgment to make."

"Well, did the fire *sound* any lighter? Did there appear to be any fewer enemy positions firing on your men?"

"The conditions on the hill, the smoke alone—"

"You couldn't tell."

"No, Sir, I couldn't."

"Captain, according to my notes here—if I don't have it right, let out a yell—on the second try at the hill, the first time all three rifle companies were committed to the attack, the assault consisted of about four hundred men backed by artillery and mortar fire. That sound right?"

"It was a little under four hundred men."

"And you couldn't break the German line. On the third and final attack, less than *three* hundred men made the assault with diminished fire support. Yet you felt the hill could still be—"

"Objection," Courie said, exasperated. "Defense is questioning Captain Joyce's judgment, but Captain Joyce did not order the attack on the hill. For that matter, neither did Major Porter! Whether or not the battalion had the preferred tactical advantages or not, the battalion was under orders to attack from higher echelons, as Colonel Voss has so carefully seen to remind us. The battalion didn't have a choice but to attack *as ordered!*"

"True," Harry agreed mildly. "Corps gave that attack order. But as Captain Courie so carefully reminds us, the order that's the basis of this trial—the order to stand and hold—was given by Captain Joyce."

"Overruled."

"Captain," Harry went on, "when Lieutenant Sisto contacted you and told you that Major Porter had ordered the assault detail off the hill, why didn't you believe him?"

"After three hard assaults we had finally gotten ourselves to a position where we had a clear opportunity to finally take Hill

399. I could not believe that Major Porter was willing to relinquish that advantage so quickly, particularly since it appeared the men had a defensible position."

"With all respect, Captain, that doesn't even qualify as a gut feeling. You had no concrete basis for that assumption, did you?"

"I became more suspicious when Lieutenant Sisto refused to put the major on the radio."

Harry referenced a note card. "'Refused'? Didn't he say something like—yes, here, you said he said something like *'You can talk about it with him when he comes down.'* "

"Something approximating that."

"Couldn't the lieutenant have been implying that the major simply couldn't get to the radio?"

"Objection. He could've been implying *anything!*"

"That's my point."

"I'm still going to sustain," ruled Ryan.

"In your experience under Major Porter's command, Captain Joyce, were all his orders always issued personally?" Harry asked.

"Of course not!"

"Messengers, radio operators, subordinates, routinely transmitted orders, just like with any other outfit. Even *you* carried orders from the major on occasion, right?"

"Naturally."

"Then what was so odd about it this time? Don't you think it's possible that Major Porter just couldn't come to the phone? It sounds like the guys up there did have their hands full."

"It seemed to be too convenient at that time. I couldn't even be sure that the major was still alive."

"You mean that Major Porter might already have been dead or wounded, and Lieutenant Sisto was lying about having orders from the major to pull out."

"I did entertain the suspicion, yes, Sir."

"And why would Lieutenant Sisto want you to believe the major was still alive?"

It was Joyce's turn to shake his head, puzzled that Harry couldn't see the obvious. "To make me think that he was under the major's orders."

"What difference would that make, Captain?"

"Obviously—"

"Hold on a second, Captain, and hear me out. Let's say—just for the moment—that Major Porter was dead. We'll give your theory the benefit of the doubt for the moment—"

"It's not exactly a theory. It was just a suspicion—"

"Please, Captain, for the sake of discussion, OK? Major Porter was dead and never gave the withdrawal order. Wouldn't it have made more sense for Lieutenant Sisto to *not* contact you at all and just pull the men off the hill?"

Meekly: "Um, yes, I see your point. As I said, it was only a—"

"Suspicion, yes." Harry took a moment, then, "The Rapido River and Lieutenant Sisto's spirited occupation of a wine cellar . . . excepting those occasions, prior to the events on Hill 399, had you ever known Dominick Sisto to disobey a direct order in a combat situation?"

Almost reluctant to concede the point: "No, Sir."

"And, in fact, even though those two incidents of misconduct would technically be considered disobedience, they were not cases of his disobeying a *direct* order, correct?"

"That's a rather narrow definition of disobedience—"

"Then by that narrow definition?"

"By that definition, no: in neither case was it an instance of disobeying a direct order."

"Hmm. 'In *neither* case.'" Joyce had pronounced it in the proper English way, *nyther*, and this was how Harry repeated it.

"Colonel Ryan!" complained Courie. "He's doing it again!"

"My apologies . . . again," Harry murmured. "Captain Joyce, let's open the question up a bit for you. Did you ever hear a rumor that Dominick Sisto might have disobeyed an order but had managed to conceal it somehow?"

"Objection! Hearsay."

"Captain Courie," Ryan said, "if you've decided to act on behalf of the defendant, I hope you'll do so with a narrower focus than Colonel Voss."

"I'm not introducing any such story as evidence," Harry rebutted. "Goes to state of mind if Captain Joyce ever heard such stories and gave them any credence."

"Overruled. Please answer, Captain Joyce."

Joyce sighed. "I'd heard stories about Lieutenant Sisto making disparaging remarks about—"

"Whatever the lieutenant's commentary might have been, other than the incidents I mentioned, you never had any cause to believe or even *suspect* Dominick Sisto had disobeyed combat orders on any other occasion, correct?"

"Yes, Sir. Correct."

"In fact, considering his rising through the ranks—*twice* thanks to his court-martial—one might say that for all his grousing and his lapses of good conduct, Lieutenant Sisto did a pretty good job of actually carrying out combat orders."

"How good a job would be a matter of opinion."

"But—"

"I have said several times that he was a good combat soldier."

"Let's move on to when the assault detail had displaced to the trench line and the whole battalion—what was left of it— was withdrawn from the hill. Who organized that?"

Wryly: "Why do you think I filed charges against Lieutenant Sisto in that regard?"

"That's what I'm trying to figure out, Captain. Lieutenant Sisto didn't contact you directly again once he'd returned to the trenches, did he?"

"I had no direct contact with the lieutenant after his transmission from the hilltop, not until he presented himself to me at the forward OP."

"So, what you know of the withdrawal, and all that went into it . . ."

"I could hear the transmissions between the rifle companies on the OP radio."

"And what? Did Lieutenant Sisto get on the horn and say, 'OK, guys, listen up! I'm taking over! I'm the new boss!'"

"He told them that they'd come down from the hilltop, and that Major Porter had ordered the battalion off the hill."

"But he made no statement that he'd assumed command of the battalion?"

"Only insomuch as he said he was under the major's orders. That gave him an appearance of authority."

Harry turned to Ryan. "Objection. That's a gross speculation."

"Sustained."

Harry returned to Joyce. "How did Lieutenant Sisto explain Major Porter's absence to the other company COs?"

"He never really addressed the issue. I heard one of the company COs ask where the major was, and Lieutenant Sisto responded that he wasn't sure, that he should've been close behind on the pullout from the top of the hill. Lieutenant Sisto said he was sending some men to look for him. But he also said he didn't think they could afford to wait, that they needed to organize the withdrawal immediately."

"Did anybody question the withdrawal?"

"No, Sir."

"Captain . . . did Lieutenant Sisto give orders to the acting King and Item Company commanders to withdraw? Now, I mean a clear, *direct* order: 'Pull out.'"

"Nothing so blatant. But Lieutenant Sisto's authority was predicated on his saying that he was under Major Porter's orders."

Harry looked up at Joyce over the top of his glasses, a disappointed frown on his face. " 'Blatant.' Captain, isn't it a fact that the communications between the three company commanders indicated that they jointly worked out the process of withdrawing from the hill? Much as they'd jointly worked out the plan of assault for that day?"

"I suppose the transmissions could be interpreted that way. There was a lot of chatter back and forth, and it was sometimes quite hard to tell exactly what was going on."

"It couldn't've been *that* hard, because you filed the charge and the Judge Advocate indicted on it."

"I said the transmissions *could* be interpreted that way. My interpretation was otherwise."

Harry nodded with a kind of melancholic air, as if he'd expected nothing else. "When you heard the company COs organizing the withdrawal, did you try to raise any of them on the radio and attempt to discourage them?"

A pause. "By then there didn't seem to be any point."

"You mean that since they'd given up the top of the hill—"

"The fight was over."

"I see." Harry flipped through his cards, seemed both surprised and relieved to see there was nothing left to address. He turned back to the defense table, moving with a weighty fatigue. He tossed that last deck of note cards on the table, dropped his glasses atop the splash of stationery, and rubbed his eyes and the bridge of his nose tiredly.

"Is that all, Colonel Voss?" Ryan queried.

After a moment's thought, Harry's head shook. "I can hear Captain Courie's objection already, but I've got to go back to this." He turned back to Joyce, but for the first time in his cross-examination, the unperturbed, blithe air was gone, replaced by a mix of anger, consternation, curiosity, frustration. "Captain Joyce. The men on that hill had limited fire support. German fire on the hill was heavy. German fire support was heavy. The Germans had retaken Schmidt, they continued to counterattack the men on the hill. Lieutenant Sisto, with over a year's combat experience, who by your own admission was an able combat soldier and who never disobeyed an order in a combat situation...he tells you the hill can't be held and you—after a few minutes' looking through your binoculars— decide he's wrong. He tells you Major Porter—a man who by *anybody's* characterization is hardly a stand-or-die commander—has ordered the battalion off the hill. But you don't believe Lieutenant Sisto." A pause.

"Captain: *what in God's name were you thinking?*"

"Objectionobjection*objection!* The question is intended to be inflammatory and argumentative! We've already covered all this ground, and to rehash it in such an *insulting* manner—"

"I read you, Captain," Ryan soothed, "and you only have to object the once. Sustained! On the *manner* of the question."

Harry nodded. "I'll rephrase." Speaking carefully: "Captain Joyce: with all these things in mind, on what basis— How could you *not* believe Dominick Sisto?"

"I simply didn't believe him. I—I don't know how else to say it."

"You know what I think, Captain? I think you didn't *want* to believe him! For the first time—for the first time—Major Porter was being the commander *you* needed him to be so you could get out from under him when he led those men up that hill! And then he started being the old Major Porter again, and you were not going to lose that opportunity!"

"Objection! This isn't cross-examination! This is the Defense's closing argument!"

Ryan was rapping his gavel. "Colonel Voss—"

But Harry crashed on: "If you could turn this thing around, well, that'd be you showing your stuff finally—"

Courie and Alth were both on their feet, banging on their table: "Objection! Objection! Dammit, objection!"

"I had to go by what I could see, and what I believed cases to be!" Joyce exploded. "I had to make a decision quickly and there wasn't time to— How much was I reasonably expected to know about everything that was going on up there?" He immediately attempted to rein himself in, his arm jerkily reached for the glass, nudged it from its perch. The crack and tinkle sounded small and lost in the arch-ceilinged chapel.

"That, Captain," Harry said glumly, "seems to be the question of the hour."

"For Christ's sake, objection!"

"Sustained!" Ryan boomed. "Strike it. Strike it all!"

The poor court recorder looked up, befuddled. "All, Sir?"

"Back to the objection!" Ryan snapped. "Strike it! The panel will disregard this entire last exchange!"

The chapel/courtroom grew quiet again. One of the MPs threw a fresh log into the fireplace, and the ice in its cracks popped and then hissed into small geysers of steam.

"Colonel Voss, do you have any further questions?" Ryan prodded.

Harry stood there in the well, looking at Joyce with—could you call that odd, almost paternal look "pity"? For a moment I thought he was going to say "I'm sorry" to the captain, who now sat slope-shouldered in the witness chair, his eyes on the floor, his last detonation having drained him.

"Colonel Voss—"

"No further questions," Harry told Ryan. "Thank you, Captain."

"Captain Courie," Ryan called, "I'd be mightily surprised if you didn't have a redirect."

"Captain Joyce, you ordered Lieutenant Sisto to hold his position at the top of the hill, did you not?"

"Yes." Lifeless.

"Flat out told him to hold?"

"Yes."

"He refused?"

"Yes."

"Cut off communication?"

"Yes."

"Didn't contact you as he should have to advise you the battalion was preparing to displace from the hill."

"Yes."

Courie nodded triumphantly. He turned toward the jury panel. "The colonel brought in so many side dishes, I didn't want anybody to forget what the main course was." He returned to his seat.

"Captain Joyce," Ryan said, "you're dismissed."

But the young captain didn't rise. It seemed to take him a moment to muster the strength, then he stood, slowly unfolding himself. He looked at the splash of broken glass and water on the stone floor. For a moment, I thought the boy was going to kneel down and begin cleaning up the shards himself.

"We'll see that that's attended to, Captain, don't worry," Ryan soothed.

Joyce brought himself to attention. He saluted Ryan, saluted the jury panel, then managed some semblance of the *faux* air of command he'd presented when he'd first entered as he made for the chapel doors.

At the defense table, Dominick Sisto had his head tilted in conversation toward Peter Ricks, while a congratulatory hand was clamped on Harry's shoulder.

But Harry's attention was locked on Whitcomb Joyce. He watched the captain walk the chapel aisle; his eyes remained on the heavy oak doors long after MP sentinels had reclosed them.

"Colonel Ryan," Courie said, "the Judge Advocate's case for the Prosecution rests."

Harry—reluctantly, it appeared—drew his attention back to the case at hand as he rose. "Defense moves for dismissal, Sir. We do not believe the Prosecution has met the burden of proof on either charge."

It was a routine request at that particular juncture of the trial, and Ryan just as routinely dismissed it, then asked, "Is the Defense ready to proceed at this time?"

"Actually, Sir, Captain Joyce has left us with a lot to consider. Might we have a recess for the afternoon?"

Ryan looked at his watch. "You know, it *has* been a long morning. And tomorrow's Sunday. I understand that Captain Courie has procured us a chaplain for services tomorrow for those so inclined. So, let's do this: I'll call it a day, we'll reconvene Monday morning. If neither counsel has an objection . . . ? Court's in recess, gentlemen, enjoy your day off," and the gavel came down.

The Military Policeman outside Dominick Sisto's quarters held the door for me as I pushed the tea trolley through, then closed and locked it behind me. I seemed to have stepped into a rather spirited debate between the lieutenant and Harry.

Harry was standing along the curved tower wall, his eyes directed out one of the narrow windows, but the frustration in his face—both with Sisto and whatever it was his eyes were waiting to see—was clear. But in opposition to Harry's stillness and quiet discomfiture, Sisto flitted and hovered like a seabird, his voice excited and raised.

"I can put this guy in the ground, *Signor!*" he was saying, oblivious to my entry.

"We already talked about this, Dominick. I told you at the beginning—"

"You put him on the ropes, but I can lay that high-hattin' sonofabitch out!"

"It's not about putting him in the ground! He's not the enemy."

"No? Who do you think put me here? Barney Google?"

I remained in the shelter of the tea trolley. "Am I interrupting something?"

"Thankfully, yes!" Peter Ricks said enthusiastically, pulling himself out of his chair and heading for the trolley. As Ricks picked his way through the sandwiches, I pointed to the coffee urn.

"I'd be after the coffee first if I were you. While it's hot. It never seems to stay that way for long in this place."

"Joyce filed the charges," Harry told Sisto, "but the *law* put you here. Well, the Army's variety of it."

Peter Ricks thrust a half-sandwich at Sisto.

Sisto pushed it away. "I don't feel like—"

With an accuracy and aplomb bred of his extensive combat experience, Ricks expertly threaded the sandwich past Sisto's moving jaws and into his mouth. "Shut...up," he said with understated calm. He directed Sisto toward the bed, giving him a final push that left the lieutenant seated atop the mattress. "Be quiet long enough to listen, OK? Right now Whit Joyce comes off in front of that jury as a snot-nosed little prick who won't dirty his hands with the doughs in the trenches or even the other officers who've got to do the heavy lifting. It's not enough he's losing on personality; he doesn't look like he's all aces at his job, either.

"But *you*? That's another story. You're the poor working stiff, a gets-his-hands-dirty GI-fightin'-Joe that Mr. Never-ends-a-sentence-with-a-preposition is always picking on, that he looks down on. But *you're* the guy who gets the job done! That wine cellar in Italy? I guarantee you, any one of those officers on the jury who spent time in Italy or France has had something just like that happen. Their troops go off on a bender, it may not make the real Bible-beaters in the bunch happy, but they understand. The Rapido River? You broke the rules going after your buddies. That's practically all-American! I'm surprised Courie even brought it up!"

"He had to," Harry said. "He had to try to discredit it, because if he didn't, he knew I'd be up there waving Dominick's Silver Star like a Dodger pennant."

"If I might ... ?" I offered. "Perhaps most important, laddie, what your colleagues on the jury saw today was that Joyce and Porter spent most of that day in November in the comparative comfort and safety of the battalion command post. You, on the other hand, were one of those few, those happy few, charged with having to fight an impossible fight ... and giving it your all."

"Add it all up, Dominick," Harry said, "and what you get is right now you look a lot like a victim. That ends the minute you open your mouth."

Which Sisto endeavored to do and was stopped by a warning finger from Peter Ricks. "All Courie has to do is get you to lose your cool just *once* and you spout off like you're about to now, and you're screwed."

Sisto was an intelligent enough boy to see the logic of it all, but that didn't stop him from being completely offended. "You don't think I can handle myself going head-to-head with Cue Ball?"

"Dominick," Harry sighed, "I know you your whole life. You're cocky. You've got a smart mouth. You can be a real wisenheimer sometimes. You don't have a lot of patience for people you think are jerks. I say this as somebody who loves you."

"Gee, a couple more compliments like that and I'm just gonna bust out cryin'!"

"I think all these little foibles of yours are part of your charm. They make you a kind of—" Harry frowned in puzzlement, then turned to me. "You're the vocabulary expert, Eddie. What would the word be? Imp?"

"Actually, by definition, I'm thinking more of a pixie."

At which Sisto humphed, and exclaimed: "Why don't you guys just call me a queer and get it over with?"

"Point is, what's colorful back home is going to play like smart-ass on the stand, and *nobody* likes a smart-ass." Harry sat by Sisto, setting a hand on the boy's shoulder. "There's nothing you can tell them about Joyce that hasn't already come out. All you'll do is make it tit for tat. It'll look personal and then they'll start thinking you're *both* full of it.

"Keep this in mind: when a defendant tells his own story, a jury always weighs the factor of self-interest. They instinctively know what the lawyers know and the judges know and everybody else knows: when the subject is yourself, everybody lies a little. But if you don't testify . . . ?"

"Then I don't lie," Sisto concluded glumly.

"If only Joyce testifies, only Joyce lies. *Ipso facto*, you end up telling more of the truth by keeping your mouth shut."

"So I don't testify."

"Say it like you mean it."

"I don't testify."

"Say it like you *love* the idea."

The lieutenant drew up an asinine grin, and with an emphatic pump of his fist against his chest bellowed, "I *don't* testify!"

Harry nodded approvingly. "Now that you love the idea, we don't have to have this discussion again. Right? Right. Eat your lunch."

I stood by Harry and offered him a cigarette.

"Listen, Harry," I said as I struck the match, "all those notes from the interviews I and the lads conducted in Wiltz...do you think I might have a look at them again?"

"Sure. Come by the room after lunch. Something up?"

"Perhaps I'm just setting a foundation to explore a few things."

He grimaced at the echo of his own courtroom performance. "That's funny. Ho-ho. Talking like that, you should be a lawyer."

One could hear the chaplain from far down the corridors, the solemn drone of scripture echoing unintelligibly along the ancient stone walls. The doors to the chapel had been left invitingly open, but I hovered about outside, telling myself I was merely curious to see who was in attendance.

There were a few from the Signal Corps and Military Police contingents. General Kerry and Colonel Bright were there, but none of the other witnesses. Of the jurymen, Pietrowski was present, and most of the others. But the members of the panel who had commanded combat troops in the Huertgen were absent.

Courie was there, and though he looked earnest enough in his attentions, I could not help but suspect he was there more to make a favorable impression on Pietrowski than out of some religious dedication. His minion Alth was present as well, no doubt in a similar mind. And that adroit, meticulous politician Joseph P. Ryan was sitting close by Pietrowski, his face calculatingly beatific.

But, to my surprise, no Harry. I had expected to see him seated toward the rear, inconspicuous but sincere in his devotions. But no, no Harry.

I turned away and bumped into Peter Ricks, loitering in the shadows of the hall.

"Peter!"

He averted his eyes, pretending to look curiously past me. "Just wanted to see who was going to show up."

Having used the same lie to myself, I nodded, allowing it to stand. "Not going to indulge in even one little prayer?"

His face grew quickly cold. "I've prayed." He held his gleaming hook before my face. "It didn't work."

Nonetheless, he lingered about in the corridor as I left.

I made my way down to the dining hall, beckoned even at a distance by a warming, appetizing scent.

"Eddie!" Harry had caught sight of me from where he sat at the long table. "Get on over here and have some breakfast!" He called to the kitchen and soon a plate piled high with American "pancakes" was laid on before me, along with a serving platter of grilled Spam and rehydrated mashed potatoes.

I took a bite of the pancakes. I was familiar with them from my travels in America, but this was quite a different concoction than I'd remembered. The enticing aroma had been misleading. Unlike the pancakes I'd remembered, these had been made with a bow toward battlefield necessity. Made from flour and powdered eggs, they had a "hearty" consistency guaranteed to exhaust the jaws without ever pleasing the palate. "Not exactly *crêpes suzette*."

"Don't be such a snob."

"Harry, I've just come from the chapel. I was surprised not to see you there."

Harry turned his attention to his plate with a shrug. "I'm Russian Orthodox."

"It appeared to be a nondenominational service."

"Saw your light on until the late hours," Harry said. "You were doing a lot of homework. Anything come of it?"

I shook my head. "I keep thinking it's there, Harry. I know I must be going right past it, but it's there."

"I've been getting the same feeling myself. Something's not right somewhere. I don't know. We've had to move so fast, get through so much material . . . This is not the way to do things." He frowned.

"Problem?"

"Dominick wants to fight it out."

"Of course."

"You don't understand. See, it never occurred to me. After you left, Pete said something . . ." He set his fork down, pushed the dish away.

"What is it, Harry?"

"If Dominick gets convicted, it means a long stretch in Leavenworth. If he's acquitted . . . he goes back up to the line. Peter said I should put it to Dominick; what does he want to do?"

"And he wants to make a go of the trial."

"Yes."

"Odd, don't you think? I mean, at the onset he seemed, oh, I suppose I'd say prosaic."

"If that means he looked ready to just let Courie roll over him, yeah."

"But now he thinks he can win?"

"Seeing Joyce up there really did something to him. Now I think he's less concerned about an acquittal than in trying to hurt Captain Joyce. And he sees an acquittal as a way to do that."

"Harry, I was wondering if you could arrange something for me. A proper transcript of the trial won't be prepared for weeks, correct? That very studious lad who keeps the record, would it be possible for him to sit with me today and read back the stenographic tape of the trial?"

"You want this guy to sit with you—"

"If I could read the tape myself, I would."

"That's a hell of a way to spend your day, Eddie."

"Can you arrange it?"

"It's supposed to be a public record. I guess I can set it up. That steno kid isn't going to be too happy about how he's going to be spending his day off. I'd consider flowers and candy if I were you."

"Aye, you're a funny thing, you are, Harry. Quite the wit."

"You really think there's something to find there?"

"As I say: I don't know. But I don't know where else to look."

Harry lit himself an after-breakfast cigarette. "Look, tomorrow you might want to bring a helmet. I think you're going to be treated to another one of Courie's conniption fits. The fur is going to fly."

"Mounting a spirited defense, are we?"

"I want to put up some of the soldiers who were on Hill 399 with Sisto, have them let the panel know what it was like up there. Courie'll object, say it's prejudicial, I'm just trying to get sympathy for Dominick, and he'll be right. If Joe Ryan doesn't let me present them, though . . ."

"What else do you have?"

"I have whatever generosity of spirit there is in that jury panel. And whatever *you* come up with."

Now I pushed the pancakes away and stood. "Then I'd best get to it, eh?"

Harry stubbed out his cigarette and stood as well. "I'll go break the unhappy news to that steno."

As we walked out of the dining hall and headed for the stairs, I asked him, "And while I'm feverishly trying to devise some method of saving your young mate, how will *you* be spending the day?"

"Me?" He clapped a sympathetic hand on my shoulder. "I'm tired. I'm going to take a nap."

Harry had been right: Leonard Courie was agitated even before court was reconvened on Monday morning. Ryan had gotten as far as announcing, "This proceeding is now—" when Courie was on his feet, charging toward him, holding aloft a sheet of paper.

"Sir! Colonel Ryan!"

"—in session," and finalized the declaration with his gavel.

"Sir!" Courie continued, oblivious to the finer points of reconvening. "Five minutes before we reconvened I was delivered an amended witness list—"

Ryan, who seemed to be girding himself for the battle royal Harry had predicted, held up his own copy of the aforementioned list. "As was I, Captain. I take it you have a protest."

"You're damned right I do!"

"As I anticipate a spirited debate, I'm going to ask the panel to withdraw so as not to prejudice the case one way or the other." Ryan ordered the MP sentries to escort the panel to the far end of that floor of the chateau to ensure they'd be out of earshot.

But Courie barely waited for the chapel doors to close behind them. "It's funny to hear the Court worried about prejudicial testimony after Saturday! What passed for testimony in this room Saturday afternoon was a joke! But this is an insult! Do you know what this is?"

Ryan's eyes had grown so narrow, I wondered if he could still see. "Why don't you go ahead and tell—"

"This is an ambush job!"

Peter Ricks stood. "Colonel, every name on that list was drawn from the Trial Judge Advocate's own Discovery list. Those are men who were either deposed or filled out interrogatories for the Judge Advocate and are therefore eligible—"

"Never mind their eligibility! And let's put aside that this Court doesn't seem to give a damn at all about prejudicial testimony! This is as cheap an appeal for sympathy as it gets! The Defense is trying to win by tonnage! Colonel, this is cumulative and repetitive testimony that only rehashes what's already been brought up in court! It's unnecessary, and its materiality is based on a foundation that shouldn't have been set in the first place!" Back to Harry: "I was led to expect better of you, Colonel Voss!"

Harry had sat stoically through the tirade, but that last,

highly personal thrust unexpectedly touched off a detonation. He threw his spectacles down on the table so hard, I feared they'd shatter, and shot to his feet. "If you mean I'm not going to roll over and let you run roughshod over this boy, then I don't feel bad about disappointing you, Captain!"

"I'm not disappointed, Colonel! I'm *outraged*! If you think I'm going to keep my mouth shut just because I can't get a judicial ruling worth a damn in here—"

Now it was Ryan who exploded: "Hold the phone, *hold the damn phone*! Both of you!" Ryan took a moment to reclaim his poise, but only barely. "Captain Courie, you can think whatever you want about how I rule! You can think I have my head so far up my ass, I look like a pretzel! And if this trial goes against you and you think anything I've said or done gives you a shot in front of a Court of Military Appeal, well, good luck to you and go get 'em! But in *this* courtroom, in front of *my* bench, *you watch your mouth*! For better or for worse, I'm the Legal Officer here, and I am also your superior officer and—in case you forgot—your *commanding* officer! One more insulting peep out of that yap of yours and I'm going to cite you for contempt, insubordination, and then I'm going to come across this table and *pop you one*! Understand?" He took a breath, which only reined him in to a seethe. He turned to Harry: "OK. Now you. You talk."

"He wants to talk about being repetitive?" Harry began. "We've been over this time and time—"

"This is all that crap about justifying a Major Porter order you can't prove was given!" fumed Courie.

"I have a problem with your characterization," Harry responded coolly, "but yes." To Ryan: "This is no rehash! The Judge Advocate has called five witnesses, but only *one* of them was actually *on* that hill! Only *one* of them knows everything those boys went through!"

Courie's head was shaking violently. "It doesn't matter what the 'boys' went through! You can give this all the context you want, Colonel Voss, but you don't get points for *context!* Context doesn't equal relevance! You can characterize this garbage however you want, but all you're doing is trawling for a defense!"

"You're goddamned right, that's what I'm doing, Captain, and why is that? Why am I digging around at the last minute, trying to find something to work with? Because last minutes is all I've been given!"

"If your client wants to change counsel on the verge of going to trial—"

"Then it shouldn't've mattered and *you know that!* We *should've* gotten a continuance, and in the interest of a fair trial, *you* should've helped push for it! I've got half a mind to be on the horn to the Inspector General as soon as the verdict gets read! You can explain to him how you cheated Dominick Sisto out of time by shanghaiing this trial out of Liège, and then disappearing for another day and a half with every bit of the Judge Advocate's Discovery finds, and why you loaded up an indictment with charges you had no legal backing to make, just so you could browbeat this kid into giving up! You're not going to have to worry about an appeal, Captain, you're going to have to worry about standing in front of the IG and answering charges of prosecutorial misconduct and—"

"*That's enough!*" Ryan bellowed, and that large-bore Irish tenor did what a gavel could not. The courtroom fell quiet. Ryan put his elbows on his table and massaged what appeared to be a growing ache between his eyes. "You know, since this thing started, there've been times I've wanted to step out from behind here and bean each of you with this gavel!" He lowered his hands from his face, and his voice grew steely even. "All right, here's how it's going to be, and I'm not opening this up for discussion.

"Colonel Voss. The Trial Judge Advocate is on point here. Besides offering some graphic details, I don't see where these witnesses can offer anything substantive beyond what's already been presented." Harry's mouth began to open. "I said this wasn't for discussion!" Ryan declared. "If you disagree, if you think there's some probative value to this parade you wanted to run through here, take it up on appeal. Now: let's get on with this. I'm going to call the panel back. Are we ready?"

Harry turned at the sound of the door at the rear of the chapel squeaking open. It was me.

Harry caught the look on my face. "With the Court's permission, a minute, please?"

Ryan brusquely ordered him to be quick about it. We conferred briefly, Harry took a moment to bow his head and consider his strategy.

"Colonel Voss!" Ryan called impatiently.

Harry returned to his table. "If it please the Court—"

"Somehow I doubt it will," Ryan said.

"We have testimony to present, but we didn't anticipate having to introduce it at this time. I'm afraid the Court's ruling today left us—"

"You want a continuance?" Ryan asked it unhappily.

"You had all day yesterday to prepare!" Courie fumed.

Ryan gritted his teeth so hard, I worried they'd crack like porcelain under a hammer. "The next time either one of you loudmouths sounds off improperly in my courtroom, I swear to God . . ." and he brandished his gavel threateningly. "Now, get away from me! Court is recessed until 0900 hours tomorrow morning and, Colonel Voss, you damned well better be ready to present!" His gavel came down. "Does anybody know where in this shack they keep the bicarb?" he said as he stormed down the aisle and out the chapel doors.

Courie was only a step behind him, angrily sweeping his papers into his briefcase before huffing an exit himself. Alth toddled along behind.

Harry took me by the elbow and began hurrying me back toward Dominick Sisto's room. "This better be good, Eddie."

"You're the lawyer, Harry," I replied. "You'll have to tell me."

CHAPTER SEVEN

★

"**Colonel Ryan, if** there's no objection, at this time the Defense would like to recall Private Avram Kasabian."

"Captain Courie?"

"No objection, Sir."

Obviously of the mind that a recall signified some misstep on his part, Kasabian walked the length of the chapel to the witness stand with the face of a student called before the headmaster. Ryan reminded the private that he was still under oath.

"Relax, Private," said Harry, smiling soothingly as he fondled a fresh batch of note cards. "I just want to clear up a point or two concerning what you testified to the other day."

"I'm not in trouble, am I, Sir?" Kasabian's dark face flinched toward the brass at the jury tables.

"No, Private, not at all."

"I told it as best I could."

"Before you get yourself worried to death, Private, why don't you wait for the questions, OK? I'm going to have Sergeant Barham read back a portion of your testimony. Just listen carefully, all right? Go ahead, Sergeant. That first piece, please."

Barham turned to a spool of paper tape already unrolled to a marked section. "'Question: Private Kasabian, you told Captain Courie that Captain Joyce threatened to relieve Lieutenant Tully and bring him up on charges?'

"'Answer: Yessir, said he'd do it right then and there.'

"'Question: But he didn't do it right then and there. He didn't do it at all.'

"'Answer: Well, the lieutenant, like I told the captain, Sir, Lieutenant Tully got killed.'

"'Question: Yes, I know. I'm sorry, Private. But Lieutenant Tully was killed later. You said Captain Joyce told Lieutenant Tully he'd bust him at that moment if he didn't move out, but he didn't.'"

"And then there was an objection from Captain Courie," Harry interjected. "Do you remember that testimony, Private?"

"Yessir, sure."

"Then, after we dealt with Captain Courie's objection, I came back to you." Harry nodded to Barham, and the recorder moved to another section of the tape.

"'Question: Check me out on this, Private, I want to be sure I've got your testimony to Captain Courie right. You told him Captain Joyce gave Lieutenant Tully the order to move out. And then you said . . . ?'

"'Answer: I said Lieutenant Tully told him to go scratch. To forget it.'

"'Question: Captain Joyce then threatened to relieve Lieutenant Tully and charge him.'

"'Answer: Right.'

"'Question: And you said the lieutenant said—'

"'Answer: Tully told Joyce to take a leap.'"

"Do you remember all that, Private?" Harry asked gently.

"Yeah, yessir, like I said. That's how it happened."

"Well, there's a discrepancy, Private."

"Discrepancy, Sir?"

"Prior to the trial, weren't you questioned by Mr. Edward Owen in conjunction with this case?"

Defensive now: "Yessir, and that's the story I told him, too!"

"Take it easy, Private. There's no discrepancy in the *actions* you described. I have here in Mr. Owen's notes, your statement—"

"Objection! *Ex parte* affidavits are not admissible evidence. I don't have the specific citation on hand—" Courie was making frantic hand motions toward Alth, who was just as frantically flipping through the reference books on the prosecution table.

"I believe the citation the Trial Judge Advocate has in mind is, ah"—and Harry took an outheld book from Ricks, which the captain was already holding to the needed page—"um, page 536 of the 1912 *Digests of Opinions of The Judge Advocate General of the Army*. The prohibition is actually intended as a protection for the accused. *Ex parte* affidavits *are* admissible with the consent of the accused. However, this was more in the order of a Q & A rather than a sworn affidavit, and, in any case, the accused is amenable. Offered into evidence as Defense Exhibit Number One."

"So entered," Ryan replied, and beckoned the bailiff to tag the report accordingly.

"I have some copies we made last night," Harry continued as Ricks began handing out carbon flimsies to Courie, Ryan, and the panel. "It was a hasty typing job and I'm afraid the carbons aren't all that clear, but if everyone would please pay attention to the marked section . . . Private, when you gave your testimony in court, you gave as Lieutenant Tully's response to Captain Joyce, well, first you said—what was it?" He turned to his note cards. "'*Go scratch. Forget it.*' Then you said the lieutenant told Captain Joyce 'to take a leap.'"

"I don't know what you're getting at, Sir."

"Well, which was it? What did Lieutenant Tully say? 'Go scratch'? 'Forget it'? 'Take a leap'?"

Kasabian shook his head. From what I could see, a number of the jury panel were equally fogged. "It's all the same thing, Sir, isn't it?"

"When you were questioned by Mr. Owen a few weeks ago, you used another phrase. Do you recall it? Mr. Owen asked you if Lieutenant Tully had given a reason for his refusal to obey Captain Joyce's order, even under the threat of arrest. And you—"

"Oh!" The young private's face glowed with enlightenment. "You mean like what were his *exact* words!"

"That's what I mean, Private. What *exactly* did Lieutenant Tully say to Captain Joyce when Captain Joyce threatened to relieve the lieutenant and have him brought up on charges?"

"The lieutenant said, 'On whose authority?' That's how I remember it. I'm pretty sure that's what he said."

"It's important, Private. How sure?"

"'On whose authority.' That's what I remember the lieutenant saying."

"I would point out to the Court that the private's recollection is consistent with what he reported in his interview with Mr. Owen. Thank you, Private. Nothing further."

Courie sat for a few seconds. He turned to Alth, there was an exchange of whispers. Both seemed unsure of what Harry was aiming at, but Courie was reluctant to let any shot from the Defense go unanswered. "Private, how come you didn't quote the lieutenant when you were asked about what went on between him and Captain Joyce here in court?"

"I got asked what happened, I told what happened. I didn't know you had to get all the words down perfect."

"But you got them perfect for Mr. Owen?"

"He was the only one who ever asked me *exact*."

Kasabian was dismissed. A look went between Harry, Ricks, and Sisto, not too unlike—I surmised—the look between soldiers before they scurry out of their trenches for The Big Push. Harry scooped up another deck of cards and got to his feet. "Sir, at this time Defense calls for a quashing of all charges and specifications in the indictment."

I girded for another detonation. Instead, there came a slow, rising, derisive laugh from Courie. He even gave a few caustic claps of his hands. "Colonel Voss, you get an E for effort. You just do not give up! Colonel Ryan, the Defense has already moved for dismissal once, and I don't see that that much has changed since then. At least not enough to warrant even *consideration* of a dismissal."

"Let me clear up a few points for the Judge Advocate," Harry said, unflustered by Courie's sarcasm. "This isn't a motion for a dismissal. I'm asking the charges be nullified. This isn't a matter of whether or not the Trial Judge Advocate has made his case. These charges should never have been brought."

"The merits of the Defense's motion aside," Courie responded glibly, "the motion is academic. The Court has no power to order a *nolle prosequi* on any charge of specification without first conferring with the convening authority. I'd be hard put to see General Cota agreeing to—"

"Excuse me, Captain," Harry interrupted, "but, um, that's not quite accurate. Once you master the complexities of criminal law, I know it must be a headache coming into the service and having to learn a whole new set of laws and precedents. But you really ought to make it your business to study these

Judge Advocate General's digests. Again, the 1912 edition, page 509, the Court *can* quash a charge of specification on its own authority in response to a plea before the bar on the grounds of sufficiency."

Courie—and good old Alth along with him—was shaking his head as if he'd not heard properly. "You're claiming . . . *insufficiency?*"

Before Harry could respond, Ryan tiredly held up his hand. "Take a break, gentlemen. Colonel Voss, do you anticipate this being another one of your dogfights with the Trial Judge Advocate?"

"Probably, Sir."

At which point Ryan ordered the panel to retire to prevent the argument from prejudicing their judgment. Once the chapel doors closed behind the last department panel member, Ryan turned to Harry with a look that warned "This had better be good, friend." "OK, Colonel. Let's hear it."

"Lieutenant Sisto had no obligation to obey the order to hold," Harry said doggedly. "The standard for disobedience—"

Courie flamed. "I know the standard, Colonel!" Alth was pushing a book at Courie, but Courie pushed it away. "*The order must be lawful; it must have been received; it must have been understood.*

"Throughout this entire trial, the Defense has tried to make an issue of both Captain Joyce's and Major Porter's judgment, but the fact is that while Captain Joyce's order may have been a bad call, that does not—by Army doctrine—*justify disobedience.* The order to hold was in keeping with the battalion's assignment. By Army standards, there was nothing unlawful about it. We know the order was received and understood by the defendant because the defendant took issue with it! I don't see where the Defense sees Lieutenant Sisto's obligation to obey obviated! Where's the insufficiency?"

Harry stood quietly in the face of Courie's blast. When the prosecutor fell silent, Harry reached behind him without looking—a wonderfully calculated effect, I must say—and Ricks placed yet another volume in his hand. "Captain Courie is correct in what he says about the standard measure of disobedience. However, *the standard presupposes that the officer giving the order had the authority to do so.* According to paragraph 134b of the *Manual of Courts-Martial, the accused in a prosecution for willful disobedience must know*—I repeat, must know—*that the subject order had been given by an officer who had the authority to give it.*" Harry placed the open book on Courie's table, then took another proffered by Ricks: "According to page 18 of the 1942 edition of the Judge Advocate General's *Digests of Opinions,* that element is a prerequisite to sustaining a conviction." He placed this second volume atop the first in front of Courie. "Regarding the second charge of the indictment, according to the Trial Judge Advocate's own pretrial argument, the act which forms the basis for the second charge was a"—now reading a quotation from one of his note cards—"'*a compounding transaction arising directly from the first.*' Consequently, the second charge should be quashed along with the first."

Courie shoved the books toward Alth to do the swot work while he angrily addressed Harry: "Captain Joyce was the executive officer of the battalion, am I right?"

"He was," Harry agreed.

"And as such Captain Joyce had the right—the responsibility—to assume command if and when his commanding officer was incapacitated or otherwise unable to fulfill the duties of his office, correct?"

"He did."

"Then where in the hell do you come up with claiming Joyce didn't have the authority—"

"If Captain Joyce had assumed command at the time he gave his order to hold the hill, I wouldn't be bringing this up! But that's not how it was. At that time, Captain Joyce believed Major Porter was still in command! Or, at the very least, he believed that Porter was *probably* still in—"

"And the basis for that is what? You have some—clairvoyance? You know what was in the captain's head at the time?"

"I have a pretty good idea."

"Oh, please enlighten us!" Courie propped himself on the edge of his table and held his head in his hands like an avid youngster at the cine. "Mind reading! My favorite!"

Harry responded with a cool firmness: "Captain Joyce didn't have command authority and he knew it. If he didn't know it on his own, Lieutenant Tully reminded him."

Courie's face brightened as he began to fit the pieces together. "That's what you were getting at with Kasabian? Just because some GI one-striper claims Tully said—"

"Joyce had threatened to relieve Tully, Tully called him on it, and Joyce backed down. We know this. You know this. Joyce didn't press the withdrawal issue when he heard the company COs on the radio trying to organize the displacement from the hill."

"Because Joyce believed they were under Porter's orders?" Now it was Ryan fitting the pieces together.

"Joyce testified on all this!" rebutted Courie.

"Yes," Harry assented, and began flipping through his note cards. "Captain Joyce says he suspected that Porter might've been dead and Lieutenant Sisto—an officer who, for all his kicking and moaning, never disobeyed a combat order—was trying to pull a fast one. But even Joyce agreed with me when I said that didn't make sense; *the lieutenant could've just not contacted*

Joyce at all and pulled his men out. And even if he wants to stick with that story, the onus is on the Prosecution to prove it." Another card: "He says he didn't try to intercede with the company COs organizing the withdrawal from the hill because *'by then, there didn't seem to be any point.'* There was a hell of a big point, and here's where all of Joyce's explanations become bunk, Captain:

"It was only *after* Lieutenant Sisto reported to him and informed him definitively that Porter had been lost on the hill— only then—that Captain Joyce announced he was assuming command and placing Lieutenant Sisto under arrest. *If he'd been so damned sure Major Porter was no longer in command while Sisto was still on top of that hill—maybe somebody can tell me why, right then and there, Joyce didn't get on the battalion frequency and say, 'Hey, Major Porter's dead! I'm in command! Listen to me!'*

"I'll go you one better! I'll call every officer and enlisted man to the stand who could hear the communications between Captain Joyce and Lieutenant Sisto and ask *them* when they thought command passed to Joyce! Because, Captain, if *none* of them believed Joyce was in command, *how do you make the case that Lieutenant Sisto should have known?*"

One could see Courie wavering, but he was far from willing to surrender: "We could clear this all up with a couple of questions to Captain Joyce."

Harry tossed his cards and spectacles tiredly down on his table. "We could." He sighed and rubbed his eyes. He turned to Ryan. "Off the record?"

Harry turned back to Courie. "He'll get up on the stand and, under oath, in front of the panel, maybe come up with some pretty good explanations for why we should accept him as having been in command early on and why nobody else in the battalion knew it. But you saw the way that boy's testimony played in front of that jury. And you know they're going to be thinking that a month after the fact, he's just looking to alibi his own conduct. It's enough he's going to come out of this looking like a screw-up as a combat commander. I'm not looking to serve Captain Joyce up as a liar. And if you put him up, that's how he's going to come across."

"Trying to bluff your way to the pot, Colonel?" Courie sneered.

Harry shrugged. "Fine. It's your case; he's your witness. I have no objection to you calling him in rebuttal."

Courie turned away to huddle with Alth. He turned to the referenced pages Harry had left for him. As the discussion proceeded, I could see Courie's shoulders sag, his head begin to drop. He may have been an ambitious and combative blighter, but he was neither dull nor incompetent. When he next rose from his chair, it was with an air of resignation. "Sir," he addressed Ryan, and the colonel signaled Barham to restart his recording, "I'd like some time to discuss these particulars with Captain Joyce."

"No objection," Harry said.

Ten minutes later, with the jury panel back in place, court resumed.

"Sir," Courie said, "in response to the Defense's motion, the Trial Judge Advocate would find a directed verdict of not guilty acceptable."

"Acceptable?" Ryan's usual poker face faded into cold anger. He signaled Barham to lay his fingers down and beckoned Courie to stand close. He had spent days—weeks, actually— presenting some semblance of objectivity, but now Ryan no longer saw the need. All his pent-up feelings regarding

Leonard Courie boiled up in a scathing seethe. It had been meant as a whisper, but I doubt there was a soul in the court who didn't catch most of it. "*'Acceptable'?* This isn't about what you consider *acceptable*, Captain! A directed verdict implies you had a *reason* to make the charge; you just couldn't make the case. But you're not getting off the hook that easy! This shouldn't have come to court; there shouldn't have been an indictment! You've got egg on your face, *Lenny*, and it's not my job or the job of the Judge Advocate's office to help you clean it off!" He waved Courie back to his seat and signaled the reporter to resume his duty. "Regarding the Defense's special plea, does either party have anything further to add to the discussion? Captain Courie, do you wish to recall Captain Joyce?"

Meekly: "No, Sir."

"In that case..." Ryan cleared his throat, carefully intertwined his fingers, and affected a pose of mature statesmanship. "I have studied the judicial citations submitted by the Defense along with the particular elements of the plea before the bar. The Court considers the arguments by the Defense valid and grants the special plea. All charges and specifications are herewith stricken on the basis of insufficiency. Lieutenant Sisto."

Sisto, a bit dazed by the rapid turn of events, rose to attention. "Yes, Sir."

"You are hereby returned to duty and ordered to rejoin your unit forthwith. The 103rd Regiment is still attached to the 28th Division, which, as I'm sure you know, is headquartered in Wiltz. You will effect transport to Wiltz at the earliest possible opportunity, and you will be directed to your unit therefrom."

"Yes, Sir."

"The business of this proceeding is now concluded. The

panel is dismissed with the thanks of the Court, and this tribunal is now dissolved."

Ryan's gavel slammed down and Sergeant Barham set his fingers in his lap.

And so, it was finished.

CHAPTER EIGHT

———— ★ ————

"And that," Peter Ricks pronounced, "as they say, is that."

From a window in Dominick Sisto's tower room, Ricks and I watched Leonard Courie's staff car head down the drive and disappear into the woods.

The trial was concluded, but its *corpus* had not quite been laid to rest. From the tower room, we could see quite a bustle about the front gate. The mess crew that Courie had brought to the chateau were loading their gear into one lorry, while at another, other hands were loading up the office accoutrements the prosecutor had been so loath to share. The higher-ranking members of the jury panel and witness list were departing in a parade of jeeps and staff cars lined up at the barbican, while the lower-ranking participants gathered by the tailgate of a deuce-and-a-half, awaiting the last of their still-packing comrades before climbing aboard. At the rate occupants were abandoning the chateau, I speculated the place would be back to its somnolent self by evening.

Dominick Sisto was now a free man. The door to his quarters

stood unguarded, unlocked, and open. The lieutenant was pack-ing his belongings into his duffel bag.

Nearby sat Harry. I puzzled over his clouded mien. He sat on a chair, elbows on knees, head low. Hardly the image of tri-umph.

His packing finished, Sisto reached for his windcheater. "Well, I guess that's it for clean sheets and hot food."

"It's a rest area," Ricks soothed. "Maybe it won't be so bad."

"Even if it's the Ritz . . . I mean, Jesus, Cap, I've been sleeping in a fucking *castle!*" He and Ricks shared a laugh. Sisto clasped the captain's hand in his. "What can I say, Captain? 'Thanks' doesn't seem to cut it. Ya know, you're not too bad at this! You might want to think about going back to it full-time."

"I'll take it under advisement."

Sisto turned to me. "Mr. O, you were the goddamned cavalry to the rescue! If it wasn't for you—"

I held up a finger for silence. "Throwing compliments my way is not unlike dropping lit matches into a pool of petrol. Your thanks are appreciated and enough said."

"I owe you big-time, Mr. O. All of you guys."

"Knock-knock!" It was Joe Ryan standing in the doorway, wearing his posh bridge coat. "I wanted to make sure I got my goodbyes in before I head out."

Harry looked up. "Where are you off to?"

"Wiltz."

"You didn't get yourself in any trouble here, did you?" asked a concerned Sisto.

"Unlike some I can name"—and Ryan playfully slapped Sisto on the chin—"I do not get into trouble. I *navigate* it. Since I hardly expect Lenny Courie to accept defeat with quiet grace, as soon as we adjourned, I shot a message off to Cota's head-

quarters, apologizing for this whole mess. I said we should forgive Courie his understandable zealousness—"

"Courie got greedy," I translated.

"—and give an allowance for his limited understanding of
military *judicata*—"

"And didn't know what he was talking about."

"—and that it was very easy for all concerned to become
persuaded by the captain's enthusiasm and give him free rein."

"A clever reminder to the general that he had signed off on
Courie's actions as much as you did." I clapped my hands. "The
maestro again demonstrates his skills in a *tour de force*. He accepts
responsibility but blames Courie, and tells a three-star general,
'This is partly your fault. Sir.' All without one undiplomatic
word. *Bravo!*"

Sisto snapped to an exaggerated attention and flashed a
British-style palm-up salute. "All hail the man in the Big
Chair!"

"Kiss my ass!" Ryan smirked and he and Sisto shook hands.
"So, now I have to go down to Wiltz and smooth everything
over and assure the general that it will never happen again."

"How do you make good on that?" Ricks inquired.

"By also assuring him that as soon as I get back to Liège, I'm
shoving a rocket up Courie's ass and sending him off to bother
somebody else. I can't decide where, though. So many appetizing options! The Aleutians, Burma. Kansas. Harry, you had to fly
through Greenland when you came over; how awful was
that?"

"Pretty awful."

"Maybe Greenland, then." Ryan now belatedly noted
Harry's less than effusive mood. "What's with the puss?"

"Just tired. Been a long couple of weeks."

"Oh, I almost forgot..." Ryan extracted a wireless message form from his pocket and handed it to Harry. "Now that everything's wrapped up, what do you want to do with this? From Corporal Thom."

"Jesus, I almost forgot about poor Andy!" Sisto said.

"You guys sent him off on some scavenger hunt to find somebody?" Ryan asked. "This came in a little while ago. Looks like he found the guy, but I guess that's moot now."

"If it's not too much trouble," Sisto asked, "maybe you could radio back to him, tell him the show's over and I'll meet him in Wiltz. That is, if it's OK with the signor."

"That OK with you, Harry?" Ryan asked.

Harry had his reading spectacles on and was scanning the brief communiqué. He seemed not to have heard. Ryan asked a second time and Harry absently nodded his agreement.

"Now listen!" Ryan was the firm *paterfamilias,* a reprimanding finger poking into Sisto's face. "You pretty much used up your ration of luck on this one, boy-o. Be nice! Particularly to people who outrank you! If you're going to call them assholes, make sure you put Sir! after it, OK?"

"OK." Then, pointedly, "Sir."

We all laughed. Except Harry. He seemed to still be considering the message from Andy Thom.

"Well," Ryan said, "Harry, there's no rush on you leaving these lush surroundings. I won't be back in Liège until tomorrow night, maybe even the day after. You and I and Captain Ricks here should meet up then and maybe talk about what's next."

"Next?" Harry still appeared in a fog.

"Once Courie's gone, that leaves my T.O. short an attorney. Captain Ricks, I can make room for two."

"We'll talk about it then, Colonel," Ricks said uncertainly.

Ryan stopped at the door. "You know, Dominick, I know I said that you had to get back to your outfit at the 'earliest possible opportunity.' Tomorrow morning qualifies."

"Thanks, but there's a new company CO, I've got almost a whole platoon of replacements to deal with...I need to get back. The guys who are heading back to Wiltz, they're holding their truck for me right now."

Ryan nodded. "You're a good kid, Dominick. Behave." A wink, a smile, and Ryan left.

Sisto turned to Harry. The older man slowly—wearily, I thought—pulled himself from his chair.

"I don't know what to say, *Signor.*"

"Just say you'll take care of yourself."

"Goes without saying."

"I mean it, Dominick."

I thought they might have embraced then, as they had that first day. But Sisto preempted, putting his hand between them. Harry took it, but then his other hand set itself on Sisto's neck. As a father might.

They stood that way a long time.

"Those guys are waiting..." From Sisto, an awkward interruption. He pulled on his garrison cap, threw his bag across his shoulder. He looked around the room at the three of us one last time. He made as if to speak but found no words.

Harry nodded that it was all right; no words were needed. "*Ciao.*"

"*Ciao,*" Dominick Sisto said, and disappeared out the door.

We crowded about the narrow windows, watched Sisto be pulled up into the back of the lorry below by friendly, helpful hands, saw the truck vanish into the shadows of the trees at the end of the drive.

When I turned away from the window I found Harry

pacing about the room, much as I'd seen him pace about the well of the court, still apparently focused on the wireless message from Andy Thom.

"What is it?" Ricks asked him.

"The reason you could never find him on any of the battalion rosters is he wasn't a member of the battalion."

"Who?"

"Your phantom radio operator who was supposedly on top of the hill with Dominick. He was with the Air Corps."

"Air Corps?" I was puzzled.

"A Forward Air Controller," Ricks guessed, and Harry nodded. "They stick these guys with the forward outfits to help coordinate air strikes," Ricks explained. "So, this poor bastard must've gone up the hill with the battalion, the weather cancels out the air strike... Now, *that's* bad luck!"

Harry mumbled something about seeing us at dinner, then abruptly left the room. A moment later, we heard the echo of the door to his own quarters slam shut.

"What the hell's that all about?" Ricks asked me.

"I don't know. I'm not sure he does, either."

Having grown quite comfortably accustomed to the tasty offerings of Courie's mess crew, it made for a rather grim repast to once again turn to rifling through 10-in-1 assortments to try to compile something resembling a meal fit for human consumption. It certainly added nothing to the meal that the kitchen stood dark and empty, and Peter Ricks and I sat alone at the long table in the great dining hall.

After some unenthusiastic pecking at his tin plate, Ricks sat back with a groan. "Not to belabor the obvious, but something's up." Without a further word, he pushed back from the table and set off out of the dining hall. I followed, and a moment later stood with him as he knocked on the door to Harry's quarters. When there was no answer, he unhesitatingly swung the door open.

Harry gave no notice he was aware of our entry. He paced about the room, his spectacles parked far down on his nose, studying the mosaic of note cards that he'd spread about the floor.

"Wasn't enough time," Harry mumbled, as much to himself as to us. "Never had time to think . . . to think . . . You have time . . . you consider what you don't *want* to consider."

"Harry?" Ricks called, but Harry's trance was undisturbed.

"It didn't make any sense as a lie," he continued to muse, "because we were wrong about *why* the lie . . ."

"Harry!" I called sharply. "What are you on about, mate?"

He stopped his perambulating, his eyes—as if he were just waking up—blinked and belatedly focused on us. He nodded toward the cards as if we could as easily glean whatever epiphany had taken hold of him. "In the beginning, I had the same suspicion Joyce did, that maybe Dominick was lying about getting the withdrawal order from Porter. The more I found out about the fight for Hill 399 . . . if he hadn't pulled them down, none of them—" Harry closed his eyes, shook his head, trying to rid himself of an ugly thought. "If it was a lie, I could've lived with that.

"But I believed him because the lie didn't make any sense, just like I brought out during Joyce's cross. Dominick didn't gain anything by it."

"You chopped up Joyce pretty nicely on that, Harry," Ricks put in, "but I always thought it was obvious. He lied that Porter had given him the order so the order would have a weight—"

"Right!" Harry jumped at the point. "*That* part made sense!"

Ricks and I were both shaking our heads, bewildered.

"What the hell're you talking about, Harry? What's the *other* part?"

"He gets on the horn to Joyce to say 'I've got this order to get the hell out of here from Major Porter.' Joyce says 'Oh, yeah? Let me talk to him.' Dominick says 'Well, I'm sorry, he's in the shower right now and can't come to the phone.' You think that gives his story about an order from Porter credibility? I think it does the exact opposite: *it's guaranteed to make the guy on the other end of the line suspicious.*

"I said it during Joyce's cross: Dominick never had to make that call. He could've claimed bad communications, commander's discretion, whatever, he never had to confer with Joyce. 'Major Porter was dead, I couldn't get through to battalion HQ, I had to act on my own.' Under the circumstances, that would've been a hell of a hard story to shake apart. *Why make the call?*

"Even if you buy the idea that Dominick hoped this little fib about getting the order from Porter would somehow give everybody the idea that he had Porter's blessing for the pullout, that all evaporates the second he gets the assault detail back to the trench line. Once they're back in the trenches, they look around, Porter's not there, everyone assumes he's dead. Command falls to Joyce, and everybody on that hill who still has a working radio already knows from the first damned message between Sisto and Joyce that *Joyce wants them to stay on the hill.* So, where is Dominick ahead? The only thing he's bought himself with a lie about Porter—maybe—is the few minutes it takes him to get the assault detail from the top of the hill back to the trenches, at which point he *does* ignore Joyce and pull the whole battalion off the hill. But . . ."

He sat heavily down on the cushy mattress of his four-poster. He tossed his glasses onto the bedclothes and blinked at us blindly. "It *does* make sense if the lie *isn't* about Porter giving the order. The lie . . . is that *Porter was still alive when Dominick made the call to Joyce.* What he was trying to buy himself was everybody believing that Conrad Porter was still alive when Dominick started taking his men off that saddle."

"What does that buy Dominick? So the krauts put a pill in Porter. What does Sisto get from hiding that?"

Harry's eyes turned to the ancient warped beams crossing the ceiling. "Nothing. Not a goddamned thing . . . as long as what killed Porter was a German bullet."

CHAPTER NINE

——— ★ ———

The home of the American 984th Fighter Group consisted
of barely more than a scattering of tents and a steel-mesh run-
way thrown across a muddy field just south of Mons.

His mates remembered Lieutenant Tyrone Compton as an
ebullient, cocky lad who wore his crushed officer's cap at such
a jaunty angle, it threatened to topple from his crest of thick,
wavy hair. But they would tell you that *that* Lieutenant Tyrone
Compton was no more.

The Tyrone Compton we found walking the floorboards of
his tent in Belgium was of a markedly different character. He
was unshaven, pale, the once bright and smiling eyes now red-
rimmed and nervous. He was huddled deep in his fleece-lined
flying clothes, shivering, although he'd stoked the woodburn-
ing stove so high, it nearly glowed red.

And he talked. His jaws worked ceaselessly, as if powered by
an abject terror of silence.

"Where'd you guys say you were from? Judge Advocate?
Whatever it is, I didn't do it!" A nervous giggle. "Just kiddin'!
'We wuz all in the back singin', Officer!' You ever hear that

one? Cop pulls over a car and there's these three drunks in the backseat and the cop says, 'All right, which one of you bozos is the driver?' and one of them says back, he says—'Nobody wuz drivin', Offisher! We wuz all in the back shingin'!'" An explosion of harsh laughter. "You never heard that one? That's a good one, huh? So, Judge Advocate—seriously, I don't know, uh—"

"You're not in any trouble, Lieutenant," Harry said calmly.

"Uh-huh, uh-huh, OK." His fingers sifted through the unkempt tangle of hair. "So, what's up, then, huh? What's the poop? Hey, anybody see my smokes?"

Harry held up the flattened packet of Lucky Strikes he found near him on the cot where he was sitting.

"Damn." Compton's hands flitted about his Irvine jacket, looking for a packet of cigarettes that wasn't there. "Can anybody here butt me? Anybody, uh, spare something? I'm just dyin'—Oh, hey, thanks, Cap."

"Keep 'em," Ricks told him.

"Good deal, thanks loads, really, thanks." Compton fumbled a ragged book of matches from his pocket but couldn't steady his hands long enough to strike one. Ricks offered the blaze of his Ronson. "Hey, thanks again, Cap, really." Compton held out his shaking hands for us all to see, apparently surprised at his inability to master them. "Do you believe this? This is somethin', huh? You know I flew thirty-two missions, I was a rock, no kiddin'. No shit. Ask anybody. Really. Thirty-two missions, didn't bring up sweat on a cow's brow with me. I know guys with half that got to practically drag themselves into the cockpit, but not me! Really! I was a fuckin' rock!" It seemed to suddenly occur to him that we had yet to get to the subject of our meeting. "Jeez, I'm sorry, fellas, I keep goin' off like that. Don't know why. I really don't. You said you were with the Judge Advocate? Whaddaya want with me?"

"Just a few questions," Harry said. "About Hill 399."

"What do you guys have to do with Hill 399? Oh, none of my business, right? Confidential and all that, right? OK, sure, I understand, sure. I mean, whaddaya want to know?"

"You were a Forward Air Controller with a battalion that tried to take the hill last month, weren't you?"

Compton let a darkly humorous chuckle bubble up. "That was a fuckin' joke, huh? I mean, the weather was never good enough to call the planes in! I mean, is that fuckin' ironic? Jeez, are you guys cold?" Compton reached for another block of wood from the pile by the stove and tossed it through the grate. "You'd think these furs would do it, huh? Keep you warm? Look at these boots! They weigh a goddamn ton! Look at that fur! I had some doughfoot once offer me fifty bucks for a set of flying boots. But they don't keep out water. You don't need to keep out water at ten thousand feet, but it rains, it snows, it gets in, then your feet are wet, you'd just as soon wear those infantry clodhoppers, you know? Really! You have a choice: you wear the clodhoppers and you're cold but dry, or you wear these and—well, I guess if your feet get wet, you're going to be cold anyway—"

"Lieutenant," Harry said.

"Oh, yeah, I'm sorry, I'm goin' off again. I'll be damned if I know why that is. I'll tell you when it started—"

"With Hill 399," Ricks sympathized.

"You're goddamn right 'with Hill 399'!" Suddenly, viciously bitter. "You know the doughs, they think everything's squeaky clean up you-know-where." A thumb jerked skyward. "But I've seen things. A guy's plane flames, you see him stuck in the cockpit, can't get the canopy open, and you see him in there . . . or he jumps, and his chute snags or something, and then it's a long, looong, bad way down . . . One time, we sometimes come in low, Cap, we come in so low I'll part your fuckin' hair—I'm down in the grass, we're raking this kraut column, the trucks start going up like a string of firecrackers, and I see this thing go by my canopy, some guy's fuckin' leg, OK? I mean still in the pants, still wearing his boot, just this leg goes sailing by . . . OK, so what I'm sayin' is I'm not some virgin. But that day at Hill 399?" Compton held out his hands for us again. "Thirty-two missions, not even a quiver. One day on that goddamn hill and this! Isn't that a kick in the drawers? You know I'm grounded? They tell you that? Because of how I was when I came back? The flight doc grounded me! Unfit, he says, unfit!"

"Lieutenant," Harry repeated.

"Goddammit!" Compton dropped on one of the cots, shaking his head. "I don't want to be like this, fellas, I really don't."

"It's OK," Ricks said.

"Fuck you, it's OK," Compton spat back.

"About Hill 399," Harry said.

"Ya know? Fuck it!" Compton clapped his hands as if sealing a bargain. He resumed his pacing. "What happened to my smoke?" At some point it had dropped forgotten from his lips. "How the hell . . . ?" He fumbled another from the packet, gestured to Ricks for another light. "I'm not talkin' about that place. Sorry, guys. There was five hundred other guys there, I'm sure one of them—" He froze, his eyes grew moist. I think the thought had fought its way to his consciousness from wherever he had it buried under all that verbiage that perhaps five hundred men may have gone up Hill 399, but five hundred didn't make it down. "I'm not talkin' about it." He turned away, pulled open the door flap, and looked out at the P-47 Thunderbolts parked across the field protectively draped with tarpaulins, their mud-splattered undercarriages peeping out underneath. A drizzle had begun, the drops churning up the layer of snow outside, making gentle pats on the peaked canvas of the tent top. Compton looked down at his shaking hands. "We wouldn'ta been flyin' today anyway..."

Harry rose from his cot with a grunt, walked over to Compton, and set a hand on his shoulder. With his other hand he took the door flap from Compton and let it fall closed. "Aren't you cold, Lieutenant?"

"All the goddamn time."

Harry steered him back into the tent, pulled a cot up close to the stove, and sat the pilot down, pulled another cot up nearby and sat across from him. "I only want to ask what happened on top of the hill. Just that."

"On top of the hill?"

"That's all."

Compton's head wavered from side to side as if he were having some inner negotiation with himself, finally agreeing. "I was with the doughs that went up the right-hand side of the hill."

"The western slope," Ricks said.

Compton shrugged. "I guess. Put me in the air, I can navigate you all the way to Podunk, U.S.A. Put me on the ground, I get lost goin' around a corner." A thin, forced smile. "They put me on that side because they thought it was safer." A short, blurted-out laugh, and he was on his feet again, moving about the tent. "*That* was supposed to be *safer*? Safer than *what*? I don't even want to know what it must've been like on the other side if *my* side was supposed to be the easy one!" He rubbed at his forehead as if to massage an ache away. "Three times we went up that goddamn manure pile, ya know."

"I know," Harry said.

"I'm no doughfoot," Compton declared. "One thing the doughs are right about is us flyboys do our fightin' on our ass!

I haven't done any PT since basic! And after climbin' up that thing three fuckin' times— Hill, my ass, that thing was a fuckin' *mountain*! Like this!" He angled an arm to illustrate the severity of the slope. "There were times guys were *draggin'* my ass up that monster! Mind you, I had to haul this goddamn radio up on my back, the one I was supposed to use to contact the 47's that never showed up, and that thing weighed a fuckin' ton! Really! I'm lugging that thing up, by that third time up the hill, *goddamn*, man, I was *dead*. I had the jelly legs, I was wheezin'. Dead. On my feet. Really. Dead! I was *crawlin'*.

"You know how that hill was laid out? There were these kraut trenches up there? By the time we got to them, I was on my belly. Seriously. I just couldn't stay on my feet.

"You talk to any of the other guys that went up that hill? They tell you what it was like? That whole top of the hill, it was like a porcupine's ass and every needle was some kind of gun! We hit those trenches, I fell in—seriously, *fell* in, that was all I could do—and just stuck my nose in the mud and hoped somebody didn't put a second hole in my ass . . ."

He took the cigarette from his mouth; it seemed to simply slide from his fingers to smolder on the floor. I noted there were dozens of burned-out butts about. Even before he had the next cigarette in his mouth, Ricks was offering a fresh light.

"I don't know how long I was down there. Bottom of the trench, I mean. A fuckin' *joke*! I *knew* we weren't gonna get any good sky over that hill that day. Thirty-two goddamn missions, you better believe I can read a little weather. Just before jump-off, I told them, I said, 'Look, you see anything but ugly clouds up there? We're not gettin' any sky in here today.' They could just as well left my ass back in the woods, I wasn't goin' to do anybody any good up there. But, 'Just in case! Just in case!' My ass 'just in case'!"

"The top of the hill," Harry gently guided him.

"Yeah, right, right, I'm off somewhere else again, huh? Really sorry about that. OK, so, I don't know how long I was keepin' my head down in the bottom of that trench, but then somebody was pullin' me up sayin' somethin' about tryin' for the top of the hill, I thought the guy was batshit loony, you know? But I looked up and there were some of our guys already on top. It was a run across open ground, but if we could get up there, hell, at least up there I thought I'd be behind the krauts."

"So up you went."

"Fast as I could, still luggin' all that goddamn hardware with me, too. I'm surprised I didn't get a fuckin' hernia with that thing. We got up there, I saw a hole, a shell hole, and in I went and right into my drill."

"Nose in the mud," Ricks said.

The two men exchanged a quick comradely grin. "Goddamn right, nose in the mud. I don't know how long it was, maybe just a minute or two, and then someone was kickin' me in the ribs and sayin' somethin' like 'He needs a radio! He needs a radio!' I looked up and they were pointin' to somebody outside the hole. Outside the hole? 'Anybody outside the hole,' I thought, 'who needs a radio? Fuck him,' I thought. 'Tell him to buy an RCA.' I was goin' to stay down there—"

"With your nose in the mud," Ricks said.

"—with my nose in the goddamn mud, you bet, where it was safe."

"Then what?" asked Harry.

"Then I got another kick in the ribs. I finally started thinkin' I should see what was what about this guy who wanted a radio before one of these doughfoot animals punctured my fuckin' lung. I stuck my head up. I was right about keepin' my nose in the mud, there was so much kraut steel flyin' around. I thought we were gonna be behind the kraut guns, but as soon as we were up in there—"

"You saw the man who called for the radio?"

"About ten yards away this guy's peepin' up at me from another shell hole. He gets a look at me and goes"—re-creating the surprised look, the confused blinking of eyes—"like he was thinkin', 'Who the fuck are you?' Then somebody else pipes up, thank Christ, somebody from back by the edge of the slope, some other radioman. I could see his antenna. I guess that's who this joker had been callin' for. So, he slips back down in his hole and runs over to that guy and me, I'm glad he stood me up because with all that steel flyin' around, one of us would've ended up a sieve."

"You saw the man's face?" Harry asked. "The one who was calling for a radioman? Did you know him?"

"Know him?" Compton laughed derisively. "I didn't even know the guys I was with! I didn't know *anybody* in that outfit! I just hooked up with them the day they got to whatever the hell that town was—"

"Rott."

"—whatever the fuck it was, I got introduced to the battalion CO—'Hi, how ya doin''—and the captain of the company I was supposed to go up the hill with, and that was it, and after that first try up the hill I never saw that captain again, he probably—"

"The man you saw," Harry pressed, "did you see any insignia of rank?"

"Oh, yeah, sure, he had a lieutenant's bar on his helmet, I could see that."

"And the other man?"

"Other man?"

"The other one in the shell hole with the lieutenant?"

"I didn't see anybody else in there."

"He was the battalion commander, a major, you said you met him."

"I don't give a shit if he was an admiral in the Turkish navy and he was my asshole buddy. There was nobody else in there."

"Maybe," I suggested, "he was too far down in the hole for you to see him."

Compton shook his head. "That part of the hill looked like this." He made a cup of his gloved hands. "The krauts were comin' in all around here." He indicated the high ground of his wrist and fingertips. "That's why it was such a shitty position. They could shoot right down into your holes. I was up here." He indicated a point partly up his palm. "That lieutenant was down here at the bottom. I could see pretty far down into his hole. This other guy you say was in there, if he *was* there, he must've had—"

"His nose in the mud," sighed Ricks.

"If he had any fuckin' sense."

Harry thanked the pilot and we all stood to leave.

Compton looked down at his hands again. "They wanted to send me home on a psycho, but I'm not goin' home that way. Thirty-two missions, I'm not goin' to get Section 8'd out, go home and fuck the thirty-two missions; you're a head case, that's all they know. Really. I feel like I just need a good night's sleep. Really. The doc gave me pills, to sleep, but I don't like the pills, somethin' about the pills scares me. I just need a good night's sleep." He looked up with a sad, puzzled look. "But I never get it."

"Well?" Harry asked.

Peter Ricks shrugged and continued to study Hill 399 through his field glasses.

The hill had a looming presence. The long forward slopes and upthrust crests gave it the impression of being higher. The wings of the hill, sweeping away from them and leading naturally into its tapered ends, fooled the eye into thinking the hill was receding into the far distance.

Neither the months since the battle for the hill nor a heavy coat of snow could soften the evidence of the great violence rendered in unbelievable concentration. From the woods line—where Harry and Ricks now huddled—out into the firebreak that girdled the hill and then on up the slopes was a moonscape so heavily acned from shellfire that craters often overlapped. That measled appearance continued unabated to the very top. The lower, forested slopes had nary a single tree standing untouched. Shattered, split, holed, stripped of bark and branches, charred. The trench line was clearly visible across the barren upper slopes which the Germans had stripped of trees to provide both clear observation of the surrounding area and a killing zone to be crossed by attackers.

Harry shivered. His calves ached, his knees were stiff. It had been a long walk from Rott, and the hours in the cold, the frozen ruts of the Kall Trail, the strain of jumping at every sigh of boughs and falling clump of snow from the shadowy depths of the forest had taken their toll on Harry.

As for Peter Ricks... Later, Harry would describe to me an air of... not calm, but serenity. Comfort. The ease of familiarity.

I was still in Rott, loitering about the mess tent in the divisional assembly area just outside of town. Ricks had returned from a scrounging expedition with field kit and weapons for two. "Have you seen the map?" the captain said to me. "No way you're making that hike with that bum wheel," meaning my dicky leg.

I had seen the map and was forced to agree. As I watched

them disappear down the Kall Trail early that morning, it also occurred to me that I would rather have limped and crawled along with them than spend that day . . . waiting.

The Americans had withdrawn behind the Kall River and as a consequence—so Intelligence officers said—the Germans had abandoned Hill 399. The hill now sat in a no-man's-land frequented only by reconnaissance and infiltration patrols.

"So, is it safe?" Harry had asked the divisional G-2 who'd briefed them.

The G-2 officer's response had been a wry smile and a shrug. "You can tell *me* when you get back."

"Sure you're up to this?" Ricks asked Harry as he continued to study the hill. "Or, as they say back home, 'Is this trip really necessary?'"

"Anybody up there?"

Ricks shrugged. "I don't *see* anything. But that's not really an answer. There's only one way to find out. Ready?"

With a grunt, Harry grabbed his carbine and pulled himself to his feet. Ricks picked up his own weapon, motioned Harry to take a position a few yards to his right, then they started out into the open ground.

The firebreak was so pocked with shell holes that a straight transit was impossible, and the two men found themselves constantly zigging and zagging until they reached the base of the hill. Ricks took another moment at the bottom of the hill, scanning the high ground again through his field glasses.

That was when Harry noticed the bodies—dark, huddled piles almost concealed by the snow, sprinkled about the forward slope.

Ricks looked to Harry, Harry nodded, and up the hill they started. Under the snow was crumbly shale, fallen branches, partially filled shell craters. By the time they cleared the tree line halfway up the slope, Harry was wheezing, and his legs were on fire.

"A little farther," Ricks urged. "And follow right in my footsteps. There's still live mines here."

Ricks led them through a path blown through the minefield and double apron wire that had fronted the trench line. Finally, they slid into the trench. Harry fell back on his duff, his face sheathed with sweat.

"Catch your breath," Ricks told him. Out came the field glasses again as he studied the crests above them. He pointed out the path ahead. "This is where it gets tricky."

A few yards beyond the trench was the foot of the spine of rock that led ramp-like to the saddle between the two crests. There was no cover, nor did the narrow dimensions of the spine allow any room for evasion. The shell-resistant stone did not even provide any shell craters for possible cover. As apprehensive as Harry was of making that walk, he could not fathom doing it under fire.

They clambered out of the trench, then stumbled and slid up the icy rock until they finally stepped onto the saddle. Almost immediately, Harry faltered. Leaning on his carbine, he winced against the pain of the cold air rasping his throat. At his feet, a shell hole, and at its bottom the desiccated bodies of two American soldiers.

"This must be it." Ricks stood by Harry's side, breathing a bit heavily himself. "That's what they said: as soon as they hit the top they jumped in a hole. Makris, Bonilla, some others." He slid down the snowy side of the crater. "Yeah! Remember? They said there was a line of shell holes, almost like a trench." He pointed to the faux trench leading off the first hole. "This must be it."

"They still have their dog tags?"

Ricks brushed aside the snow, fumbled inside a collar with his one good hand. "Beaudrie," he read.

"And Wardell," Harry recalled. "This is it." He slid down the side of the crater and followed Ricks through the shell holes. The snow at the bottom was deeper than elsewhere, and it was an effort to wade through it. They came to the end of the line of holes almost at the midpoint of the saddle.

Ricks shook his head. "If this is it, he should be here."

"Maybe the Germans took the body—"

"And left all these others?"

"—or maybe he was just wounded and taken prisoner."

"The Red Cross doesn't have his name. Dammit . . ." Frustrated, Ricks pulled himself out of the hole and began to scout the other craters that had churned up the saddle.

From the crater, Harry could easily see the well-positioned dugouts all along the high ground. Huddled in the low ground between the two crests, Dominick Sisto and the other men had been right to view holding the position as tantamount to suicide.

"There's more bodies here," Ricks called. He was standing near a crater partway up the saddle's sloping side. "This must be where the Item Company men came up. They jumped in here. Compton said he saw the assault detail below him." He frowned. "This has *got* to be right. So where the hell's Porter?"

Harry was slowly moving about at the bottom of the crater. "How far down into this hole can you see?"

Ricks crouched to approximate the view Compton might have had. "Better than halfway down the far side. Nearer to me, you have to be down a good two feet before I can't see the top of your head."

Thunk. Harry's boot collided with something metallic. He gave a push with his toe and a helmet popped free of the snow in a burst of powder. Harry found himself looking at the officer's bar painted down the back of the helmet. "I think I've got something."

He picked the helmet up, dusted off the clinging snow. At the front of the helmet was a major's bronze oak leaf. Just below and a bit to one side was a hole nearly an inch across. He turned the helmet over to look inside. The front of the liner around the hole was discolored with a dark, mottled stain. Along the side, just above the rim, in small, neat white letters was painted PORTER, CJ.

"What've you got?" said Ricks, skidding down the side of the crater. He took the helmet from Harry's gloved hand, quickly glanced inside, then turned to study the hole. "See the way the metal puckers out? This is an exit hole. It looks angled up. No entrance hole. You'd have to be pretty far down behind him . . ." He tossed the helmet away and looked about the shell crater. "Where the fuck could this joker be?"

He went down on his hands and knees, his good hand sweeping over the hard ground beneath the snow cover along the lower part of the crater. "There wasn't time to bury him. Couldn't've done more than shove him somewhere and pull some mud down on him."

Harry began following Ricks's example, searching the opposite side of the crater. "There's no chance Porter was hit by the Germans?" he asked, not believing it himself.

"The bullet went in low and came out high," Ricks explained. "If it was the krauts, you'd expect it to be the other way around. The only way they could've put a pill through Porter's head at that angle was if he had his back to them, his head was between his knees, and he was practically kissing his own ass. Ah! I believe the word is 'Eureka!'"

Harry helped him clear the snow away from an area near the

floor of the crater. The corpse lay on its right side, legs tucked up underneath. Ricks's presumption had been correct: most of the body was covered with only a thin layer of frozen mud. As Ricks brushed the body clear, Harry saw a major's oak leaf visible on the windcheater shoulder. The captain drew his K-bar from its scabbard and began chiseling away at the frozen ground around the corpse's head.

Harry turned away.

"Exit wound here in the front," Ricks observed. "Lines up with the helmet."

Harry glanced quickly toward the captain, saw the fingers of his good hand feeling around the discolored, leathery skin at the base of the skull, turned hastily away again.

"Right there!" Ricks declared. "There's the entrance wound. He must've just missed the rim of the helmet." He stepped away from the body and brushed his glove clean on his trouser leg. "Are you ready to head back?"

Harry picked up Porter's helmet and nodded. "What do we do about him?" He nodded at the body at their feet.

"What do you mean?"

"Feels funny just leaving him like this."

"He's got plenty of company up here, Harry." Ricks stopped at the end of the trench, looking down the slope. "Too goddamn much company if you ask me." He spat into the snow, then, without waiting for Harry, he started back down the hill.

CHAPTER TEN

— ★ —

"I can't seem to get warm," Harry said.

He and I were seated at a table near one of the petrol heaters in the dimly lit mess tent in the assembly area outside Rott. Except for the mess crew bustling about their stoves and tables, preparing for the following day, we were the only occupants that night. We leaned close in to the heater, our gloved hands wrapped about tin cups of coffee that seemed to lose their heat as soon as they'd been poured.

Conrad Porter's helmet sat on the table behind Harry. I could not tear my eyes from the ragged exit hole near the major's leaf.

A rustle of the tent flaps announced Peter Ricks's return. He slipped his hook through the handle of a tin cup on the mess counter, then crossed to us, carefully setting on the table a haversack he'd had hanging from his shoulder. "How're you doing, Harry?"

"I'm starting to feel my toes," Harry replied, "and now they hurt."

"I think the doctor has just the remedy." Ricks reached into the haversack and brought out a bottle of cognac. He poured a fair-sized dose into Harry's cup, held the bottle out to me. I saw him pause then, holding the bottle over his own cup. He saw me watching him, smiled, set the bottle down, and poured himself some coffee.

"I got us a place to stay in town for the night," he said, parking himself on the table. "So now the question is: what about tomorrow?"

Harry drank from his cup and stared deeply into the glowing grill of the heater. He shook his head, unsure.

"You were up there today, Harry," Ricks said. "You saw what it was like. If they'd stayed, they'd all be dead. Dominick and the rest of them. You're going to put him against the wall for that?"

"He murdered a man, Pete."

"People were getting murdered on that hill all day, Harry, so pardon me if I don't cry over this one. You want to put somebody up for murder? Try Porter. Try Joyce. Try whatever genius at Corps came up with the whole fucked-up operation. But not this kid. Shit, Harry, if I'd been up there, I would've pipped him!"

Harry turned to me.

I shrugged. "I don't know how to judge, Harry. I truly don't. I've seen too much. I think we all have."

"Could you live with this?"

"You mean dropping this?" I stacked Dominick Sisto's failing against the twenty-odd years of human foible, frailty, and failure I'd catalogued and turned into grist for after-dinner reads. "Aye."

"Walk away from this, Harry," Ricks urged. "I'm begging you."

Harry shook his head.

"Why not?"

"I helped raise that boy."

"Then save him," Peter Ricks said harshly. "Don't hang him."

Harry stared into his cup for a moment, took a deep draft. "I have to hear what he has to say about this."

Ricks sighed in exasperation. "You're hoping he'll 'do the right thing' and turn himself in. That'll get you off the hook; you won't have to decide. What if he doesn't? What if he decides—"

"I don't know."

"You don't know. And if he *does* turn himself in?"

"I'll defend him."

Ricks laughed. Wryly. Cruelly. "And that'll make everything square with you? You'll feel good about that, will you?"

"No." Harry drained his cup, then tiredly got to his feet. "I'm going down to see him, Pete. I'm going to hear what he has to say. If you don't want to come along, fine. You've got qualms about how I'm handling this? Sit it out. But if you come"— growing as chill as the air in the mess tent—"you-keep-your-goddamned-mouth-shut! Now," Harry said, "where's this place we can bunk for the night? I'm beat."

At 28th Division Headquarters in Wiltz we were briefed on the disposition of the division's combat elements in the sector. Broken into company- and platoon-sized units, the division was spread thinly through their operational sector of the Ardennes, primarily in small villages along what the troops called Skyline Drive, a road running along high ground overlooking the Our River, which followed a roughly parallel course one to two miles beyond. Love Company of the 3rd/103rd was stretched along a line of outposts along the western banks of the Our.

Dominick Sisto's partially reconstituted platoon was emplaced about a small stone bridge below Heinerscheid. On the Luxembourg side of the bridge was a customs station with a small attached barrack, a bus depot, and a café, all long since abandoned by the natives. We arrived well into the early evening, were waved to a halt by a sentry who looked barely old enough to shave.

Harry showed the lad his identification and asked for Sisto.

"He's not here right now, Sir," the youngster said.

"Where is he?"

"I don't rightly—"

"Colonel!"

We turned at the cry and saw Andy Thom striding toward us from the café. We clambered out of the jeep, exchanged greetings and warm handclasps before he led us inside and sat us by a warm blaze in the dining room. Most of the tables had been pushed clear, and the room was littered with sleeping bags and the usual clutter of a GI bivouac. When I glanced at the troopers—all as youthful as the guardsman who'd halted us—engaged in the usual barrack pursuits—here a card game, there a letter writer, over there a peruser of a copy of *Yank*—I decided the room carried more the air of a school dormitory than a military post.

Voss flicked a thumb at the set of bright new buck sergeant's stripes on Thom's sleeve. "Where'd you get those, Andy? Box of Cracker Jacks?"

"Them and a decoder ring," Thom replied, grinning. "The lieutenant, he wangled these for me." Glancing across the room at his young charges, his grin faltered. "I like the pay raise, but I'd just as soon somebody else was doin' the baby-sittin'."

"Andy, where's Dominick?" Harry asked.

"We've got one squad at an outpost a couple hundred yards south of here, another one north. He's just checkin' in with them." But Thom's worried look betrayed the innocuousness of the duty.

"What is it, Andy?" Harry probed.

Thom hesitated, then nodded his surrender; he knew he'd been caught out. "He isn't right, Colonel. Ever since he came back, he isn't right."

"How so?"

"He'll check the outposts. He'll check our position here. He'll check the outposts again. He'll go out to bring in the night patrol, back to the outposts, he comes in here, catches a catnap, checks in with them all on the radio, then he's out makin' rounds again. He's like some ol' lady keeps thinkin' she left the gas on. He wants to be everywhere, Colonel, 'n' be there all the time. He's gonna wear himself out. I'm glad it's quiet around here 'cause he's got me worried what he's gonna be like if we have to go into action again."

Andy Thom's appraisal seemed to particularly resonate with Peter Ricks. He turned to Harry, his look in part questioning and in part accusatory, as if to demand, *Are you sure you want to go ahead with this?*

Then a fresh concern filled Andy Thom. "Colonel, you mind me askin' what you all're doin' here?"

"Later, Andy. When Dominick comes back."

"Might not be for a long while."

"We'll wait."

The clock ticked, it grew late, one by one Andy Thom's squad drifted off to sleep. We heard a jeep heading in our direction from downriver.

A small sighing moan from Harry. "Aw, hell . . ."

I would dearly have loved to know what went through Dominick Sisto's head when he stepped into the café and saw us sitting around the hearth—Harry, Peter Ricks, Andy Thom, and me—like a tribunal awaiting his appearance before the bar. He stood in the doorway for a moment, Juan Bonilla just behind his shoulder. There was the smallest bit of a smile from the lieutenant—not in amusement or welcome, but an empty, perfunctory hullo. Then he stepped up to Andy Thom, and the rest of us might just as well not have been there.

"Where's security, Andy?"

"I've got a man at each end of the street."

"You should check on 'em. I didn't see 'em. They might be off in some warm place. When was the last time you rotated 'em?"

Thom checked his watch. "An hour ago, right on schedule."

"Radio messages?"

"Nothing, Lootenant."

I caught Bonilla's eye. He shook his head in dismay, turned for the kitchen, returned with two cups of coffee, handed one to Sisto.

"Juan," Sisto said, "why don't you check on those sentries for Andy? I think him and the rest of these gents need a word with me." He waited for Bonilla to leave, then turned to us with another smile—a sad, expectant one this time—and said, "I imagine you guys'd like some privacy."

We followed him up a staircase to a suite of rooms, living quarters, I guessed, for the previous owners of the café. He led us into the cozy little bedroom, a featherbed, a few deep-cushioned chairs, and some heavy wood furniture taking up most of the floor space. Sisto tossed his helmet on the bed, sat by the night table, where he set his cup. After a long silence: "Well, Signor, not that it's not nice to see you again . . ."

"I know why you didn't want the Irishman to bring me in to handle your case," Harry told him. I don't remember seeing the helmet in his hands up to that moment, have no idea of when he'd stepped out to the jeep to retrieve it, but that's when he tossed Conrad Porter's bullet-holed headgear onto the bed.

That sad smile of Sisto's again as he glanced at Porter's helmet. "You've been getting around, Signor."

"Porter never ordered a withdrawal."

Sisto took a sip of his coffee. "Hell, he was about to order Tully's men up the hill." He said it as offhandedly as if he'd been discussing a bad play at last week's cricket match. "You've been there; you saw how it was laid out up there. The krauts were filling in their positions on the high ground. I figured we had a couple of minutes and then we were gonna be just a bunch of mommas' memories. Porter wouldn't listen." He thought back on it, his brow knitting in recollection and puzzlement. "Of all people, I never would've put money on him being the guy to want to stick up there. Maybe because we were already on top . . . Maybe he thought this was his one chance to . . ." He shook his head. "Aw, who the fuck knows what he thought?" He turned to Harry, his face . . . he wasn't pleading his case; he knew what he knew and he hoped it would be as clear to us. "We were all gonna be dead, Signor. You believe that?"

"Yes."

Another sip of his coffee. He patted his pockets, produced a cigarette and matches. "I didn't even think twice about it. I was down in the bottom of the hole, trying to keep from catching a bullet. Porter was up there at the top, Christ knows what he was looking at. All the kraut lead flying around up there, why that stupid ass didn't catch one . . ." He shook his head, amazed. "I didn't argue with him. I told him once, he told me to shuddup and make the call for Tully, I pulled my .45. It was the thing to do. Even right when I pulled the trigger . . . You know what's funny? The second my pistol jumped in my hand . . . I wanted to take it back."

"Take it back?" asked Ricks. "Why?"

He looked at Ricks, then shook his head, not quite understanding himself. He turned back to Harry. "Who else knows?"

"Just us."

"What happens now?"

"I imagine we're all a wee curious in that regard," I said, directing it at Harry.

Harry paced about the room. "I can't judge it, Dominick. I can't judge you. I'm not . . . I just . . . can't." He looked to me, smiled ruefully, perhaps at how much his own sentiment had come to echo mine. He stood by the bed, near Sisto. "It's up to you. You say so, I'll forget it. Pete, Eddie, and me. Andy, too . . . right, Andy? We'll head back to Liège, see you back home when it's all over. But . . . if you want to turn yourself in . . . I'll go in with you."

The sad grin again. "You won't forget it." He swung his legs onto the bed and stretched out, closing his eyes. "Man, I'm tired. Can we talk about this in the morning?"

As we turned and started for the door: "Signor . . . you stay. OK?"

"I'll see you all in the morning," Harry said to us.

I followed Andy Thom and Peter Ricks out. As the door was closing, I heard Harry ask, "Jesus, Dominick, why couldn't you have just hit the guy over the head?"

"Because they don't give us clubs, Signor. They give us guns."

CHAPTER ELEVEN

★

It was the mark of my exhaustion from the days on the road—from the chateau to Mons to Rott, then here to the Ardennes—that it was not the thunder of artillery crashing down along Skyline Drive that roused me from my sleep on the floor. Rather, I was stirred by a soldier's boot treading none too lightly across my kidneys. Then, groggy, I heard the distant cannonading, the nearer crash of the falling shells, the buzz of frightened voices and frantic scuffling as the troopers stumbled about in the darkened café.

Juan Bonilla's voice cut through the chaos like a whip crack: "Awright, awright, awright! It's a big noise, OK, now gear up 'n' fall in! Le's go! *Now!*" The firm orders gave them focus, the panicky grumbling subsided.

I found Harry kneeling by me, helping me to my feet.

"What the bloody hell's going on?" I asked.

A Coleman lantern flared across the room; by its light, I saw Harry's frightened, puzzled face.

Another noise, in its way more unnerving than the artillery. In the few lulls between detonations: small-arms fire. Close by.

From north of us along the river, and also due south of us. Sisto's two outposts were under attack.

The Coleman sat on the café bar where the platoon wireless had been set. Sisto had impatiently pushed the rookie operator aside and was now manipulating the controls himself as he yelled into the handset. *"This is Blue Two to Little Blue North, Blue Two to Little Blue North, do you read me, Little Blue North? Say again, say again, I can't get a clear signal."*

His voice was ragged, desperate. The light from the Coleman picked up a golden jewel of sweat coursing down the side of his face.

"Little Blue North, are you there? C'mon, Danny, this is Dominick, answer me!"

A breathless Andy Thom running in from outside. "Lootenant! They got the whole fuckin' ridge lit up!"

The handset slid from Dominick Sisto's hand and clattered on the bar. "Oh, Christ . . ." He leaned against the bar as if dizzy.

"What did you see?" Calm. As casual as asking a bird-watcher what he'd noted that morning. So calm measured against the palpable fear in that room, it seemed almost comic. It was Peter Ricks. Again: "Andy—what did you see?"

Andy Thom forced himself to think clearly. "Looks like shells coming down on every position up on the ridge. Go see for yourself."

"Sarge," Ricks said, turning to Bonilla, "you better get them outside. They're blind in here." To Sisto: "That all right with you, Lieutenant?"

From whatever soul sickness Sisto had been slipping into, that eerily relaxed voice seemed to drag him back. He took those few strands left—the pieces of Dominick Sisto that hadn't been left strewn halfway along the Italian boot, or sheared off on Hill 399—and used them to bind himself back together. "Yeah, yeah." Shaking off the daze. "Juan, hold back one fire team as a reserve. One team covers the southern approach, one team the north, the last one I want holding the road open."

"I'm going out for a look-see," Ricks told Sisto. "You should try to get your battalion CP."

"What about my two outposts?"

"I'd try to get your battalion CP while you still can."

"Yeah," and Sisto turned back to the wireless set. *"Rainbow, Rainbow, this is Blue Two, do you read me? Over . . ."*

Harry and I joined Peter Ricks outside. It was unbearably dark, only the barest bit of moonlight behind a thick blanket of clouds. East of us, we could see the bright flashes of the shells coming down—as Andy Thom had said—at points all along Skyline Drive.

"This isn't harassing fire and it isn't a probe," Ricks concluded. "This is a push. Listen . . ."

The gunfire we'd heard . . . north of us it was thinning, growing sporadic, like a faltering heartbeat. South of us . . . nothing.

A flare arced skyward from a point no more than ten or twenty yards south of us. I couldn't tell if it was from Sisto's fire team or the enemy. The flare sputtered to brilliance, began its slow, pendulating descent beneath its little parachute, and the ground around us became a jigsaw puzzle of stark shadows and flickering swaths of eerie bluish-white light.

I found myself stunned by the sudden break in the darkness, and was thus completely surprised when Peter Ricks forcefully threw me to the ground. Harry was already lying in the snow beside me, and in that flickering light I saw his eyes wide with fear.

I looked up to Ricks to ask him what the bloody hell he was

doing, but saw him bringing up his carbine. Flame spat from the muzzle as he snapped off a half-dozen rounds. He seemed satisfied with the result, helped us to our feet, and pushed us back toward the café door. I glanced hastily over my shoulder in the direction he'd been firing: two huddled shapes in white snow camouflage capes lay on the ground.

"Let's not dawdle, folks!" Ricks snapped, and gave us another shove toward the door. Once inside, he grabbed a man from the reserve detail. "Go find Sergeant Bonilla. Tell 'im he's got krauts inside the perimeter. Tell 'im to pull everybody back into the buildings. Go!" He sent the boy out with a swat on his buttocks, then turned to Dominick Sisto, who still sat at the wireless set.

"I can't raise Blue Six and I think my outposts are gone," Sisto was saying glumly into the handset. "I expect to get hit any minute."

"You're getting hit now," Ricks pointed out. "They're already on your inside."

Sisto's eyes screwed tightly shut as if Ricks's information sparked a sharp physical pain. "What can you get to us?" he asked into the handset, and I could hear the struggle for him to hold an even tone. Whatever he heard by way of response struck him stone still. After a long while, either they'd finished or he'd heard all he could bear, he stood, letting the handset slip from his hand to clatter on the bar. He walked . . . without direction, without purpose, shuffling idly about the dining room.

"Give it to us, Dominick," Ricks said.

The lieutenant sighed, almost a moan. "They're already across the river all through the sector. Where the artillery prep is letting up, they're attacking. All along the ridge. It's not just the division. They have reports from the 9th Armored south of us, and the 4th Infantry up north. They're opening up the whole front." Then, a thought: something—some little thing—for him to hold on to. He grew still, and certain, and decided. He turned to us, his face now completely composed. "The road to Heinerscheid is still open. I don't know for how long. Depending on how hard they hit us, I can maybe keep them pinned here a half hour, maybe more."

"What're you talking about, Dominick?" Harry asked, alarmed. "You're not thinking of staying? You *can't* be—"

Sisto was not waiting for a debate. He grabbed his helmet, his carbine, and started ushering Harry, myself, and Peter Ricks toward the door. "I've still got time to get you out of here."

Harry strove to push the lad off, but Sisto would have none of it. He grabbed the older man about his arms. To me, it looked like an embrace. "*Signor!* You wouldn't even be here if it wasn't for me. None of you. I've got enough to carry around in my head. *Prego, Signor,* don't put this on it, too." Harry was shaking his head, but the lieutenant finished firmly, brooking no argument: "*Signor,* I'm not *askin'* you."

Outside, the flare faded. Bonilla was in the street, pushing his charges toward the buildings, ordering them to take positions at the windows, to fire at anything that moved. The artillery bombardment along Skyline Drive was ebbing, but in its stead we could hear heavy small-arms fire in every direction.

Sisto herded us toward our jeep. "Just give it the gas and don't stop till you hear English."

At the jeep I stepped aside to allow Peter Ricks to take his usual seat in the rear. Another flare sparked in the night, and I saw him smiling. "I'm staying."

"Pete . . ." It was Harry. Pleading.

"It's OK, Harry. Really. I'm afraid I have a talent for this." Ricks gave Harry's shoulder a squeeze, turned, and disappeared into the shadows down the street toward where we could hear Bonilla still shouting orders to his men.

Dominick firmly took Harry by the elbow and put him behind the wheel of the jeep as I clambered in the other side. "Time for you to go, Signor. When you get home, give my regards to the missus and those boys of yours. You take care of those boys, Signor. And when you see my mom"—he smiled in a helpless, hapless way, very much the boy at a loss—"tell her . . . tell her something."

"Dominick . . ." I heard the sob in Harry's throat.

Sisto stepped back into the shadows. "Go." He turned and ran off after Ricks.

Harry punched the starter with his foot, and the cold engine coughed and spluttered to life.

Rifle fire now, from the other end of the street.

"Harry!"

He wiped at his eyes, then put the jeep into gear, whipped us onto the road, and headed us east.

In just moments, the little cluster of buildings disappeared into the darkness behind us, but the sounds of gunfire followed us all the way to the top of the ridge.

Within an hour, it was silent down there in the dark by the river.

CHAPTER TWELVE

———— ★ ————

The Germans' winter offensive in the Ardennes—what the Americans would come to call the Battle of the Bulge—had been raging for three days by the time Harry and I finally arrived in Liège. It had been a time spent battling along roads choked with retreating soldiers and refugees, and still other American units moving forward, trying to stem the growing enemy penetration. Time and again we found our passage north blocked by the deep thrust of the German spearheads, and we found ourselves skirting the spreading front of the battle as we endeavored to get back to familiar territory.

The city was in chaos. The Americans were convinced that the enormous supply caches about Liège would draw the resource-starved Germans in their direction and were preparing their defenses. Meanwhile, thousands of civilians were taking to the roads heading north and east. They'd suffered through one German occupation and were not about to risk a second.

It was under such circumstances that we appeared at the offices of the Judge Advocate General's Bureau: unshaven, unwashed, exhausted, cold, hungry, eyes only half open and red. After his immediate reaction of "Where the fuck have you meatballs *been*?" Joe Ryan took us into his office, set us down on an abused but comfortable sofa, and ordered us hot food and coffee.

While we waited for the food, he dug a bottle of cognac out of his desk drawer and poured us each a stiffening jolt.

Harry—in a surprise to both Ryan and myself—beckoned for a second, taller ration of the stuff, and when it was gone, he told the story to Ryan: from his suspicions back at the chateau to the trip to the Huertgen and his discovery there, and then to the little post on the Our and Dominick Sisto's confession.

As the story progressed, Joe Ryan sat back in his desk chair, his chin on his chest, in a pose of deep contemplation. There was no sign of his feelings on the matter.

"Where's Peter Ricks?" he asked when Harry had finished relating his tale.

"He stayed."

A small, unsurprised nod from Ryan. "Besides Ricks and Andy Thom, who else knows about this?"

"Just us."

Ryan took a deep breath. He rose from his chair, stood at his windows, looking down at the civilians loading their possessions onto everything with wheels, from Citroëns to bicycles. He watched MPs try vainly to organize the desperate flood.

"You see any reason for it to be otherwise?" But Ryan wasn't asking. He turned and faced me. "Does it seem all that newsworthy to you?"

"In light of the coming end of the world, it would seem to be of particularly little notice," I replied.

He turned to Harry. "You're the one that's always a bug about the truth and all that. Conrad Porter died a hero's death.

So did Dominick Sisto. And they both got what they deserved. Short of breaking a wife's and a mother's heart, is there any gain to taking this further?"

There was a knock at the door.

"Come," Ryan called, and in came one of his office staff, carrying a tray of food. Ryan reached for his hat and coat. "I'm going to find someplace for you guys to bunk. Tomorrow, I'll see about arranging transportation out for you. Maybe it's time for you to go home, Harry."

And he left.

The two of us stood at the edge of the airfield—the same one where I'd met Harry on his arrival barely a month before—and watched our flight leave and head east, toward England.

"Master Ryan'll be quite perturbed when he finds us still here," I told Harry.

"Dominick's listed as missing. So is Pete. When I know—" He could not say the words. "When I know, it'll be finished."

We turned and looked about the airfield for someone who could take us back toward the city.

ACKNOWLEDGMENTS

As always, I find myself deeply indebted to others, without whose help this book could not have been produced.

Once again, I owe thanks to the team at Bantam, as well as to my agent. I'm afraid I gave them all a rather hard time on this one. It was only through their considerable efforts that this book happened at all. In light of their contribution, I'd be shorting them not to say that The Defender is, in many ways, more their book than mine.

This work also earns my wife, Maribel, a special mention. As I say, there was a hard time on this one, and if she hadn't been there keeping me sane, it's doubtful it would've gotten done.

For their assistance as well as support, more special thanks to the following:

The Hon. Robert S. Armstrong
Richard Herman
Mark Peters, Esq.
Robert Shanahan, Esq.